PRAISE FOR THE WORK OF RAY VILLAREAL

"This wonderfully moving novel alternates between humor, tenderness and insight about what it means and takes to become a man." —*KLIATT on My Father, the Angel of Death*

"A San Antonio teenager hooks up with a fast-living pro wrestler and discovers the downside of hanging out with risky companions in this sequel to *My Father, the Angel of Death*."

—*Kirkus Reviews on Body Slammed!*

"This stand-alone sequel to Villareal's earlier novel, *My Father, the Angel of Death* (2006), tells a taut and believable story about a young man's coming-of-age and the choices he must make. The material about professional wrestling will be of special interest to boy readers." —*Booklist on Body Slammed!*

"A solid glimpse at seventh-grade life from a writer who understands the age—biography reports, friendships made and lost, crushes, misbehavior and sometimes quiet heroism. The story of these three Latino boys with Stephen King-ish imaginations ought to find a wide audience."

—*Kirkus Reviews* on *Who's Buried in the Garden?*

"An intriguing tale that will capture readers' imaginations. [Readers] will also like the lighthearted humor and wrestling antics that have been integrated into the story. The sprinkling of Spanish words reflects Joshua's Hispanic neighborhood in Texas."

—*School Library Journal* on *Who's Buried in the Garden?*

"After saving the life of a famous model, a 14-year-old Mexican-American boy learns the pressures of popularity and the definition of true heroism. The third-person narration follows Rawley's journey as he learns who his real friends are and the difference between comic-book and real-world heroes. A good story with some unexpected twists."

—*Kirkus Reviews* on *Don't Call Me Hero*

"Villareal takes on several important themes including illegal immigration, bullying, parent / teacher relationships and bilingualism. Ultimately, many of the characters—and readers—learn that there can be more than one truth, more than one point of view."

—*School Library Journal* on *Alamo Wars*

"The loss of his mother catapults a young teen and his father into homelessness. Villareal paints a believable picture of what can happen to a family when a crisis hits and how such events can ripple throughout every aspect of an adolescent's life."

—*Kirkus Reviews* on *On the Other Side of the Bridge*

"Villareal has written a grimly realistic story about the plight of the homeless in America."

—*Booklist* on *On the Other Side of the Bridge*

CHRONICLES ★ OF A ★ LUCHADOR

RAY VILLAREAL

PIÑATA BOOKS
ARTE PÚBLICO PRESS
HOUSTON, TEXAS

Chronicles of a Luchador is funded in part by a grant from the Texas Commission on the Arts. We are thankful for its support.

Piñata Books are full of surprises!

Piñata Books

An imprint of
Arte Público Press
University of Houston
4902 Gulf Fwy, Bldg 19, Rm 100
Houston, Texas 77204-2004

Cover design by Mora Des¡gn Group
Credit photo: sdstockphoto

Library of Congress Control Number: 2021943484

∞ The paper used in this publication meets the requirements of the American National Standard for Information Sciences—Permanence of Paper for Printed Library Materials, ANSI Z39.48-1984.

Printed in the United States of America

October 2021–November 2021
Versa Press, Inc., East Peoria, IL
5 4 3 2 1

For my grandson, Christopher David Villareal

CHAPTER ONE

Why is it that when you're a kid, teachers always ask you what you'd like to be when you grow up? And of course, you're supposed to answer with a career that sounds impressive and important.

"I'm going to be a doctor."

"I'm going to be an astronaut."

"I'm going to be President of the United States."

The last time a teacher posed that question to one of my classes was when I was in the seventh grade. We had to respond to it in the form of an essay. I wrote about wanting to be a police officer, which was usually my go-to answer. My friend Eric facetiously wrote that he wanted to be a slumlord. I got a B on my paper. Eric got an F on his, with our teacher calling his essay "distasteful."

Grilling little kids about their future is pointless because most of them will never follow through on their childhood aspirations.

I sure didn't plan to.

The only reason I used to say I wanted to be a cop was because at one time, my father considered applying to the San Antonio Police Department, and I thought it'd be a cool profession to get into. Though as I grew older, the idea faded.

At any rate, my father never joined the SAPD. Instead, he became one of the most popular wrestlers on American Championship Wrestling—the six-foot, seven-inch, three-hundred-twenty-pound, skeleton-faced monster known as the Angel of Death.

My father began his wrestling career in the independent circuit. First, going under the name of Mark "The Mangler" Baron, as he was known by his fans and teammates when he played defensive tackle at the University of Texas. Later, he wore a black and silver mask and called himself The Annihilator.

When he signed with the ACW, Frank Collins, the company's booker and promoter, gave him the gimmick of a supernatural figure who'd rise from the lower regions of the Netherworld to vanquish his mortal enemies.

To help create his new persona, my father let his hair grow past his shoulders. He painted his face to look like a skull, and he wore black tights, a black sleeveless shirt and black boots. For a final touch, he entered the ring wearing a black hooded cloak, and he carried a long-handle scythe.

My father traveled across the country and around the world, performing before sellout crowds in arena after arena. And everywhere he went, fans mobbed him, wanting to take photos with him and begging for his autograph. His image appeared on posters, backpacks, T-shirts, baseball caps, coffee mugs, you name it. Plus, you could find Angel of Death action figures in the toy section of most department stores.

As exciting as my father's career may have been, I'd never given any thought to becoming a professional wrestler, mainly because I'd also seen the dark side of the business.

Most fans know that pro wrestling is scripted, so any time a wrestler is presumably hurt, they figure it's part of the show. But on many occasions, without realizing it, they watched my father suffer concussions, broken bones, tears to his knees and shoulder separations, among other injuries, for which he had to take pain medications that often left him in a foul mood.

Not only that, the amount of time he spent on the road put a tremendous strain on our family. My mom was constantly harping on him to give up wrestling, but he refused. Eventually, his career led to my parents' divorce, and it wasn't until he retired that they decided to remarry.

Nevertheless, there I was, standing in front of my mirror, dressed only in a pair of black underwear and my father's Annihilator mask, imagining myself wrestling before a packed auditorium as the crowd chanted my name. Except they wouldn't be yelling, "Jes-se! Jes-se! Jes-se!" Not if I had on a mask. I'd need to come up with a cool ring name.

I puffed my chest and flexed my biceps, then switched to other posedowns. At eighteen, I'd grown to an even six feet, with a two-hundred-thirty-five-pound body of solid muscle. I'd gained my physique by working out regularly in the fitness room at the Ox Mulligan Pro Wrestling Factory, a wrestling school my father bought after he retired.

While I was admiring my reflection, my phone chimed a text alert. The message was from my girlfriend, Wally.

Hola, Jessup. You home? I have something for you. Can I stop by?!!

Sure, come on over. Where are you?

Outside your house.

Okay, give me a minute.

I peeled off the mask and put on my jeans and T-shirt. Then I hurried down the stairs to the foyer and opened the front door. Wally was standing on the porch with her dog, Samson. I greeted her with a kiss and invited her and the dog inside.

My mom looked up from the dining table where she was sitting, grading her English I students' compositions. "Hi, Wally," she said. "I'm sorry. I didn't hear the doorbell ring."

Wally waved and smiled. "It would've been spooky if you did, Mrs. B., because I didn't ring it."

"She texted me to say she was here," I explained.

Wally handed me a rectangular box wrapped in newspaper with a ribbon and a bow drawn on it with a red marker. "I decided to give you your graduation present early," she said. "That way, if you get the same thing from somebody else, I can say I gave it to you first."

"What is it?" I asked.

"Well, unless you've got x-ray vision, you'll have to open it to find out. And be careful with the wrapping paper. I spent a ton of money on it."

Ignoring her, I ripped off the newspaper and removed the lid from the box. Inside was a burnt-orange University of Texas polo shirt. I took it out and pressed it against my chest. "Thanks."

Wally frowned. "Geez and crackers, Jessup. Don't lose control of your emotions over it. If you don't like it, I can always…"

"No, no, it's fine. I mean, it's great."

"That's very thoughtful of you, Wally," my mom said. "I know Jesse appreciates it."

"You don't have one like it already, do you?" Wally asked, eyeing me skeptically.

"No, I just got my acceptance letter last Friday, remember? So, I haven't bought any UT stuff yet." I slipped on the shirt. "Thanks," I said again, this time with more enthusiasm and a kiss.

"I don't know if Jesse's told you this, Wally, but his father and I are both UT grads," my mom said. "So is my dad. And he was very excited when I told him that Jesse finally heard from UT, and that he's thinking about majoring in mechanical engineering, like he did. As you can probably guess, we're die-hard UT fans around here." She gestured a "Hook 'em Horns" hand sign, but I didn't say anything to confirm that I agreed.

"Let's go to the porch," I told Wally, when I noticed my mom staring disapprovingly at Samson. She didn't like having animals in the house.

We sat on the front steps, and Wally extended the leash on Samson's collar to let him move about the yard.

"Okay, Jessup," she said. "My Spidey sense is tingling. What's the deal with you and UT?"

"What are you talking about?"

"You tell me. I mean, I gave you this fabulous shirt, and you acted as if I was offering you a bowl of worms. And the other day, when you called to let me know that you'd been accepted by the school, you didn't sound particularly thrilled. Even now, you seem ambivalent about it."

I wrapped my arm around her and drew her close. "Sorry if I came across as ungrateful. I really do like my shirt."

"Then what is it?"

Wally and I had dated for a while, and we often shared secrets. Still, I was reluctant to reveal this one, feeling she'd be disappointed in me. I hesitated before answering, "I'm not sure I'm ready for college just yet."

"Is that it? *Phew!*" she said, brushing her fingers across her forehead. "For a second, I thought you were going to say something god awful, like you'd rather go to the University of Oklahoma."

"Come on, Wally, I'm serious."

"Me, too. I can't stand the Sooners."

I separated myself from her and looked away.

Realizing she was being insensitive she looped her arm around mine and reeled me back in. “Hey, there’s nothing wrong with wanting to wait awhile before you start college,” she said. “Anyway, who says you can’t?”

“Nobody. I’m just expected to go. You heard my mom. My whole family’s big on education, especially her, since she’s a teacher.”

Samson did his business next to one of the trees. Then he trotted up to Wally and sat at her feet. As she stroked his ears, she asked, “So what are you thinking about doing instead? Getting a job somewhere?”

“Not exactly.”

“Okey doke, then that leaves Option C. Sitting at home all day doing nothing. Is that your big plan?”

“Forget it,” I said, “because it’ll never happen. The reality is that I’ll be going to UT, whether I want to or not. And I’ll major in mechanical engineering because that’s what my grandfather wants me to do. Then I’ll graduate and work for a large company. End of story.”

Wally nodded, feigning concern. “Hmm, that *does* sound horrible. I’ll bet it ranks up there with Sisyphus having to spend eternity rolling a giant boulder up a hill.”

I couldn’t help but chuckle at her sarcasm. Wally’s unique sense of humor was what first attracted me to her. The rest of her quirkiness, which included preferring to be called Wally, rather than Ann, her middle name, and her hairstyle choice, a boyish undercut, faded and dyed turquoise blue, took me a while longer to get used to.

“Well, if Sisyphus had to take calculus and physics, he might decide that pushing a rock up a hill isn’t so bad,” I countered.

“Touché,” she said.

We sat quietly, staring at the row of two-story houses across the street. Finally, Wally asked, "So are you going to tell me what Option D is?"

"Nah, there's no point, because like I said, it's never going to happen."

She got up and tugged at Samson's leash. "Let's go, boy. Jessup's keeping secrets from us."

"No, I'm not. It was just a crazy idea I had, that's all."

"I'm messing with you, love," she said. "You don't have to tell me if you don't want to. But I do have to go. I can hear my homework calling me."

"Let me get my keys, and I'll give you a ride."

"That's all right. Samson's getting a little chunky. He needs the exercise." Wally kissed me goodbye. "Hasta Laredo," she said, before heading down the sidewalk.

I waited until she disappeared from my view. Then I returned to my bedroom and picked up the Annihilator mask from my dresser.

All my life, I'd felt like a marionette, with my strings being pulled this way and that. For instance, because of my father's career, we had to move a lot, so I was always switching schools. By the time my parents settled here in San Antonio, where they'd grown up, I'd attended ten different ones.

And when I was in the sixth grade, my mom forced me to take band, even though I didn't want to. The director stuck me in the percussion section, which I hated, so I never learned to play the drums well.

Then in high school, my father made me sign up for football, saying it could lead to a college scholarship, and I sucked at that, too.

Now I was supposed to go to the University of Texas to study mechanical engineering. But given my track record, I wouldn't be surprised if I bombed out my first year.

Recently, I'd had a revelation about my future, but like I told Wally, it was a crazy idea. It came to me while I was working out at the Ox Mulligan Pro Wrestling Factory. As I watched the wrestlers rehearsing their matches, I felt I could be just as good or better than any of them.

I'd been around pro wrestling my whole life, so I was familiar with most of the holds and moves. Also, because of the intensive weight-lifting and cardio exercises I'd been putting myself through, I knew I had the strength, quickness and stamina to handle myself against anyone in the ring. And if my father were to train me, I had no doubt that someday soon, I could be a top competitor in the ACW.

But after the toll the profession had taken on him, physically and emotionally, I knew what he'd say if I were to tell him I wanted to pursue a career in pro wrestling.

I slipped the Annihilator mask on the Styrofoam head and placed it back on my bookcase.

If only.

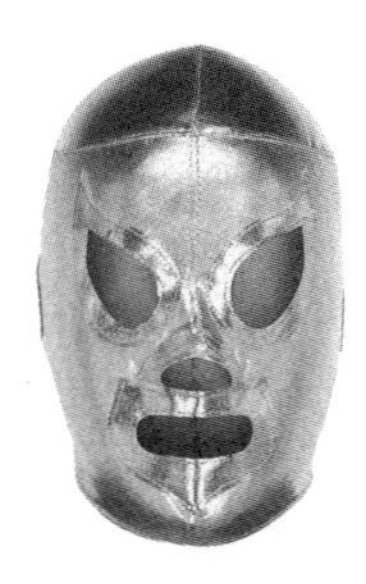

CHAPTER TWO

The Ox Mulligan Pro Wrestling Factory stood at the edge of the Starlight Shopping Center. The building used to be a furniture warehouse, but it had been vacant for years, until Mike Mulligan, a former pro wrestler, bought it and converted it into the wrestling school. He also formed an independent wrestling promotion, where his students could hone their skills. When my father took over the business, he kept the name in honor of his long-time friend.

Inside the makeshift arena, large banners with images of famous wrestlers, past and present, including the Angel of Death, dangled from the ceiling. The words OX MULLIGAN PWF in red, with a picture of an ox in white standing on top of them, were painted on one of the walls. A jumbo screen, on which vignettes were shown to introduce new wrestlers, was attached to another wall. The ring had a black apron with the PWF logo on it and was stationed in the middle of the room, with a lighting truss hanging above it to illuminate the action. The ring was surrounded by a security barricade to separate it from the folding chairs and bleachers that encircled it. At the far end of the arena, a steel frame with stage lights, blue curtains and a metal ramp, made up the wrestlers' entranceway. Three practice rings were located on the other side of the curtains, as well as a fitness room, showers and lockers.

During the week, my father held classes, and every other Saturday, he staged wrestling events. Around five hundred people usually attended them. Scouts from bigger promotions also turned up on occasion, looking to sign up prospects.

In addition to the regular programs, my father held events four times a year at larger venues and invited bigger-name stars to headline them. He didn't have a TV contract, but his shows were aired on YouTube.

On Saturday nights, I manned the ticket counter, partly to pay back my father for letting me use the fitness equipment. Plus, I enjoyed the time we spent together, after years of being apart from him, due to his career.

At six o'clock, fans began trickling into the Factory, and by the time the show started at seven-thirty, the arena was filled nearly to capacity.

First on the card was a match between Travis "Mace" McKeon and Alonzo "The Bombardier" Barclay.

Travis, a ring veteran, and one of the trainers at the Factory, was a long-haired, bearded bull of a man. He dressed in a black sleeveless shirt with a picture of a skull on it, black and gray camouflage shorts and black boots. His eyes were masked with white Halloween contact lenses.

By contrast, Alonzo was a skinny nineteen-year-old, who epitomized what wrestling legend, Freddie Blassie, mockingly referred to as a "pencil-neck geek." Alonzo had on a brown leather bomber jacket, a red scarf and a pair of aviator goggles, to go with his stage name.

Clyde Conner, a car salesman, who worked the shows as the announcer, stood inside the ring, microphone at his mouth. "*Ladies and gentlemen, the first bout of the evening is scheduled for one fall, with a twenty-minute time limit. Introducing first, weighing in at two hundred, fifty-eight pounds, from Dallas, Texas . . . Mace McKee-e-e-o-o-o-n!*"

The crowd booed, knowing that Travis, a familiar figure at the shows, was the heel, the bad guy in the match.

"And his opponent, making his wrestling debut, weighing in at one hundred, sixty-seven pounds, from Shreveport, Louisiana . . . Alonzo 'The Bombardier' Barcla-a-a-y!"

This time, the audience applauded mildly for the unknown rookie.

Doug Fletcher was the referee for the bout. Doug had trained to be a wrestler, but after a few matches, discovered his body couldn't handle the punishment. He was ready to leave the business until my father offered him the role of referee.

Doug called the wrestlers to the center of the ring to go over the rules. He patted them down, then sent them to their respective corners to wait for the bell.

Alonzo removed his accessories and handed them to Clyde, who doubled as the ring attendant. Without them, he looked even scrawnier.

Joe Ellis, another trainer, served as the timekeeper. At Doug's signal, he rang the bell.

The men opened their match with a standard, collar-and-elbow tie up. Just the way they had rehearsed it.

Alonzo got the upper hand by grabbing Travis in a side headlock, then flung him against the ropes. When Travis bounced back, Alonzo flipped him over with a back-body drop, followed by two hip tosses. Just the way they had rehearsed it.

Travis slid out of the ring to escape the attack, but the "Bombardier" wasn't done. Getting a running start, he hopped on a top turnbuckle and launched himself at Travis with a Corkscrew Senton.

This was *not* the way they had rehearsed it.

Alonzo misjudged the distance and missed Travis by a mile. He landed on his back, hitting his head on the concrete floor. Travis picked him up by the hair and leaned into him, probably asking him if he was okay. Then he threw him inside the ring and held him down with a rear chin lock. Doug pretended to make sure Travis wasn't choking him but was actually assessing the situation. Seeing the glassy look in Alonzo's eyes, he must've told the wrestlers to "take it home," because Travis skipped to the planned finish.

He allowed Alonzo to get to his feet and slip out of the hold. Alonzo hit him with a forearm to the face, which Travis shook off, then retaliated by kicking him in the stomach. Next, he whirled him around with a Spinning DDT and slammed him on the mat. He pinned Alonzo's shoulders, and Doug counted to three for the fall.

"The winner of the bout, in two minutes, forty-six seconds," Clyde Conner bellowed, *"Mace McKee-e-e-o-o-o-n!"*

The fans jeered at the announcement. As Travis made his way to the back, they continued to hurl insults at him.

Moments later, Doug helped Alonzo out of the ring and escorted him up the ramp. I left my post and followed them, wanting to make sure Alonzo was all right. I didn't know him well, but we chatted sometimes, whenever we ran into each other at the Factory.

Backstage, my father confronted the men. "What the hell happened out there?" he barked.

"Sorry, Mark," Travis said. "I didn't know the kid was going to do a senton."

My father glared at Alonzo, waiting for an explanation.

"I thought the crowd was kind of dead, sir," he said. "I was only trying to get them into the match."

"No, you weren't! You were showing off. I told you not to try any high-risk spots, like that 'Dive Bomber' thing you insist on doing. Not until you've had more experience. Are you're trying to impress someone?"

Alonzo hung his head. "Sorry, Coach Baron. It won't happen again."

"Safety first, son, remember that. How is your opponent supposed to protect you if he doesn't know what you're going to do? From now on, just stick to the script, you hear me? I don't want you improvising anything."

My father's temper softened enough to tell Nic Slade, the athletic trainer, to check him for a possible concussion.

After Nic had completed his examination, I asked Alonzo how he was feeling.

"I'm all right," he said. "I ain't got a concussion or nothing. I don't know why Fletcher had to stop the match. I coulda kept going. And Coach McKeon knew I might do the Corkscrew Senton. We'd practiced it before."

"I'm sure you did," I said. "The problem wasn't that you tried it. It's that you didn't call the spot, and Travis wasn't expecting it. I wouldn't worry about it, though. This was only your first match. You'll get better as time goes on."

Despite Alonzo's botch, I envied him. At least he'd gotten to wrestle in front of an audience.

He headed to the showers, and I went back to watch the rest of the matches. The show ended just after ten, with the main event featuring a "no-disqualification" title bout between Hondo Kelly and Steve Dalton. Hondo was the PWF heavyweight champion.

The men put on a brutal performance, attacking each other with kendo sticks, folding chairs and even a cheese grater and a cookie sheet, at one point. The match went on for almost thirty minutes, until Hondo caught Steve in his finisher, the Texas Cloverleaf, and forced him to tap out.

After the wrestlers and the ref had cleared the ring, Clyde Conner took the microphone and thanked everyone for coming, saying he hoped to see them again in two weeks.

As always, my father had put on another entertaining show that sent the crowd home happy.

CHAPTER THREE

Following the matches, my father and I went to eat at Romo's. The owners of the pizzeria, John and Mona Romo, used to run an indie promotion called Southwest Wrestling Association, and my father wrestled for them briefly during his "Mangler" days.

The first time I ate at Romo's was when TJ Masters, an ACW wrestler, brought me after one of my football games. He claimed that the restaurant had the best pizza in town—coldest beer, too—and offered to buy me one, even though I was only sixteen. I didn't think the Romos would serve me a beer, and I don't think TJ did, either. He just wanted to see how I'd react.

Mona came around the register to greet us. "There they are," she said. "My two favorite men. And I hear that somebody's graduating from high school pretty soon."

"Well, it isn't me, so it must be this guy," my father said, clapping me on the shoulder.

"Congratulations, Jesse," she said. "Me and Johnny are very proud of you. We'll definitely be at your party."

I looked at my father. "What party?"

Mona cupped a hand over her mouth. "Oops. Did I let the cat out of the bag?"

"That's all right," my father said. "I was about to tell him anyway."

She picked up a couple of menus. "Follow me, darlins. I'll give you the best table in the house." At near closing time, the place was almost empty.

After we were seated, I asked my father about the party.

"You're about to reach a big milestone, and we need to celebrate it," he said. "We're planning on having it the day after your graduation. Mom's checking out caterers. She's also thinking about getting Rick Dunham to DJ it. We'll have the party in the back, so feel free to invite as many of your friends as you want."

Our yard had plenty of space and a large swimming pool. Maybe if the weather was warm enough, we could make it a pool party.

Mona stopped by a few minutes later with a pad and a pen. "Y'all know what you want?"

"Sure," my father said. "We'll each have a Calzone Supreme and a Coke."

"Um, can you make mine diet?" I asked.

"Honey, we don't have diet calzones," Mona said with a straight face.

"No, I mean . . ."

She flashed my father a wink. "I know what you meant, darlin. I'll bring your food right out."

Since it was late, I had thought of having only a small Caesar salad, but my father was treating, and I didn't want to order something different. Besides, a calzone wouldn't kill me. According to TJ, most foods were okay, as long as you ate them in moderation.

"All right, so we've got the party," my father said. "Mom has some other ideas, too. But let me ask you, Jesse. Is there something in particular you'd like for graduation?"

Nothing came to mind. I had everything I wanted or needed, including the black Dodge Challenger he'd given me for my seventeenth birthday.

"A special trip somewhere," he suggested. "Maybe to London or Paris."

London sounded awesome. My parents had been there several times with the ACW, but I never had.

Suddenly a thought struck me. "Actually, there *is* something I want, but I don't think you'll go for it."

"Well, I hope it isn't a Learjet because that might be a little bit out of my price range," he joked.

"I want you to train me to wrestle."

My father stared at me for a few seconds. Then he said, "I've been wondering when you were going to bring that up."

"You have?"

"I know you're dying to get in the ring. I see it in your eyes every time you go to the Factory. I hadn't mentioned it because I wanted it to come from you."

"Will you do it?" I asked, my heart racing.

"Sure, why not? I can have Mace show you how to run the ropes, take bumps, stuff like that."

I couldn't believe it. If I'd known it'd be this easy, I would've approached him about it a long time ago. "So how soon do you think it'll be before I have a match?" I asked, thinking of Alonzo Barclay as a possible first opponent.

My father's cheerful disposition vanished. "Hold on, I never said anything about letting you wrestle."

"What? But you just told me you would."

"No, I said I'd let Mace teach you the basics."

"Yeah, but . . . then what's the point in training me if I'm not going to wrestle?" Somewhere in the back of my head, I could hear the old advertisement warning: *If it sounds too good to be true, it probably is.*

"The point is that you'll be in top physical shape," he said. "And isn't that the reason you started going to the Factory in the first place? Because you wanted to get in shape?" Then in a jab that was totally unnecessary, he added, "And isn't that why you used to spend so much time with your buddy, TJ?"

"*My* buddy?" I snapped. "Dad, he was your buddy first, remember? You're the one who introduced me to him."

Mona arrived with our drinks. "Everything okay here?" she asked.

"We're just talking," my father told her.

She gave us a questioning glance, then left.

"Anyway, you know my policy," he said. "I don't put anyone in a match until they've had at least four or five months of training, which you won't be able to complete, because you'll be living in Austin by then."

Up until that time, I'd been tentative about sharing my thoughts on college with my parents, but I felt my hand being forced. "That's the other thing, Dad. I'm kind of thinking about waiting a year or two before I start school."

"What for?" he said sharply. "So you can stay here and wrestle? Absolutely not. You get your degree, Jesse, you hear me? You get your career going. *Then* you can come back and talk to me about wrestling."

Mona was tending to two geezers at the bar. She and the geezers turned and stared at us, but my father dismissed their concern with a shake of his head. Softening his voice, he said, "Look, everyone on my roster's got a regular job. Steve's a software engineer, Mando's a security officer, Kendric works for a printing company . . . I could go down the list, but you know what I'm getting at. Wrestling's a hobby for them. They're weekend warriors, if you will. Most of them don't have any real expectations of going beyond the indie circuit."

"But you did," I said. "And you made it big. I mean, the whole world knows who you are."

My father leaned back and crossed his arms. "I see. So that's what this is about. You want to be famous."

"No, Dad, it's just that wrestling's the one thing I honestly believe I can be really good at. And if I were to hold off going to school, I could focus on developing my skills and . . ."

"And what? Become the ACW heavyweight champion? Listen to me, Jesse, I got lucky, plain and simple. I also happen to have a degree in criminal justice. And if things hadn't turned out the way they did for me, I would've been proud to have gone into some field of law enforcement."

The difference between my father and me was that he'd studied criminal justice because he wanted to be a cop. It had been his dream since he was a kid. Wrestling was something he stumbled onto by chance, when he met a former pro wrestler who saw potential in him and recommended him to people he knew in the industry.

I didn't particularly want to be a mechanical engineer. Or a teacher, as my mom had suggested. Or anything else. The only future I could see for myself was as a pro wrestler.

My father continued to lecture me about how I needed to make college my first priority, retelling the stories I'd heard a million times before: how he and my mom had struggled financially, trying to live on her substitute teacher's salary, while he was getting beaten up in rec halls and high school gyms all over the country for pennies; how he used to have to work as a bartender to help make ends meet; how even after he signed a lucrative contract with American Championship Wrestling and made more money than he'd ever imagined, his grueling schedule forced him to spend most of his time on the road, leading to his and my mom's divorce; how at age forty-seven, his body was a wreck, with injuries that would never heal completely.

I resisted asking him why he was operating a wrestling school if he thought the profession was such a bad one to get into, but I knew the answer. It was fine for everyone else, just not for me.

"Here's what I'll do for you, Jesse," he said at last. "I'm having tryouts on the first Saturday in June. Then the following Monday, I plan to start a beginners' class. You're welcome to participate in the sessions until the fall, but I'm not putting you in a match. Take it or leave it."

Texas had plenty of other wrestling schools where I could train, but I didn't want to cause a rift by defying my father and enrolling in one of them. So, I agreed to his terms. For now. Maybe after he saw what I could do in the ring, he might change his mind.

Mona came by with our food. "Enjoy your calzones, darlins," she said, but the bubbliness that had been in her voice earlier was gone.

For a while, we ate in silence. Finally, I looked at my father and said sheepishly, "Can we still go to London?"

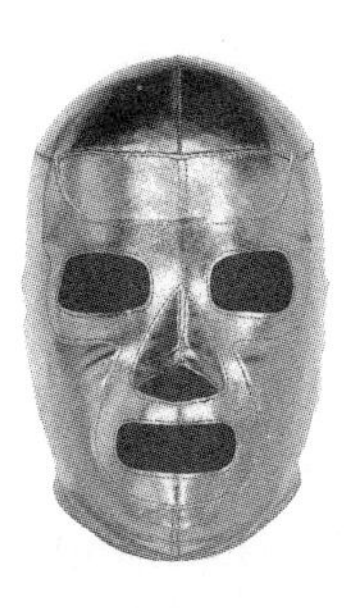

CHAPTER FOUR

You might think that being the son of the Angel of Death would make you super popular at school. And for the most part, you'd be right. Kids used to latch onto me the minute they found out who my father was. I even had a teacher who set up a home visit and a bogus parent conference for a chance to see where her favorite wrestler lived.

Thankfully, the novelty wore off, and by the start of my sophomore year, I was just another student at Erastus Deaf Smith High School. I still had lots of friends who I planned to invite to my graduation party, but my inner circle consisted mainly of three guys: Abel "Goose" Guzmán, Wendell Cooley and Bucky Henderson.

I'd known Goose and Wendell since middle school, when my family and I moved here from St. Louis. At first, I didn't care for them much because they were huge ACW marks, so I thought I knew why they wanted to hang out with me. But after a while, I realized they liked me for who I was, not necessarily who I was related to. Bucky joined our group when the four of us played on the Sidewinders football team.

I'm not sure why I remained friends with those guys. We didn't have a lot in common, and we often got into arguments. Wally described our relationship as "symbiotic," which was her way of saying that people with opposite personalities can still get along.

Lately though, Goose had been talking about how after graduation, we'd be going our separate ways and probably wouldn't see each other anymore. He brought it up again while we were standing on the school steps, waiting for Wally, so I could give everyone a ride home.

"Before you know it, you'll be moving to Austin," he told me. "Wendy will be in Dallas at SMU, and Bucky's gonna go to that girl's school in New York."

"It's not a girl's school!" Bucky cried. "It's a culinary school. And it's one of the best in the country."

"Oh yeah, I forgot," Goose said, smirking. "So what are they gonna teach you at that cooking school, Bucky? How to make nachos and lemonade?"

"Leave him alone, man," Wendell said. "At least he's getting a degree in something he wants to do, instead of mowing lawns for the rest of his life."

"Hey, I ain't gonna do that forever," Goose shot back. "I'm just helping my uncle till I make enough money to pay for my graduation stuff. After that, I'm gonna look for a better job."

Goose had always done poorly in school, yet had somehow managed to pass each grade. As a senior, however, he'd been facing the possibility of not graduating. Only recently had he learned that he'd be walking across the stage with us to receive his diploma. Even so, he didn't have any real plans for his future and may have been bummed that we did.

While we were talking, Wally showed up.

"You ready?" I asked her.

"That's okay, love," she said. "I don't need a ride today. I just came to tell you that I'm staying late for rehearsal." She ran her hand gently across my chest. "By the way, you look positively wicked in your UT shirt."

"Thanks," I said, making sure to sound appreciative. Then I told the guys that she'd given it to me.

"Man, I wish Yolanda would give me something besides a pain in the *nalgas*," Goose complained. "She says that her last name is Benavides, but I really think it's Whiner, 'cause she whines about *every* little thing. What do you say, Wally? You think I should dump her?"

Glaring at him, she replied, "If you want my advice, you'll have to see me during business hours, which are between 'Not Interested' and 'Don't Care.'"

"Oooh, burned," I said, making Bucky and Wendell laugh.

Wally turned her attention back to me. "I also want to remind you about my play Saturday night. Please say you'll come."

"Yeah, sure. My father doesn't have a show this weekend, so I'll be there."

"You boys are invited, too," she said. "Our play is called *Las Soldaderas*. It's about the Mexican Revolution. We'll be performing it in the auditorium."

"Man, I'd love to go to it, Wally, but my business hours are . . ."

"Sorry, Goose, gotta run," she cut him off and left.

As we watched her go back in the building, Goose remarked, "That chick's got an attitude, you know that? No offense, Jesse, but I've always thought you could do better than her."

"That's because you're intimidated by girls who are smarter than you," I said.

"Oooh, burned!" Bucky cried.

The four of us made our way to the parking lot and climbed in my car. I drove to the corner, made a left turn, then headed toward my first stop, the Harvest Hills Apartments, where Goose lived.

If he was concerned about the possible loss of our friendship after high school, I was even more troubled by what would become of Wally and me. She had another year to go before she graduated, and once I moved to Austin, I didn't know when I'd see her.

The logical thing would be for me to break up with her. After all, it wouldn't be fair to expect her not to date other guys while I was gone. But how do you tell someone you care about that it's time to end the relationship?

I hadn't forgotten the heartache I felt when Sara Young dumped me for that arrogant jackass, Riley King. What's strange is that Sara never gave me a reason for why she decided to break up. She just ghosted me—stopped talking to me one day, and that was it. The next thing I knew, she was snuggling up to Riley. I hate to admit it, but I cried a lot, trying to figure out what I'd done to drive her away.

Now I was contemplating doing the same thing to Wally.

Funny, but when I first met her, she was the last person in the world I thought I'd date. I mean, I didn't find anything attractive about a tall, skinny girl with a weird-looking haircut, who called herself Wally. She lived with her mom in a house that looked like a small castle, and she had a parrot named Orpheus that could whistle "The Star-Spangled Banner."

As for similar interests, we were worlds apart. Wally listened to music from bands I'd never heard of, like the Jamaican Rudeboys and Yells at Eels. She read epic poetry, which I found boring. She loved musicals and plays, and she enjoyed watching artsy-fartsy foreign films.

Yet, she and I connected, somehow. We could spend hours talking about the most mundane things—places we'd been, books we'd read, favorite and least favorite foods to eat, TV shows, movies (including the artsy-fartsy ones), and our views of the world.

I shared with her what it was like growing up as the son of the Angel of Death. She told me about her dad, an orthopedic surgeon named Wallace Morúa, who'd been killed in a car accident right before she was born, which was how she'd gotten her first name. And about her stepdad, who cleaned out her mom's savings before abandoning them. Wally helped me with my English lit homework, and I tutored her in math and science.

Talk about a symbiotic relationship.

Oddly, one of the things that brought us together was that Wally was a mega wrestling fan. Each week, she watched *Monday Night Mayhem.* She explained that she had a fondness for the theater, and to her, professional wrestling was the ultimate stage production. "It's the sweetest action on television," she said.

While my mind was on Wally, I missed out on some of what the guys were talking about. I tuned back in when I heard Wendell suggest to Goose that he should consider enrolling in a trade school.

"You could learn to be an electrician or a plumber," he said.

"I don't know, man. I've heard that those trade schools are real expensive."

"You can always join the Army," Bucky said. "That's free."

"Nooo, thanks."

"How about becoming a professional wrestler?" I asked.

The guys laughed.

"Seriously. My father's planning to start a new class in June. You ought to think about signing up for it."

Bucky leaned forward from the backseat. "Do it, Goose. Then maybe someday you'll be the ACW women's champion."

Ordinarily, Goose would've responded with a snarky comment, but I could tell that he was running the idea through his head.

"Football season just ended a few months ago, and you look like you're still in good shape," I told him. "What do you weigh? About one eighty-five? One ninety?"

"Something like that. So what would I have to do, exactly?"

"Well, first you go to the tryouts. You'll have to pay a thirty-five-dollar fee to get in. Then, if you decide you want to take the course, it'll cost you around four thousand bucks."

"Four thousand? Man, that's a lot of money!"

"No, it isn't."

"Easy for you to say. You're rich."

"I mean, compared to college tuition," I said, wishing Goose wouldn't bring up my family's wealth, which he often did, to justify why he thought his life was rougher than mine. "My father will let you pay it in installments if you need to do it that way."

He looked at the guys. "What do y'all think?"

"I think it'd be awesome," Wendell said. "If I didn't already have a scholarship to SMU, I might consider doing it, especially with Jesse's dad training me."

"And you'll get paid for running around in your underwear," Bucky teased.

"Now, I'm not going to promise that you'll ever be a top star in a promotion like the ACW and make a ton of money," I said. "Some guys spend their entire careers wrestling in the independent circuit for next to nothing."

"But I have a chance, right?" Goose said, growing more excited.

"Everybody's got a chance. It all depends on how much effort you put into it. That, and a few lucky breaks here and there."

"Me, a wrestler," he mused. "You know what? I'm really gonna think about it."

I pulled into the parking lot of his apartment complex and let him out. "Talk it over with your parents," I said, before driving off.

While it may have appeared that my motivation for encouraging Goose was to give him something to look forward to after high school, I wondered if, subconsciously, I wanted to live vicariously through him, by helping him with a career I thought I'd never have.

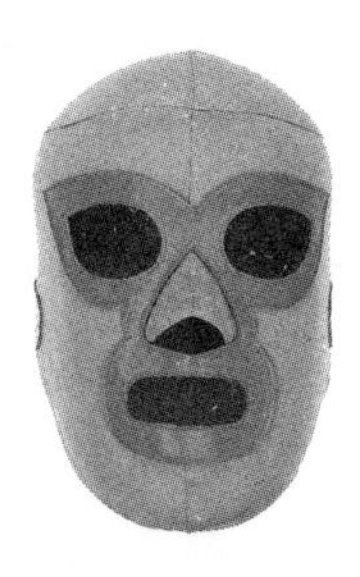

CHAPTER FIVE

Las Soldaderas was an end-of-the-year theater arts project Wally and her group had written for their final. It was one of three short plays scheduled to be presented Saturday night. *Wrongful Death* and *After Hours* were the other two.

Not surprisingly, Wally was the one who'd come up with the idea of writing a bilingual play about events that took place during the Mexican Revolution of 1910, as told from the perspective of *soldaderas*, female soldiers. She was a history buff, and unlike me, she spoke Spanish fluently.

When I entered the auditorium, I spotted Wally's mom sitting in the front row with two other ladies. I thought about joining them, but since I was planning to break up with Wally soon, I didn't want to get any chummier with her mom than I had to. So, I sat alone, toward the back.

First on the program was *Wrongful Death*, a creepy story about a popular high school girl named Ashley Wilson, whose body is found floating in a creek by a fisherman. She's the fourth girl from the same school who's been murdered in the past few weeks.

The narrator tearfully explained how he'd had a crush on Ashley for years and couldn't believe she was gone. In the end, the narrator turned out to be the murderer. He'd been killing girls from his school who rejected him, and mistaking Ashley, the only girl who was ever nice to him for someone else, unintentionally strangled her.

For a play written by juniors, I thought *Wrongful Death* was great, especially the twist ending.

After a ten-minute break, the Mexican revolutionary song, "La Adelita," began playing, and the curtains opened. Wally and her fellow *soldadera*s appeared onstage, wearing sombreros and long, flowing skirts, with bandoliers strapped across their chests. Each girl held a prop rifle. Behind them stood a paper-mâché wall painted to look like stone, with a Mexican flag attached on top.

Las Soldaderas told the story of the women who helped the male revolutionaries topple the dictatorship of Mexican President Porfirio Díaz. A lot of the dialogue was in Spanish, so I didn't fully understand everything that was said. Fortunately, Wally had told me beforehand what the play would be about and I could follow along.

Las Soldaderas ended with a final battle scene, then a victory celebration. As the performers took their bows, green, white and red confetti rained on them.

Wally's play didn't have the shocking effect of *Wrongful Death*, but I thought it was just as good, if not better.

After Hours, in my opinion, was the weakest of the three plays. It was about teens dealing with grief and depression. Watching it made me feel depressed, too.

Midway through it, Wally entered the auditorium from the back and started down the aisle. She was headed toward her mom, but when she saw me, she took the seat next to mine.

"You rocked," I told her.

She put a finger to her lips, then pointed to the stage. I got the hint. *After Hours* may have been a downer for me, but the students were Wally's friends, and she wanted to watch their performance uninterrupted.

To close the show, Ms. Telchik, the theater arts teacher, called the actors and tech crew from the three plays to the stage for a final round of applause.

Then, as the audience began exiting the auditorium, I made my way to the front to catch up with Wally. She was talking to her mom and guests, who were introduced to me as her aunts. Wally's mom introduced me to them as Wally's "special friend."

"We're going to grab a bite to eat," Wally told me. "Want to join us?"

I pulled her aside and whispered, "I was hoping you and I could go out by ourselves."

"Sure, no problem." Wally turned to her mom. "If it's okay with you, I'm going to pass on your invite. Jessup says he wants to buy me dinner at Belmondo 51."

Belmondo 51 was one of the fanciest and most expensive restaurants in San Antonio.

"Actually, I was thinking more in terms of Taco Bell," I said.

"That's fine," her mom told her. "Have a good time, and don't be out so late."

Wally went to the restroom to change. She came out a few minutes later, wearing faded blue jeans, a black Aquabats! T-shirt and a pair of red, high-top Converse sneakers. She dropped her costume off backstage, and we headed to my car.

Before we got in, she asked, "Do we have to eat at Taco Bell?"

"No, I just thought that since you were in a play about the Mexican Revolution, you might want to have Mexican food," I said.

"I would. But *real* Mexican food. Not that pseudo junk."

"Pick a place then."

"Have you ever eaten at Casa Guanajuato?" she asked.

"I don't think so."

"Jessup, my man. You're in for a treat."

Wally had been to the restaurant before, but she didn't know how to get there, so I GPSed it on my phone. The directions took me to a run-down neighborhood on the South side that could easily be mistaken for a Mexican border town, with many business signs written in Spanish.

Past a row of old houses and apartments, a grocery store, a used car lot and an Exxon gas station, stood Casa Guanajuato, a white building with a red tile roof. The green, white and red neon sign displaying the restaurant's name flickered in spurts, as if it were gasping for breath. The parking area was cratered with potholes, and I worried about possible damage to my car as I drove through them.

The stucco walls inside the restaurant were painted Pepto-Bismol pink. Multicolored Christmas tree lights hung across the ceiling, along with *papel picado* banners and piñatas. A large TV in the middle of the room was airing a news program on Telemundo with the volume turned off, and a mariachi group was playing and singing their hearts out.

The restaurant was packed, mostly with large families talking loudly to hear each other over the music. Some of their kids were running around the tables, chasing each other.

I wished we'd gone to Taco Bell.

"I've eaten at hole-in-the-wall joints before," I told Wally. "But this one's a rat's nest."

"Don't act so bougie," she said, frowning. "Casa Guanajuato may not be Belmondo 51, but the food here is amazing."

A big man with a thick black mustache welcomed us in Spanish, then took us to a booth and handed us a pair of menus.

"How'd you hear about this place?" I asked Wally, surprised by her restaurant choice.

"My tías, Gloria and Irene, the ones you met at school, recommended it to my mom. We love it here."

I skimmed through the menu, but nothing grabbed my attention. "So, what are you going to have?" I asked.

"I think I'll go with the Tacos de Cochinita Pibil," she said. "They're Yucatán-style pork tacos. They serve them with rice and beans and a cup of *sopa de conchas.*"

"Sounds good. Go ahead and order it for me, too."

Wally sighed. "*Ay, Jessup. ¿Cuándo vas a aprender hablar español?*"

"I can speak Spanish," I said indignantly. "When I have to. Right now, I don't have to."

My parents were fluent in Spanish, but they'd never made much of an effort to teach me the language. The little I knew, I'd picked up mostly from my grandparents and from a class I'd taken at school. But unless I was in a situation where I was forced to speak it, I stuck with English.

A server came by to take our order. As I expected, she asked us in Spanish what we wanted. I could've told her easily enough, but conversing with a native speaker always made me uncomfortable. I looked at Wally. She gave me the eye, then ordered for the both of us.

While we waited for our food, she talked at length about her play, which she'd also done on the way to the restaurant. Both times, I listened patiently, knowing how much work she'd put into her project.

Finally, during a lull in the conversation, I said, "Listen, I need to discuss something very important with you."

She grinned. "You're nominating me for a Tony?"

What are you doing, Baron? This is Wally's big night. She's in a great mood. Don't spoil the evening by telling her that you should break up.

"Never mind," I said. "We'll talk about it another time."

"No, now you've got me curious." Wally folded her arms on the tabletop and leaned into me, as if I were about to reveal a big secret. "What is it?"

"I . . . um . . ." *Come on, come on. Think of something.* "I . . . I need to know if you're still planning to go to the prom with me so I can buy tickets."

Wally sat back. "Geez, I don't know. Bruno Mars called and said he wants to take me to dinner that night. I told him I'd have to think about it." She giggled. "Of course, I'm going to the prom with you, silly. No worries. I'll just tell Bruno . . ." She stopped, and her face grew pensive. "Wait. This isn't about the prom, is it?"

Wally had an uncanny knack for reading me, so I didn't try to deny it. "No," I muttered.

"I know what you want to talk about. You're wondering what's going to happen to us after you graduate, right?"

"Why do you say that?" I asked, stunned by her accuracy.

She tapped a finger against her temple. "Spidey sense, remember? And also because I've been down this road before. I told you about Andrew Albits, my first boyfriend. Well, after he graduated from Deaf Smith, he enrolled at Arizona State, and . . . poof! That was the last I saw of him. So, I've been waiting for you to do the same."

"Believe me, Wally," I said. "I don't want us to break up. But you need to be free to date other guys when I leave for college, and I don't want to be in the way."

She shrugged. "I wasn't looking for a boyfriend when I met you, and I don't expect to be in the market for another one after you're gone. Look, Jessup, I love you. More than you'll ever know. I enjoy every minute I spend with you, and I miss you when we're not together. But hey, nothing lasts forever. Everything we have in this world is on loan from God. So I'm grateful for what He lets me have, even if it's only for a short while." She shrugged again. "I learned that from my mom, I guess. That's how she was able to cope with my dad's death."

Wally tried to sound indifferent, but her glistening eyes exposed her true feelings. She dabbed them with her napkin, swallowed hard, then continued. "Somebody once said, 'All the world's a stage, and all the men and women merely players. They have their exits and their entrances.'" Despite her pain, she managed to crack a smile. "It might've been Shakespeare. Either him or Kermit the Frog. I get those two mixed up."

Thank goodness for her quirky sense of humor.

"But this isn't just about me, is it?" she said. "I know you want to be able to date other girls, so . . ." Her voice trailed off.

"That's not it, Wally. I want to keep seeing you. The thing is, I'll probably be so busy with school and everything that I won't get to come home whenever I want."

She raised a hand to stop me when she saw the server coming with our food. "Hold that thought, Jessup. I'd rather break up on a full stomach than on an empty one."

I don't know if *love* is the word I would've used to describe how I felt about Wally at the time. But she was, without a doubt, the most incredibly fascinating girl I'd ever known. For a seventeen-year-old, she had the wisdom and knowledge of someone far older. Would it be possible to keep our relationship going while I was in college? Would she want to?

"Holy cats!" she cried, when she bit into one of her tacos. "I forgot how yummy these bad boys are. Try yours, Jessup. You'll think you died and went to Heaven."

The only decision Wally and I made that night concerning our breakup was to not discuss it anymore, not until we both felt the time was right. I did assure her that since Austin is less than an hour-and-a-half's drive from San Antonio, I'd do my best to come home as much as possible, and that I'd stay in constant communication with her.

What I didn't realize was that within a month, she'd no longer be my girlfriend.

CHAPTER SIX

The guys and I were hanging out in my bedroom waiting for *Monday Night Mayhem* to start. I was sitting on my bed, strumming chords on my guitar. Wendell and Bucky were on the floor, playing one of my video games, *Sun Gods II*, and Goose was slouched in my desk chair, compiling a list of possible ring names he might use once he became a wrestler. So far, he'd come up with Maximilian Guerrero, Salvador Balboa and Angelo Carrasco. And so far, we'd rejected each one.

"What about Jonathan Justice?" he asked, adding the name to his list. "I could wear Captain America-type shirt and blue tights."

"Seriously?" I said. "Jonathan Justice sounds like a superhero in a low-budget movie."

Goose sighed, then deleted it.

"Why don't you just go by Goose Guzmán?" Wendell asked. "I mean, that *is* your nickname."

"Naw, man. Nobody's gonna be intimidated by a guy called *Goose*."

"How about Gorilla Guzmán?" Bucky suggested. "That sounds scarier."

"Yeah, that would work . . . *if I was hairy and weighed four hundred pounds!*"

Goose came up with other names: Crusher Chacón, Osiris Orozco and Cuauhtémoc the Aztec Warrior. We said *no* to those, too.

"Let me give you some advice, Goose," I said. "I agree that eventually, you'll need a catchy ring name. But when you go to the tryouts, the best thing to do is to introduce yourself as Abel Guzmán. Don't even call yourself Goose. My father tends to frown on people who show up on the first day with a gimmick. He thinks they're more interested in becoming a star than in learning the craft."

"You're probably right," he said. "But I'm still gonna work on some names."

I could appreciate Goose's enthusiasm. Ring names I'd considered for myself when I fantasized of being a wrestler were the Angel of Death, Jr., or a variation of it—the Death Angel. Another idea I had was to dye my hair red and call myself Jesse "The Red" Baron.

Goose brainstormed a little longer. Then he got up and walked around my room, looking for something else to do. He removed my father's Annihilator mask from the Styrofoam head and asked if he could put it on.

I told him he could.

He pulled the mask over his head, tied the laces on the back, then stood in front of my mirror and flexed his biceps, the way I'd done many times before.

"Maybe when I become a wrestler, I'll wear a mask," he said.

"Good. That way, people won't have to see your ugly face," Bucky wisecracked.

"Hey, nobody's talking to you, Betty Crocker!"

Goose turned back to his reflection. Seconds later, he snapped his fingers. "I know what I'll call myself. Cyclone

Suárez. Suárez, because that's my mom's maiden name, and Cyclone . . ."

"Because you're a walking disaster?" Wendell interjected.

Bucky tee-heed. "That's a good one, Wendell. A walking disaster."

"I think that's a great name," I said. "It's strong, it has a nice ring to it, and it's easy to remember."

"Cyclone Suárez," Goose said to himself. "Or maybe Ciclón Suárez if I wear a mask and promote myself as a *luchador*."

He picked up my hairbrush from the dresser, and using it as a microphone, yelled into it, *"Ladies and gentlemen, introducing first. Weighing in at one-hundred-ninety pounds, from Mexico City, Mexico, the greatest* luchador *of all time . . . Cicló-ó-ón Suá-re-e-e-z!"*

The guys and I booed and made thumbs-down gestures as Goose paraded around my room, blowing kisses to his imaginary audience.

He stopped and posed in front of the mirror again. "You know what would be so cool? What if the four of us were to go to the prom wearing *lucha* masks?"

"Are you insane?" Wendell said. "In this day and age, do you really think we'd be allowed to walk into the ballroom of the Hilton, wearing masks? Security would be all over us in a second. Besides that, nobody in charge of the prom is going to let us wear them. They're picky enough as it is about the dress code."

"Hey, man, calm down," Goose said. "I'm just talking." He took off the mask and combed his hair with my brush.

Goose's idea was absurd, to say the least. Nevertheless, I thought Wally would get a kick out of me taking her to the prom wearing my father's mask. She thrived on doing things that set her apart from everyone else.

"I think we ought to do it," I said. "And we can if we get permission. Dr. Ríos is a huge wrestling fan. I'll bet that if we explain to him that we'd wear the masks strictly for laughs, he might go along with it."

Wendell wasn't swayed. "I don't know, man. Even if he lets us, I'm not sure Stacy would want to go to the prom with me if I told her I was wearing a wrestling mask."

"Yeah," Bucky said. "Ramona and her friends have been shopping for dresses, and I've heard them talking about who's going to do their hair and makeup and stuff. If I were to show up at her house with a mask on, she'd probably tell me to get lost and go to the prom without me."

The guys had a point. I hadn't thought about their dates.

"How about Yolanda?" I asked Goose. "What do you think she'll say?"

"Aw, you know her. She'll whine about it, like she does every time I wanna do something fun. But I'll still do it if the rest of you will."

We stared at Wendell and Bucky, hoping they'd reconsider.

"We won't keep the masks on all night," Goose said. "Maybe just when we first walk in. You know, to make a grand entrance. And after people take pictures of us . . ." His face lit up. "That's it! That's how you can talk your dates into it. Tell them that they'll be in more pictures than anybody else at the prom, even the king and queen. They'll love it. I know for sure Yolanda will. She's a photo hog."

"We *would* look awesome, wouldn't we?" Wendell said, now giving the idea a second thought.

"Hell yeah, we would!" Goose said. "We'll be the freakin' highlight of the evening. Imagine the four of us, dressed in tuxes and masks. We'll look like a *lucha libre* faction from CMLL or AAA."

"All right, I'll ask Stacy and see what she thinks."

We waited for Bucky.

"I guess Ramona will be okay with it," he said. "As long as she knows that she and I will get our pictures taken without me wearing a mask, too."

Goose slapped his hands together. "Let's do it then! We'll give everybody at the prom something to talk about for a long, long time."

I didn't want to douse the fire, but I had to remind the guys that we still needed to get permission from the principal, although I didn't foresee a problem. The gag was totally harmless.

"So where are we going to get the masks?" Wendell asked. He looked at me. "Do you have some we can borrow?"

"No, but there's a shop at El Mercado that sells them," I said. Seeing Goose's face souring, I added, "Don't worry. They aren't very expensive."

* * *

At eight o'clock, I turned on the TV.

With the roar of the live audience in the background of the Staples Center in Los Angeles, American Championship Wrestling commentators, Simon Graham and Moose McGirk, welcomed viewers to another exciting presentation of *Monday Night Mayhem*. They showed a recap of last week's matches, including a clip of Butcher Murdock attacking John Henry Sykes during Sykes' title bout against the ACW heavyweight champion, Solomon Grimm.

Grimm was disqualified due to Murdock's interference, but he still remained the champ, because according to ACW rules, a title can't change hands on a disqualification.

An enraged Sykes, having been cheated of his title opportunity, and wanting retribution, challenged Butcher Murdock to a match, setting up the evening's main event.

"I can't stand that guy," Goose said of Sykes. "I hope Murdock beats the crap out of him."

"That's good," I said.

He frowned at me, thinking I was being sarcastic.

"It doesn't matter whether you like him or not," I said. "John Henry Sykes got a reaction out of you, and that's what's important. As a wrestler, the last thing you want to hear when you step inside the ring is crickets chirping. I mean, if all you get from the audience is dead silence, I guarantee you, you won't last long in the business."

Graham and McGirk gave a rundown of the scheduled lineup. After that, Thunderbolt Jake Cassidy's music began to play. Cassidy ran out, high-fiving the audience as he made his way to the ring.

"I don't like that guy, either," Goose said. "He's always so happy."

"He's supposed to be happy," I said. "Cassidy's young and good looking, so the ACW has him playing a baby face. His character is meant to appeal more to little kids and soccer moms than to hardcore fans."

Next, Prince Romulus' music sounded. Immediately, the crowd began to boo. The boos became deafening when Romulus, accompanied by his manager, Lord Sterling, appeared onstage. The Prince, arms crossed, head held high, gazed arrogantly around the room. Lord Sterling wasn't nearly as composed. He paced back and forth on the entrance ramp, screaming like a maniac at the audience for jeering his client.

"If you play a heel, that's exactly the kind of heat you want to get," I told Goose.

Bucky tee-heed. "You'd be good at it, Goose, 'cause nobody likes you, anyway."

"Aw, go play with your Easy-Bake Oven," he said, and threw a pillow at him.

"When you start training, my father will teach you how to use ring psychology to tell stories," I said. "Because that's what pro wrestling's all about. Telling stories. You do it through your words, your moves, your facial expressions and your body language. You want to make the audience believe that everything you're doing is real, even if they know it's not."

In the past, I'd shared a lot of information about the inner workings of professional wrestling with the guys. But now that Goose was planning to become a wrestler, I wanted them to see the business from a different perspective.

As the match got underway, Prince Romulus pummeled Thunderbolt Cassidy with heavy rights and lefts. Then he swung him against the ropes with an Irish Whip. When Cassidy bounced back, the Prince threw another punch, but this time, Cassidy ducked and hit him with a clothesline. He followed it up with a standing dropkick. Lord Sterling quickly jumped on the ring apron in protest, distracting the referee. Meanwhile, the Prince thumbed Cassidy in the eye, and once again, took control of the match.

I continued to explain to the guys how the men were furthering their story through their actions. And the more I talked about it, the more my desire to become a wrestler grew.

Cassidy and Romulus may have learned their craft at a wrestling school, but I was born into the business. The way I saw it, wrestling was my birthright. I deserved the chance to step inside the ring and compete. The question was, how badly did I want it? And was I willing to go against my father to fulfill my dream?

The match came to an end when Cassidy caught Romulus with a roundhouse kick to the jaw, causing him to spin, cartoon-like, before collapsing. While the ref was checking on the Prince's condition, Cassidy climbed on a top turnbuckle and got ready for a Frog Splash. As he did, Lord Sterling snuck up behind him and pushed him off. Cassidy landed awkwardly on the mat, twisting his ankle. Romulus took advantage of the situation and locked his submission hold on him, the Procrustes Stretch. Cassidy struggled for a few seconds, then tapped out.

I figured Prince Romulus was going to win. He'd once defeated my father for the ACW heavyweight title, so he had more star power than Thunderbolt Cassidy. Still, I thought they'd put on a great match.

"Man, I can't wait to be a wrestler," Goose said, when the show went to a commercial break.

How I wished I could say the same thing.

CHAPTER SEVEN

Since I was the one who had suggested asking Dr. Ríos for permission to wear wrestling masks to the prom, I was the one chosen for the job. I tried to get Goose to go with me, reminding him that the mask idea was his to begin with, but because of the failing notices he'd gotten throughout the year, he was too embarrassed to meet with the principal.

Dr. Ríos smiled when I told him about our idea. "I'm surprised no one's thought of it before," he said. "Then again, we've never had a student whose dad was a world-famous wrestler."

My father had made an appearance at our school earlier in the year for Career Day. Knowing that Dr. Ríos was a wrestling fan, he gave him an autographed photo of himself as the Angel of Death. Dr. Ríos framed it, along with one he took of my father and him shaking hands. Both photos sat on his bookcase behind his desk.

"I won't be at the prom," he said. "But Ms. Kahn will. She'll be at the door, checking for tickets and dress-code violations. I'll let her know what you plan to do so she can tell the other chaperones about it."

"Thank you, sir," I said.

He came around his desk and walked me out the door. "You be sure to take lots of pictures, you hear? I'll see to it that they get posted on our school's website."

I had a feeling that one of those photos would soon join the other two on his bookcase.

* * *

After school, I drove the guys to Market Square, a popular San Antonio attraction, more commonly known as El Mercado.

The plaza was filled with tons of shops, where visitors could buy Talavera pottery, hand-woven blankets and leather goods, in addition to endless curios and souvenirs. There were also lots of places to eat at in the area, including the renowned Mexican restaurant, Mi Tierra Café. I loved their food, but Wally didn't like going there, calling it too "touristy."

Not far from Mi Tierra stood a vendor's booth that sold *lucha libre* masks and Mexican wrestling action figures. I'd browsed through there last time my parents and I ate at Mi Tierra but didn't buy anything.

The guys were astonished by the colorful masks hanging on the walls and racks, and sitting on tables.

"This place is awesome," Wendell told me. "Why haven't you brought us here before?"

"I don't know. I'm not much of a *lucha libre* fan. Although . . ." I stopped when I saw a Mil Máscaras mask hanging in a corner. I hadn't noticed it the last time I was there. The mask was a duplicate of the one TJ Masters gave me the first time I visited his apartment. It was silver, with black jagged trim around the eyes, nose and mouth, and a red M in the middle of the forehead. I didn't get to keep the mask long, though. Later that night, as a rib, TJ dared me to put it on the Deaf Smith statue at school.

The following morning, when the kids showed up, they laughed and took pictures of Deaf Smith, who now looked like a *luchador*. Unfortunately, Dr. Ríos confiscated the mask. I don't know what happened to it, but I would guess he had it somewhere in his house.

"Could you bring down that mask for me, please?" I asked the vendor.

He was a little guy with stringy hair. He appeared to be in his late thirties or early forties, but he had a thin mustache that looked like the type a fourteen-year-old might grow.

"*¿Cuál?*" he asked, looking in the direction where I was pointing.

"*La de Mil Máscaras*."

He picked up a pole, unhooked the mask and handed it to me.

"How much is it?" I asked "*¿Cuánto?*"

"*Treinta*," he said.

I gave it back to him. "Forget it. That's too much money. *Mucho dinero*."

I'd seen similar masks at a flea market that sold for fifteen dollars, so I figured I could get him to come down in price.

"Why do you want to buy a mask?" Goose asked me. "You already have your dad's."

"I know, but I told you what happened to the Mil Máscaras mask TJ gave me. I'd like to have another one."

"*Bueno, entonces veinticinco*," the vendor said.

"*Quince*," I counter offered.

"Twenty," he said in clear English. "That's my final price. Twenty, plus tax."

I got a little irritated with him for leading me to think that he couldn't speak English. Maybe it was a tactic he used with non-Spanish speakers so they wouldn't try to haggle with him.

"No tax," I said. "Twenty even."

He gave me a weasel-like grin. "Okay, you win," he said, although I had a feeling, he still thought he'd come out ahead on the deal. Sweeping his hands over his merchandise, he announced, "Special price today, my friends. All masks, twenty dollars."

While the guys looked them over, the vendor continued with his sales pitch. "These masks are imported all the way from Mexico. Handcrafted. Very fine quality." My father's Annihilator mask was custom designed, made of Lycra and leather. These were made out of much cheaper fabrics. But what did I expect for twenty bucks? Anyway, they'd be fine for the prom.

Goose decided on a mask of Último Dragón, Wendell, one of Octagón and Bucky chose a mask of El Audaz.

The vendor pulled a wad of bills from his pocket and added our money to it without giving us a receipt.

"Come back and see me, amigos," he said, grinning his weaselly grin again. "And be sure to tell your friends about my store."

I didn't care for that guy.

* * *

My mom insisted on going with me to rent a tuxedo, saying she wanted to make sure it fit properly. I was eighteen and about to graduate from high school, but in her eyes, I was still her baby. She drove me to Bloomberg's Formal Wear, a shop she found on the internet that had excellent ratings.

Evidently, she wasn't the only one who'd read the reviews. The store was bustling with clerks tending to guys my age, also needing prom tuxes. I felt embarrassed being the only one in there with his mom. Lucky for me, none of those guys were from my school.

A kindly old man with a head of wavy white hair and rosy cheeks introduced himself to us as Alvin Bloomberg, the store's owner. My mom explained why we were there. Then, like a magician who can make playing cards appear in his hand, Mr. Bloomberg whipped out a tape measure. He measured my height, my chest, the length of my arms and legs and my waist. Next, he showed us what he had available in my size.

My mom steered me away from the gaudy tuxedos, which wasn't necessary. The guys and I had decided to go with a James Bond look—a plain black tux, white shirt and a black bowtie. No cummerbund. No vest. Our *lucha* masks were all we'd need to stand out.

I selected a tux I liked, and Mr. Bloomberg took me to a dressing room to try it on. When I came out, my mom had me button the coat and turn around.

"How does it feel?" she asked.

"Okay, I guess."

She looked at Mr. Bloomberg. He tugged the front of the coat, then the pants waist. "I think it's fine," he said.

He also suggested that I rent a pair of dress shoes. "You don't want to go to the prom looking like a GQ model, with scruffy shoes, do you?"

He measured my feet, then brought out a pair of black patent leather shoes. I tried them on. They felt almost as comfortable as my sneakers.

Before changing back to my regular clothes, I asked my mom to take my picture. The guys hadn't rented their tuxes yet, and I wanted to show them what I'd chosen, so they'd know which style to get.

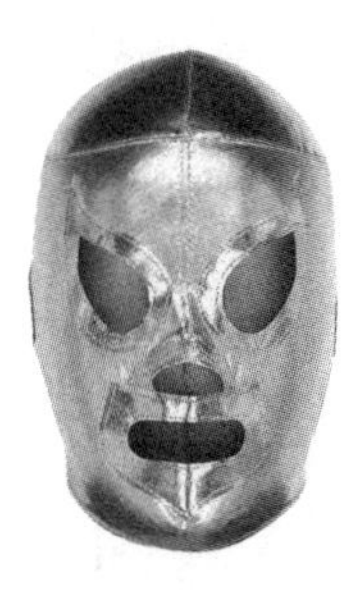

CHAPTER EIGHT

The week of the prom was full of senior activities. Some of them were stupid, such as dressing up like a kindergartener one day and a senior citizen the next. We had Retro Day. We had Western Day. Thursday, we attended Senior Luncheon, which sounds fancy, but it was just fajitas grilled by some of the PTA parents. The luncheon was held at Salazar Park, down the street from our school.

Friday night was the prom.

I had planned on driving Wally to it, but my parents surprised me by renting a limo for my friends and me. I told the guys and their dates to meet at my house at seven.

Wally was the first to arrive. Her mom came with her to visit with my parents and to help with the after-prom dessert party they were hosting for us. I think the limo and the party was their way of ensuring that we didn't go anywhere or do anything inappropriate after the dance.

Wally wore a short, sequined, turquoise-colored, form-fitting dress, with a gold bolero jacket and gold high heels. She also had on makeup, which was rare for her. In fact, I don't think I'd ever seen her with makeup other than when she was performing on stage. Or jewelry, for that matter.

My parents gushed over how glamorous she looked and how her dress matched beautifully with her blue-green hair. Her mom, in turn, raved about my appearance. They took photos of us. Then they went to the living room to chat, while Wally and I waited in the den for the others.

Once we were alone, I kissed her and said, "You look amazing. I feel like I'm taking Cinderella to the ball."

"Meh," she replied, brushing off the compliment. "It was my mom's idea to paint my face. She picked out this dress, too. And the pearls and earrings. But I'm still going to wear these." Wally opened her green messenger bag to show me her red, high-top sneakers. "If I'm going to dance all night, I'll need something more comfortable than these stripper heels I have on. They're another torture device my mom forced me to wear. I'll change shoes when we get in the car."

Wally would never admit it, but I had a suspicion that, secretly, she enjoyed dressing up. No one could look as stunning as she did and be unhappy about it.

She adjusted my bowtie and smoothed down the lapels on my coat. "You're not bad looking yourself, Jessup. You sort of remind me of . . ."

"Bond," I said, in a deep, smarmy voice. "James Bond."

"No, I was thinking about the Penguin from the *Batman* comics."

"Quack, quack, quack," I said, imitating Burgess Meredith in the old *Batman* TV series.

"Jesse?" my mom called. "Don't forget to give Wally the . . . you know what."

"I was just about to do that!" I shouted back. "She's such a mom," I complained to Wally. "Come on, let's go to the kitchen. I have something for you."

I opened the fridge and took out a plastic box that contained a wrist corsage of gold and white roses and a matching boutonniere.

"Geez and crackers," Wally grumbled. "So in addition to all this nonsense, I have to wear a plant, too?"

"You might as well get used to it," I said. "Because you'll be doing it again next year, when you're a senior."

Our moms followed us into the kitchen. When Wally's mom saw the corsage, she said, "Oh, how lovely. And it goes perfect with your bolero jacket, and your . . . wait. Where's the clutch purse I bought you?"

"No worries. I have it right here." Wally took out a small gold purse from her messenger bag.

"*Ay, muchacha.* I don't understand why you're dragging that ugly messenger bag around," her mom said. "You should've left it at home."

"I told you. It's for my comfy shoes, in case these high heels start hurting my feet, and I have to change out of them. But I'll leave my messenger bag in the car. I promise."

What Wally didn't mention was that the "comfy shoes" were her sneakers.

Her mom helped her with the corsage, and my mom pinned the boutonniere on my lapel. She kissed me on the cheek and said, "You look so suave and debonair, Jesse. I'll bet that if some Hollywood producers were to see you right now, they'd want to cast you as the next James Bond."

I smirked at Wally. "See?"

She stuck her tongue out at me.

At ten till seven, the guys and their dates began arriving, and by five after, everyone was there.

Stacy, Ramona and Yolanda, like Wally, were elegantly dressed and had wrist corsages. Goose, Bucky and Wendell wore tuxedos similar to mine.

When Wally saw the guys and me together, she said, "I didn't know they were holding auditions for the new *Batman* movie at the Hilton."

Goose looked at her, puzzled. "What's that supposed to mean?"

"Ask Jessup. He'll tell you," she said, and walked away.

Goose turned to me.

"Nothing," I said, smiling.

"*Está loca*," he muttered.

My friends' parents came, too, to take pictures. And man, did they ever. They took photos of us as couples. Of the girls. Of the guys. As a group. Individually. Each guy and girl with their parents.

The wrestling fans asked my father if he'd pose with them, and he gladly obliged.

The one photo no one took, however, was of the guys and me in our wrestling masks. We didn't want to have to explain why we were wearing them to the prom, so we kept them hidden inside our coats, folded over the waists of our pants. We knew our parents would eventually see pictures of us with the masks on, but by then it wouldn't matter.

The paparazzi-like photo frenzy continued outside as we stood next to the white limo, which had been parked in our driveway for about fifteen minutes.

The driver introduced himself to us as Malcolm. He dressed in a black suit, a white shirt and a black-and-white striped necktie, with a black chauffeur's cap and black gloves. He opened the doors for us, and we climbed in.

Before he drove away, my father walked over to him. "Remember what I told you, Malcolm. I want you to stay in the Hilton parking lot the entire time. If my son and his friends need to leave early, I don't want them having to wait for you."

"Yes, sir, Mr. Baron. I'll take real good care of them. And thanks again for the Angel of Death picture. My kid went crazy over it when I gave it to him. Like I told you, you're his all-time favorite wrestler."

The limo came equipped with WIFI and a terrific sound system to which I was able to connect my phone, and we could listen to music. It was also stocked with soft drinks, juices, water bottles, chips and cookies.

As we rode, we snacked and took selfies, then posted our photos on social media. Wally took off her "stripper heels" and put on her sneakers.

Goose fiddled with the sunroof button but couldn't get the panel open. "Hey, Malcolm, can you open the sunroof for us so we can stand up and look out?"

"Well, normally, I don't do that. You know, for safety reasons," he said. "Tell you what. I'll open the sunroof when we stop at a red light. You can poke your heads out then. But the second the light turns green, you need to come back inside. Everyone clear on that?"

We agreed.

"Just so you don't freak out, Malcolm," I said, "my friends and I are going to put on wrestling masks."

He laughed. "Why am I not surprised?"

The guys were wrong about the girls. They loved the idea of us wearing masks to the prom.

"People are going to think we're dating real wrestlers," Ramona said.

"We'll look like we're going out with superheroes," Stacy added.

Yolanda was fine with Goose wearing a mask—except for one complaint: "I wish you'd worn the mask of a wrestler that kids'll recognize, like Rey Mysterio, or somebody like him."

"Man, quit your whining, Yolanda," he said. "Nobody's gonna care whose mask I have on."

I didn't expect anyone to recognize my father's Annihilator mask, either, but I decided to wear it, because after trying on the Mil Máscaras one, I found my father's mask to be much more comfortable. Still, I was glad I'd bought it. TJ used to have a wall in his apartment covered with all kinds of wrestling masks, and I'd often thought about starting my own collection.

At the first red light, Malcolm slid open the sunroof panel. Goose and I stood up, but the street was empty.

"Wait till we get downtown," Malcolm said. "There'll be a lot more traffic there."

He kept driving until he reached a busy intersection. As soon as the light turned red, Goose and I stuck our bodies through the opening. We pumped our fists in the air and began chanting, "Lu-cha! Lu-cha! Lu-cha!"

The drivers around us smiled and waved, perhaps thinking we were actual Mexican wrestlers.

Wendell and Bucky did the same thing at the next light.

When we stopped again, Goose started to get up, but Wally yanked him back down. "Come on, Goose. Give us a chance. We want to look out, too."

"That's right," the girls said.

"Whatever," he mumbled, and stayed in his seat.

Wally and Yolanda pulled themselves up. They waved and hooted at pedestrians and drivers. A lot of them waved back, but one idiot crossing the street began shouting obscenities at them. Yolanda fired back with two middle fingers and a few choice words of her own.

We laughed hysterically, but Malcolm didn't think it was funny. When Stacy and Ramona took their turn at the following light, he cautioned them not to do or say anything that would anger people.

Soon, we neared the Alamo. I asked Malcolm if he'd stop for a few minutes so we could take pictures in front of the historic landmark. Malcolm parked the limo next to the plaza, and we got out, the guys and me in our masks. Visitors and tourists strolling through the grounds began taking photos of us. We stopped and posed for them, but Malcolm interrupted us, saying, "If you want me to take pictures of you in front of the Alamo, I've gotta do it fast, 'cause I'm parked illegally."

For the sake of time, I told the group to let Malcolm use my phone and that I'd send the photos to them. He took several shots, then herded us back to the limo. From there, we rode to the Hilton.

* * *

Couples and groups, dressed in tuxedos and prom dresses, congregated outside the hotel. The moment Malcolm pulled into the entrance driveway, they stopped talking and stared at the limo's tinted windows, trying to see who was inside.

Wendell told us, "We'd better take off our masks. I don't want us getting in trouble with security when we go in."

"Naw, man," Goose said. "It's prom night. We've got the girls with us. Nobody's gonna think we're terrorists."

Goose was right. The whole purpose of wearing wrestling masks was to attract attention. Why wait until we went inside the ballroom?

I had an idea.

"Malcolm, can you do us another huge favor?" I asked.

"Name it, and I'll try."

"Will you pretend to be our bodyguard? You know, like movie stars have, and act as if you're keeping our fans away from us?"

Malcolm stood over six feet and weighed at least two hundred and fifty pounds. He actually could be a bodyguard.

"It'll be my pleasure." He took his sunglasses out of the console and put them on to project a more intimidating image.

To the guys, I said, "When we get out, let's act arrogant, the way Prince Romulus does. Don't talk to anybody until we reach the ballroom. It'll make us look cooler."

"What about the girls and me?" Wally asked. "What do you want us to do?"

"You're in theater arts," I said. "I'm sure you'll think of something."

"Gotcha. Okay, ladies. Follow my lead."

I could understand why my father enjoyed being a celebrity. It was exhilarating having strangers marvel at you. I'd felt it at the Alamo, and now, as I gazed through the windows at the prom goers waiting with anticipation to see who was going to come out of the limo, I felt the same rush sweep over me.

Although I'd denied it to my father, one of the reasons I wanted to be a wrestler was because of the fame that came with it. I'd always been shy and tended to keep to myself. Part of it had to do with my having to switch schools a lot, which made it difficult for me to make close friends. Also, I was never at a school long enough for teachers to notice anything special about me. To them, I was just another transient student who'd be gone soon.

The only thing I'd ever been known for was that my father was the Angel of Death, and that didn't do me any good when I played football. Despite my father and grandfather talking to Coach Blaylock about putting me in the games more often, I spent most of the time standing on the sidelines. No wonder I sucked as a player.

If I was an ACW wrestler, things would be different. I'd be on television, in magazines, and all over the internet. People would idolize me. They'd beg for my autograph and try to get their picture taken with me. As for possibly getting injured, I figured the risks weren't any different from the ones athletes in other sports took. My father was right. I *did* want to be the

ACW heavyweight champion. More than anything in the world.

"You ready?" Malcolm asked us.

"Yeah," we said.

"Wait for my signal."

He stepped out of the limo and shut the door behind him. Standing rigid, he swiveled his head slowly, as if scanning the area for possible threats. The prom goers, intrigued by the imposing figure, followed his movements. Malcolm stopped momentarily, appearing to zero in on something suspicious. Some people shrank back, ready to run and hide in case the danger was real. He took one more look around. Then he opened our doors and gave us an all-clear nod. We exited the limo, with him standing in front of us, arms outstretched like a protective barrier.

It took only seconds for everyone to realize the whole thing was a charade. The guys and I were masked, but our dates weren't, and we were easily identified.

"That has to be Wendell Cooley because Stacy Hobbs is with him."

"And the little guy with Ramona Allen is probably Bucky Henderson."

"I'll bet you that's Jesse Baron 'cause he dates that junior with the weird hair."

"Hey, Yoli! Is that Goose with you?"

Sam Morales laughed and clapped. "That is such a freakin' awesome idea. Man, I wish I'd thought of it. Way to go, guys!"

Without acknowledging anyone, we puffed our chests, locked arms with our dates and filed into the hotel behind Malcolm. Out of the corner of my eye, I caught a glimpse of the girls. They had their noses in the air and were flicking their hands as if they were shooing away onlookers. All the while, people took photos of us—dozens and dozens, it seemed like.

Masked, I felt completely uninhibited. I wasn't boring old Jesse Baron, graduating senior. I was a *lucha libre* superstar!

I thought back to the time when TJ invited me to a Halloween party at his apartment complex. Because I was underage, I wasn't allowed inside the clubhouse where the party was being held. So TJ let me borrow a brown wrestling mask and introduced me to everyone as a veteran ACW wrestler named Sweet Brown Coffey.

The mask gave me the confidence to flirt with a woman who was at least seven or eight years older than me. I could tell she liked me—until I was forced to take off the mask, and she found out I was just a high school kid. Needless to say, she became disgusted, not only with me, but also with TJ, for making her think I was a lot older. Still, with the mask on, I became a different person, same as I was tonight.

"Give them room!" Malcolm barked at the guests. "Let them through!"

We walked across the lobby to the escalator and rode it to the second floor.

At last, we made it to the ballroom. A rustic wooden sign hanging on a stand outside the doors read, THE ENCHANTED FOREST, the prom's theme.

Malcolm gave me his business card. "I'll be in the parking lot. Text me whenever you're ready, and I'll bring the limo to the front and wait for you there. Or if you'd like, I can come back up here and escort you to the car."

"Thanks," I said, "but we don't need for you to pretend to be our bodyguard anymore. We'll meet you outside. Listen, Malcolm, we really appreciate everything you've done for us."

"That's what I'm here for," he said, with a tip of his cap. "Y'all enjoy your evening."

After he left, we formed a line in the hallway like a wedding processional. The group decided that since my parents had rented the limo, Wally and I would go in first.

The ballroom was decorated with artificial foliage and trees to simulate a forest. It had animal topiaries, oversized toadstools, statues of elves, a lamppost, a wishing well and an arched, wooden bridge. Fairies and giant butterflies hung from the ceiling, in between strings of white twinkling lights.

The DJ was playing a Kat Martin song, and some people were dancing to it. Others were either eating or milling about, visiting with friends and taking selfies.

Whatever they were doing, they stopped and gawked at us the minute we entered the room. Then they broke into spontaneous cheers and applause. Somebody started a "*lucha*" chant, and within seconds, almost everyone joined in. "Lu-cha! Lu-cha! Lu-cha!"

We pumped our fists in the air and chanted along with them. "Lu-cha! Lu-cha! Lu-cha!"

I thought the chaperones were going to stop us, but they just smiled and waited for the noise to die out.

Ms. Kahn, one of our assistant principals, called us to the table where she and Ms. Delaney, a guidance counselor, were checking prom tickets.

"Dr. Ríos told us to expect some masked wrestlers," Ms. Kahn said good-naturedly. "You guys look great. And you girls are absolutely gorgeous."

We thanked her and presented our tickets. Ms. Delaney handed us programs of the evening's activities. "Be sure to get your pictures taken," she said, pointing to the professional photo booth. "And don't forget to vote for king and queen."

By that time, we had dropped our act. We chatted with friends who'd gathered around us to talk about how ingenious we were for coming up with the mask idea. Tommy

Kaliszewski put his arms around the guys and me and told Lydia Martínez, his date, to take our picture. Alberto Chapa scooted in for the next one. We took a few more. Then we made our way to the photo area.

The back wall of the booth had a forest scene to match the prom's theme. When the photographer saw us, she said, "In all my years of doing proms, I've never seen this before. You guys aren't real wrestlers, are you?"

"Not yet," Goose said. "But I will be, pretty soon."

She took photos of us as a group, then as couples, with the guys and me masked and unmasked. After that, we decided to keep our masks off for a while.

Early in the week, seniors were encouraged to nominate candidates for prom king and queen. The student council had tallied the numbers, and the names of the finalists now appeared on ballot cards, which Mrs. Dowell, the teacher in charge of the voting table, gave us to mark.

"Hey, did you guys see who's on here?" Wendell asked, pointing to Riley King's name.

"Yeah," Bucky said. "And did you notice that he's with Darlene Willis, and not Sara Young?"

"I heard they broke up," Ramona said. "But Sara's here. I saw her sitting with Pauline Garrett and Alma Flores and some other girls when we came in. She's over there somewhere."

"*Ay, pobrecita*," Yolanda said derisively. "Couldn't find a date for the prom." She elbowed me in the ribs. "That's what she gets for what she did to you, right?"

I wished I still had on my mask because I could feel my face reddening.

"Are you talking about Jessup's ex-girlfriend?" Wally asked.

"Yeah. Sara dumped him for Riley 'cause she thought she was too good for him, and now Riley's dumped her for that *cara de burra,* Darlene."

"Come on, Yolanda," I said. "That happened a long time ago. Sara doesn't mean anything to me. Wally's the only girl I care about."

Wally fluttered her eyelashes at me. "Oh, Rhett, you *do* give a damn."

Wendell chuckled at her *Gone with the Wind* reference, but I don't think anyone else got it.

"Those two deserve each other," Stacy said. "They're both stuck up and full of themselves."

I didn't have a problem with Darlene Willis, but the girls did. Riley King, though, had made my life miserable the entire time I was on the football team. He was the star quarterback, and I was a lousy backup center, and he never missed an opportunity to remind me of it. Even as recently as last month, he kept staring at me while he was bragging about his football scholarship to Ohio State.

"Hey, you know what we ought to do?" Bucky said, smiling mischievously. "Let's vote for Riley and Darlene for king and queen."

Wendell scowled at him. "What's the matter with you, man? Didn't you hear what we said? We can't stand either one of them."

"That's exactly why. If they win, we'll put on our masks and take the attention away from them when they have the Coronation Dance."

"I like how you think, Bucky boy," Wally said. She looked down at her sneakers. "I've got my stompers on. Jessup and I will burn circles around those two posers."

We decided to go along with Bucky and cast our votes for our least favorite couple on the ballot.

From there, we headed to the buffet line. The food was mostly appetizers: veggies and fruits, cheese and crackers, pastas, Swedish meatballs, mini eggrolls, quesadillas and chicken strips, plus iced tea and lemonade.

We served ourselves, then found the table that had been reserved for us. While we were eating, friends stopped by to say hi. Jerry Patrick and Rashaad Williams asked if they could borrow our masks, but we said no. We didn't want anyone taking credit for our idea.

After a while, Wally and I made our way to the dance floor. The DJ's music was a mixture of pop, classic rock, Latin hip hop, rap and *bachata*. I wasn't much of a dancer, but with so many people around us, I don't think anyone noticed.

At the scheduled time, Mrs. Dowell stopped the music and stood in the middle of the room to announce the prom king and queen winners. We were a little disappointed that Riley and Darlene's names weren't called. The honors went to Greg Evans and Helen Chu. They were a nice couple, and I was happy for them. Mrs. Dowell presented Greg and Helen with cheesy crowns and sashes, then turned the floor over to them for the Coronation Dance.

Following their number, everyone was invited to join them. The minute Riley and Darlene got up to dance, the guys and I slipped on our masks, and we and our dates danced as close to them as we could.

Our strategy worked. No one paid any attention to Riley and Darlene—and regrettably, neither to Greg and Helen. As Goose had predicted, we became the "freakin' highlight of the evening."

I happened to glance over at Sara Young. She was sitting with her friends, looking downcast, perhaps wishing she'd stayed home. I have to say that I took satisfaction in knowing I'd gotten the last laugh on her and Riley.

I tried not to dwell on it, though. They were part of my past. What mattered most to me was that I was having the time of my life at my senior prom with Wally Morúa, the only girl I'd ever . . . loved?

CHAPTER NINE

As tired as I was from the night before, I got up early Saturday for a quick breakfast and my regular morning jog. I tried to run at least four or five times a week. Wally called it a discipline, but I didn't think of it that way. Jogging was such a part of my life that any time I didn't run, I felt an emptiness inside.

After my jog, I drove to the Factory to continue my workout. My father was putting on a show that evening, so some of the wrestlers were already there, going over their matches. Oona Sifuentes, whose stage name was Oona the Enchantress, and Janiya Jenkins, who went by Sparkle, were inside the main ring, practicing moves and counter moves. Steve Dalton and King Jordan Crabtree were discussing possible finishes, and Travis McKeon was sitting with Kendric Scott and Xavion Strange. They were watching a video of Kendric and Xavion's last match, and Travis was offering them pointers on how to sell their punches better. The rest of the roster would come in throughout the day. My father wouldn't get to the Factory until around four.

I greeted everyone, then went to the fitness room to begin my drills. I started on the dip station to work my upper body. Next, on the Hammer Strength machine. Halfway through my sets, my phone chimed a text alert. When I saw who the message was from, I flinched in surprise.

Awesome pics of you wearing your pop's mask to your prom. I'm gonna be in town tomorrow. Let's get together for lunch.

I hadn't heard from TJ Masters in over a year. And the last time I saw him in person, he was lying unconscious in a Mexican hospital, hooked up to all kinds of machines.

TJ wanted to go to Nuevo Laredo to buy steroids, but he needed a translator. He figured that since I'm Latino, I spoke Spanish fluently. I told him I only knew a few words and phrases. He said that was good enough for him, and he talked me into driving with him to Mexico to help him get what he wanted. While we were there, a bunch of thugs attacked and robbed us in an alley. I managed to survive the assault with a few bumps and bruises, but TJ was so badly beaten, he wasn't able to wrestle for months.

I'd been aware that the ACW was bringing *Monday Night Mayhem* to San Antonio, and I assumed he was going to be on the show, but I didn't think he'd want to see me. He must've known that my family still hadn't forgiven him for taking me to Mexico without their permission. What especially angered my father was that he'd recommended TJ for a job with the ACW and had helped him get adjusted after the company hired him. He saw TJ's negative influence on me as a betrayal of that trust.

Wally had never met TJ, but I'd told her stories about him. Like the time we were pulled over and I was almost arrested, after TJ, who was drunk, got mouthy with the police officer and tried to pick a fight with him. And about the time he got us kicked out of the Alamodome during an MMA event, when he shoved one of the fighters and challenged him to a match.

Wally referred to him as a "nogoodnik," and she was right. TJ was wild and reckless and had huge problems with authority.

But until the incident in Mexico, I'd never had as much fun as I did when I hung out with him. TJ used to let me drive his car, even though I only had a learner's permit. He went to my football games, something my father never did. He took me to the UFC fights and bought me dinner. He invited me to work out with him in the fitness center at his apartment complex, and he taught me which vitamins and supplements to take to boost my strength and energy.

I read his message again.

Awesome pics of you wearing your pop's mask to your prom.

The only way he could've seen my photos was if he followed me on social media, which made me feel flattered, knowing I was still on his radar.

I'm gonna be in town tomorrow. Let's get together for lunch.

Although I was excited to hear from TJ, I wasn't sure I wanted him back in my life. I knew my parents would be upset with me if they found out I'd been in contact with him.

Then I thought, what can be the harm in seeing him for a couple of hours? It wasn't as if I was going to start hanging out with him again. TJ didn't live in San Antonio anymore. Tuesday morning, he'd either catch a flight home, wherever that was, or travel to the next city, if he was booked to wrestle at a "house show," an untelevised event.

The problem with getting together with him on Sunday afternoon was that my parents would expect me to go to church with them and then out to eat. Church was non-negotiable, but I could skip lunch if I told them I'd made plans with Wally.

If I decided to meet with TJ, it'd have to be at a place where neither my parents nor Wally were likely to show up. After mulling it over, I wrote back.

It's good to hear from you, TJ. Let's have lunch at the Taco Bell near my school at 1.

He answered right away.

I didn't know you had a taste for fine dining. OK, Taco Hell it is. See you there.

TJ's texts made me lose interest in exercising, so I called it quits for the day and drove home.

When I walked in the house, I found Frank Collins from American Championship Wrestling sitting in the living room, talking to my father. He'd been in town, making preparations for *Monday Night Mayhem.*

"Good gracious!" he exclaimed. "Jesse, is that you?" He rose from the couch and shook my hand. "I hardly recognized you."

"It's been a while since you've seen him," my father said.

Mr. Collins squeezed my biceps. "Man, what do they feed you around here? Iron and steel?"

"I try to stay in shape," I said modestly.

"I can tell. Are you planning to follow in your old man's footsteps and become a wrestler, too?"

Before I could answer, my father jumped in. "Maybe after he finishes college, Frank. But not anytime soon."

I think Mr. Collins caught on that he'd asked a touchy question because he changed the subject. "Guess what, Jesse? I just talked Mark into appearing on our show Monday night."

"Really? That's great," I said, but I wasn't surprised. With *Monday Night Mayhem* coming to town, it seemed only natural for Mr. Collins to want to involve my father in it. "Who are you going to wrestle, Dad?"

"Nobody. I'm a little too rusty for that. I'm just doing a spot with Gunnar Brooks. Frank's idea is for me to . . . well, I won't spoil it for you. Let's just say that Gunnar's going to wish he'd never gotten in the ring with the Angel of Death."

"Have you told Mom?" I asked, thinking about the fights they used to have over his career.

"Not yet, but she won't mind. It's just a one-shot deal. As a matter of fact, Frank wants to use her in our segment, somehow."

Whatever they had planned, I knew the fans would go bat crazy over it. The ACW still received tons of emails, asking when my father was going to wrestle again.

"Mr. Collins?" I said. "Would it be possible to get tickets to the show for my girlfriend and me?"

I had wanted to take Wally to *Monday Night Mayhem*, but I waited too long to buy tickets, and the event was officially sold out.

"Of course. I have a handful of promo passes left. I'll be glad to give you a couple of them. It's the least I can do, considering that Mark's appearing on our show and he's letting us use his building."

"I'm opening the Factory tomorrow," my father said. "That way, the ACW boys and gals can work out in private, instead of having to use their hotels' fitness rooms."

Whenever my father used to be out on the road, he'd exercise at his hotel or at a local gym. But if he was in town, he always used the facilities at the Ox Mulligan Pro Wrestling Factory.

"I'll text everyone to let them know about your offer, Mark," Mr. Collins said. "I'll also write to Shirley and Connie and tell them to bring your outfit and makeup kit."

Shirley Washington sewed the wrestlers' ring gear and was responsible for storing them. Connie Herrera headed the makeup department.

"Tomorrow after church, I'm going to need for you to go to the Factory with me to help out," my father told me. "We'll pick up burgers on the way."

I'd already set the time to meet with TJ at one o'clock, and I didn't want to change it. "Sorry, Dad, but Wally and I are getting together for lunch," I said.

"That's fine. When you're done, bring her to the Factory. I know she'll love meeting the wrestlers."

"I . . . I can't. I mean, Wally's going with her mom to the hospital to visit a sick aunt as soon as we finish eating."

"Ah, that's too bad. Well, on Monday, I'll invite her backstage and introduce her to everyone."

When he said that, I realized I couldn't take Wally to *Monday Night Mayhem*. If I did, my father would likely mention the Factory to her, saying how he was sorry that she couldn't watch the wrestlers prepare for their matches. And he'd want to know how her sick aunt was doing. I didn't want to ask Wally to cover for me because of her attitude toward TJ.

It occurred to me that the problem I used to have when I hung out with TJ Masters was the same one I was dealing with now—having to lie to my family about him.

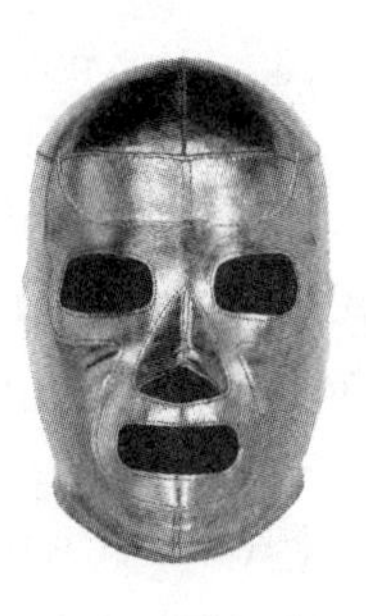

CHAPTER TEN

TJ was sitting in his car when I pulled next to him in the Taco Bell parking lot. We got out and exchanged greetings and hugs.

"Damn, you've hulked up," he said. "I know you didn't get that way eating here."

I'd put on almost twenty pounds of muscle and grown two inches since the last time he saw me. "I hit the weights as much as I can," I said. "And I jog almost every day."

"Well, whatever you're doing, it's working." TJ ran his hand across the hood of my Dodge Challenger. "I see you've also developed the same taste in cars as me."

"My father gave it to me for my birthday," I said. "He knew how much I liked your car, so he bought me one like it."

"Outstanding. I wish I was driving mine right now, instead of this cheap rental," he said, looking at his blue Ford Fiesta. "C'mon, let's go inside. I'm starving."

While we were standing at the counter studying the menu board, one of the ladies in the back pointed to TJ. She mouthed something to her coworker that made her smile. TJ caught the women staring and winked at them.

"They know who I am," he said. "They just don't know how to approach me 'cause I'm a jobber. That's what I do these days, job to whoever the ACW puts in front of me. Monday, it'll be Jumbo Jefferson."

TJ wasn't exaggerating. I watched *Monday Night Mayhem* every week, and I couldn't recall the last time he'd won a match.

He ordered the Nachos BellGrande, plus six beef tacos and a Coke. I'd had a big breakfast, so I kept my meal light, with three chicken tacos and an iced tea. The cashier brought our food, and we found a place to sit.

My tacos were okay, but they couldn't compare to the incredibly delicious ones I'd eaten at Casa Guanajuato.

"I guess you heard that my father retired and bought the Ox Mulligan Pro Wrestling Factory," I told TJ.

"Yeah, I knew that. And of course, Collins sent everybody a text about how your pops has opened the Factory for us today. I'd like to go 'cause that's where I did my training when Ox was running the school, but I don't think your pops would appreciate it if I showed up."

I wanted to tell him he was wrong, except that I'd be lying. If TJ were to go to the Factory, there was a possibility my father would confront him and cause a scene.

"I'm sure you'll have plenty of time to go over your match with Jumbo at the Alamodome," I said.

TJ chuckled. "Hey, remember when we got kicked out of there? Now I'm wrestling in the same arena where the cops threw me out. Kind of ironic, ain't it?"

"I guess," I said, hating being reminded of that scary episode. "So, what have you been up to? I mean, since you left San Antonio."

"Well, after the thing in Nuevo Laredo, I moved in with my parents in Amarillo to recuperate," he said. "I live in Albuquerque now. In the meantime, I lost the minor push the ACW was giving me. They were planning to have me fight

Judson Tanner at a pay-per-view, but that went down the toilet real fast once I got hurt. I even heard a rumor that your pops tried to get me fired."

"That's not true," I said. "My father doesn't do things behind anybody's back. He's not that kind of person."

"Whatever. Anyway, even if they wanted to, the ACW couldn't 'cause I was still under contract, but that didn't mean they had to continue my push. So as soon as I was cleared to wrestle, they put me back on jobber status."

I understood where TJ was coming from. In his time with the company, he'd been used primarily as enhancement talent. Most wrestlers start out that way, but eventually, they want to move up and perhaps get a title run.

"The good thing is that Mr. Collins uses you a lot," I said. "Even in squash matches, which means that he sees potential in you."

"Hey, don't get me wrong. I ain't complaining. I'd much rather be part of the action than part of the audience."

As we visited, I learned that TJ decided to move to Albuquerque because he was a fan of the TV series, *Breaking Bad* and *Better Call Saul*, and he wanted to live in the city where the shows had been filmed. He also told me he was dating Jeannie Stone, an ACW wrestler, but that she hadn't made the trip with him because she wasn't going to appear on *Monday Night Mayhem*.

He finished his Nachos BellGrande, then started on his tacos. "Before I forget," he said, "I want to congratulate you on your graduation."

"Thanks. The ceremony will be in a couple of weeks."

"I'll have to buy you a present. I'll pick up a gift card for you on the way out. Is five bucks, okay?"

I couldn't tell if he was joking because he looked and sounded serious. Then he grinned, and we both cracked up. Same old TJ, I thought. Easy going and fun to be around.

I told him about my parents getting remarried. I also told him about Wally and my school year and about getting accepted to the University of Texas. TJ acted surprised, but if he followed me on social media, he knew everything, because I posted stuff all the time.

"So what was the deal with the wrestling masks?" he asked. "I can't believe they let you wear them to the prom."

I laughed. "It was something my friends and I did for a gag. My principal watches wrestling, and he gave us permission to wear them."

"Man, I wish I'd been able to do that at mine," he said. "You know, when I saw your pics, I wondered if you and your buddies were making a statement."

"Like what?"

"That y'all were gonna get into pro wrestling."

"My friend Goose is," I said. "After graduation, he's going to start training with my father at the Factory."

"Outstanding. How about you?"

"I'd like to, but . . ."

"But what?"

I looked down at the remnants of lettuce left over from my tacos and flicked them aside with a finger. "My father doesn't want me to wrestle. He says I need to go to college first."

"Oh, brother," TJ groaned. "I used to hear the same song from my pops. He wanted me to go to Texas Tech to study law like him, so you can imagine how he reacted when I told him I was gonna be a wrestler. Well, guess what, Jesse? Even as a jobber, I make more money than he does, and he's the chief felony prosecutor in Amarillo. Look, I know you respect your pops and everything, but you're an adult now. You can't let him run your life for you."

"It's not just him," I said. "My mom and my grandparents and a lot of my uncles and aunts, they have college degrees, and they expect me to get mine, too."

"Second verse, same as the first," TJ said scornfully. "Let me straighten you out on something, Jesse, and I'm speaking from experience. College ain't for everybody. It sure as hell wasn't for me, and it might not be right for you, either. Besides, no matter what kind of degree you get, you'll never make as much money with it as you would if you were wrestling for the ACW. I mean, there's no way your pops could've made millions working as a cop." Chortling, he added, "Unless he was on the take."

"Yeah, but even if I decide to wrestle, there's no guarantee that I'll ever get hired by the ACW," I said.

"Of course there is! Your pops is the freakin' Angel of Death. Collins would sign you up in a second. I started wrestling when I was your age and look at me now. So just think where you'll be in six years with the connections and background you have."

I didn't know why I was arguing with TJ. My dream had been to become an ACW wrestler. Yet, something about his rationale and the way he was being so insistent didn't seem right.

As he continued talking, I realized he was indeed the same old TJ. The one who used to make me do things that went against my better judgment. The one who turned me against my friends. The one who almost got me killed in Mexico.

My father told me that TJ wasn't well liked backstage, and that Bronko Savage once kicked him out of the locker room, calling him an egotistical jackass. Maybe that was the reason he'd sought me out from the beginning, because he didn't have any friends in the ACW, and he figured he could win over an impressionable sixteen-year-old, who'd make him feel important.

Well, I wasn't sixteen anymore, and for the first time, I saw TJ for what he was; a manipulative, insecure loser. Was he even dating Jeannie Stone, as he claimed? I followed a lot of wrestling websites, and I'd never read anything about them being together. How convenient was it for him to use the fact that she wasn't traveling with the ACW as an excuse for why she wasn't with him?

My gut instinct—my Spidey sense, as Wally would call it—was now screaming at me to get away from him.

"I hate to cut our visit short, TJ," I said. "But I have to go. My father's waiting for me at the Factory."

"Yeah, all right. I've got things to do, too. Hey, it's been good seeing you, Jesse. Let's stay in touch, okay?"

I told him I would, but as soon as I left the restaurant, I was going to block him from my phone and social media, so he wouldn't be able to contact me anymore.

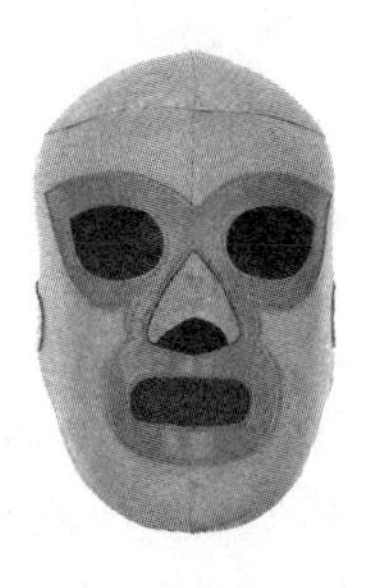

CHAPTER ELEVEN

Two front-row passes. That's what Mr. Collins had offered me for *Monday Night Mayhem*. I would've loved to have taken Wally to it, but in my eagerness to get together with TJ, I cheated her of an opportunity to watch the show in person and to meet the wrestlers backstage.

I didn't attend the event, either. Otherwise, I would've needed to come up with a reason for why Wally couldn't go with me. My father had bought the first excuse, about her not being able to visit the Factory. But knowing what a fan she was, he would've become suspicious if I'd told him that she'd also turned down a ringside seat.

When I got home from school on Monday, I made up another lie, this one about how I must've eaten something in the cafeteria that made me sick. I told my parents I had a bad case of the runs and didn't want to take a chance of having an accident in front of Wally. They understood. After all, who hasn't gotten the runs at one time or another?

My mom took my temperature to make sure I didn't have a fever. Then she gave me some Pepto and told me to drink plenty of water.

"I'm going with Dad to the Alamodome," she said. "If you want, I can call Aunt Gracie to stay with you while we're gone."

"Nah, I'll be fine. I just need for whatever's upsetting my stomach to run its course," I said.

My father snickered. "Run its course. That sounds about right."

"Don't be gross, Mark," my mom scolded him. "Jesse doesn't feel well."

I felt great, but I couldn't tell my parents that, so I stretched out on the couch in the den and pretended to be miserable. My mom kissed me goodbye and said she'd call later to check on me. My father's segment wouldn't take place until the second hour of the show, but he needed to arrive early to be fitted for his Angel of Death gear and for Connie to apply his makeup.

I lay on the couch awhile longer and eventually fell asleep. When I woke up, I went for a swim. The temperature outside was around eighty-five degrees. In a couple of weeks, it would probably climb to the low nineties. My friends already knew about my graduation party. I just needed to tell them to bring their swimsuits.

After my swim, I rinsed off and got dressed. Then I went to the kitchen to look for something to eat. I found a Styrofoam container in the fridge with my mom's Sunday lunch leftovers—chicken and rice—so I zapped it in the microwave. When the food was ready, I carried it to the den and sat in my father's La-Z-Boy and ate, while I watched *Monday Night Mayhem.*

The show opened with Elijah Nightshade and the Assembly cutting a promo in the ring about how they were going to punish Iceman Jacob Sloane for his "vile and wicked ways." They'd been feuding with him for several weeks, leading up to Nightshade's match against Sloane later in the evening.

The phony-preacher gimmick was originally given to my father, when Mr. Collins decided to get rid of the Angel of Death character, saying it had become stale and outdated. Thank goodness, my father retired before having to appear as Elijah Nightshade.

The gimmick was then passed down to Marvin Snider, who'd previously wrestled as "Demented" Devlin Dredd. Carlos Montoya, a *luchador* known as El Azteca Dorado, took off his mask to become Brother Jeremiah. Brother Luke was the former "Lone Wolf" Luke Mauldin, and Cassandra Richardson, who used to accompany my father to the ring as his valet, Spirit, made up the third member of the Assembly, Sister Ruth.

Behind them, I spotted my mom sitting in the front row with Melba Montoya, Carlos' wife. The Montoyas lived in New Braunfels, a city outside of San Antonio. Mr. Collins must've given them the passes that should've gone to Wally and me.

Following Elijah Nightshade and the Assembly's promo, Jason Cage squared off against Tashira Nagasaki in a rare, face vs. face bout. The men put on an incredible display of their wrestling abilities. I can usually tell who's going to win a match, but with this one, I had no idea, because they were equally skilled. Finally, after a series of near pins from both men, Nagasaki caught Cage in his finisher, the Cross-Face Chicken Wing, and forced him to tap out. The fans showed their appreciation by giving the wrestlers a standing ovation.

Next, the ACW tag-team champs, Lance Redwine and Red Lassiter, also known as Crimson Crush, successfully defended their titles against the Minnesota Maulers, Wayne Corbin and Blaine Colt.

Cameras then took viewers backstage, where Penelope Precious conducted an interview with the Ice Man, in which he vowed, "Tonight, I'm gonna put an end to the Assembly, and expose that charlatan Elijah Nightshade for the fraud and coward he is!"

Back in the ring, TJ faced Jumbo Jefferson in what hardcore wrestling fans disparagingly refer to as a "bathroom-break" match, so called because it's obvious to them who's going to win, and they don't care to watch it.

Clint "Jumbo" Jefferson had been out of action for months, recovering from a knee operation. When he returned, the creative team felt they needed to reestablish him as a monster heel, which was why they'd been putting him against jobbers like Chris Choate, Roderick Armstrong, and now, TJ.

To no one's surprise, in just under two minutes, Jumbo Jefferson bounced off the ropes and dropped his massive weight on top of TJ with the Jumbo Splash. The referee counted to three, and Jumbo was declared the winner. All the while, TJ lay flat on his back, looking like he'd been run over by a Mack truck. I figured he was all right, though. He always was. Still, I wondered what would've happened if Jumbo had landed wrong, and TJ sustained serious injuries and couldn't wrestle anymore?

Wrestlers try their best not to hurt each other, but freak accidents happen from time to time. Raven Starr, for instance, was forced to retire at a young age because of a severe neck injury he suffered in a match against Kenny Houston. "Mean" Dean Anderson also had his career shortened, due to a number of concussions. And poor Jon Silverman became a quadriplegic, after Vernon Harper botched a running powerbomb and dropped him on his head.

If TJ's career came to an end unexpectedly, as it almost did when we were attacked in Mexico, what options would he have for earning a living? My father had made wise investments and was able to retire on his own terms. But if TJ was as irresponsible with his finances as he was with his life, he could wind up like Bruce "The Bruiser" Brannigan, who blew every cent he made with the ACW. Bruce now worked at a Home Depot, barely able to make ends meet. My father helped him out by inviting him to wrestle at his shows, but he couldn't pay Bruce a fraction of the money he'd once earned. I could only hope TJ wouldn't turn out the same way.

In another predictable bout, though not a total squash like the one between Jumbo and TJ, John Henry Sykes defeated Tyrone Cannon with his finisher, the Derailer. I knew John Henry was going to win because he was a title contender, while Tyrone, although a decent worker, was strictly a mid-card performer.

Monday Night Mayhem went to a commercial break. When it returned, Gunnar Brooks's entrance music sounded, and he walked out to a chorus of boos and jeers. Gunnar, a recent addition to the ACW roster, played a loudmouth heel who'd been winning his matches by knocking out his opponents with a pair of brass knuckles he pulled from his trunks when the ref wasn't looking.

On his way to the ring, Gunnar shadowboxed and danced the Ali Shuffle, imitating the late, great, heavyweight boxing champ, Muhammad Ali. He continued his routine when he climbed inside.

"Boo me all you want," he told the audience. "But I have the most powerful hands in the world, and there ain't a man alive who can beat me. You know it, and everyone in the locker room knows it."

He looked down at my mom, who was on her feet, heckling him. "What'd you say to me, lady? That I'm a cheater? That I use brass knuckles? You'd better get your eyes checked 'cause all I need are these." He held up his fists. "That's why nobody wants to fight me, 'cause they don't wanna hafta eat their food through a straw with their mouths wired shut. And just to prove to you that I'm right, I'm making an open challenge to anyone in the back who has the guts to get in the ring with me. Anybody. C'mon, who's it gonna be?"

At that moment, the arena grew dark, illuminated only by a bluish glow, after which the sound of unmelodic organ music rang out. Recognizing the tune, the stunned but nonetheless overjoyed crowd jumped to its feet and began chanting, "Death! Death! Death! Death!"

A booming explosion echoed throughout the room, columns of flames shot up on each side of the ramp and smoke billowed from the stage entrance. Then out of the mist he appeared—my father, the Angel of Death.

The chants instantly switched to, "Welcome back! Welcome back! Welcome back! Welcome back!"

My father, in his skeleton face makeup and black attire, thrust his scythe in the air and unleashed a primal roar. "Aaagghh!"

The TV cameras panned across the arena to show the fans' reactions. Some of them had tears in their eyes, and everyone looked as if they'd just won the lottery.

My father sauntered down the aisle toward the ring. As he passed by my mom, she reached out to touch him, but in keeping with his Angel of Death persona, he tried not to show any affection. Still, I noticed him give her a tiny wink.

He stepped through the ropes and looked around the packed Alamodome as the crowd continued to pop for him. I think he was genuinely choked up by the response he was receiving. Then, in a low, raspy voice, he spoke in a poetic style that had long been part of his gimmick.

"From the depths of darkest regions in the Netherworld's domain,

The Angel of Death hast returned at last to the land he once didst reign.

But now he finds this braggart who speaks with wanton hubris,

Of victories and conquests, which in truth are false and fruitless.

Who art thou, transgressor? Account for what thou hast done,

Lest ye shalt face the wrath of the Netherworld's anointed son."

Gunnar eyed him up and down. "So you're the big, bad, boogeyman," he replied in a mocking tone. "I've heard about you for years, how you're supposed to be this unstoppable fiend. Well, let me tell you something, big man. I don't scare easily. I've knocked out everybody the ACW has put in front of me, and I'll knock you out, too. All you've gotta do is get rid of that scythe and face me, man to . . . whatever you are."

My father gazed deeply into Gunnar's eyes, using the "mystical power" the Angel of Death possessed to hypnotize his opponents. Gunnar's face went blank for a few seconds, but he managed to shake off the effects and looked away, as my father laughed maniacally at him.

Then, as my father turned to lean his scythe against a corner, Gunnar pulled his brass knuckles out of his trunks and swung at him. My father dodged the blow just in time and hit him with a devastating clothesline, sending the brass knuckles flying out of his hand. He lifted Gunnar, flipped him upside down and finished him off with his signature move, the Death Drop Piledriver.

"Death! Death! Death! Death!" the fans chanted.

My father raised his scythe victoriously in the air. "Aaagghh!"

He misses it, I thought. He claims he doesn't, but I know he loves being the Angel of Death. How can he not? And why can't he understand that I want the same thing?

After meeting with TJ, I was willing to concede that my father was right about my going to college, and that there was no need for me to be in a hurry to become a wrestler. My father didn't enter the profession until he was twenty-three, and he'd been at it for almost twenty-five years.

But once I got my degree, could I honestly count on him to help me launch my career? When he told me to wait until after I graduated from college before talking to him about wrestling, I suspected it was just something he said to get me to drop the subject.

Then there was my mom. With everything she'd endured as a wrestler's wife, I knew she'd be totally against what I wanted to do.

I'd just about decided to put aside my dream of becoming a pro wrestler and focus on a more sensible career path, until I saw the Angel of Death on television, and I got worked up all over again.

One of these days, that's going to be me.

CHAPTER TWELVE

Graduation Day began on Friday morning with Senior Breakfast. Except that instead of the usual cafeteria fare, we were treated to catered breakfast tacos and croissants, fresh fruit, Danish pastries, yogurt, cereals, milk, orange juice and coffee.

When we finished eating, we were taken on buses to the Freeman Coliseum to rehearse graduation procedures.

Ms. Delaney seated us in rows of chairs that had been set up for the ceremony. She reviewed the process for entering and exiting the floor, as well as walking across the stage. She also went over graduation dos and dont's.

"You may use your phones before and after the ceremony, but not during it," she said. "Gentlemen, you need to wear dark pants, white dress shirts and ties. Ladies, your skirts or dresses should not be longer than your gowns. As for your regalia, you cannot add any decorations to it, other than your recognition sashes and cords."

"Aw, man," Goose whispered to me. He had planned on writing CYCLONE SUÁREZ in silver glitter on his mortarboard.

"When you're on the stage, I don't want anyone striking poses, making hand gestures or dancing," Ms. Delaney said. "You've all worked very hard to get to this point, so don't ruin your special moment by doing something stupid." She stared coldly at us to make sure we understood she was serious. "And finally, to maintain the dignity of the ceremony, please tell your friends and family members not to bring air horns, noise makers, signs, beach balls, Frisbees or any other items that can cause a distraction, because security will make them take them back to their cars."

Following her lecture, we were escorted to the hallway and lined up alphabetically. Then, as the band played "Pomp and Circumstance," we walked back to the rows of chairs, according to how we would be called, and waited until we were given the signal to sit down.

Mr. Pritchard, another guidance counselor, was in charge of announcing our names. He gave us cards on which we wrote them down, both the standard way and with the phonetic spelling, so he wouldn't risk butchering the pronunciations.

The entire rehearsal went without a glitch. Mr. Pritchard read our names correctly, even rolling the r's in the Spanish ones, like a native speaker. We climbed the steps to the stage, shook hands with Ms. Kahn and Mr. Harris, the other assistant principal, then walked toward Dr. Ríos. We shook his hand, while acting as if we were holding our diploma covers, and posed for an imaginary commercial photographer, who would take our photos that evening. We pretended to move our tassels from the right side to the left, and then returned to our seats.

The rehearsal ended at noon, and we were driven back to school. Dr. Ríos reminded us to be at the Freeman Coliseum no later than five o'clock. After that, we were allowed to leave.

A bunch of my friends were going to have lunch at the nearby Chili's. They invited me to join them, but Aunt Gracie had volunteered to get our backyard ready for my party, and I told her I'd help her as soon as rehearsal was over.

A large white truck with red and blue letters that said STARKEY'S PARTY SUPPLIES & RENTAL was blocking our driveway, so I had to park on the street. Two delivery men were taking tables and chairs out of the rear of the truck and carrying them to our backyard. Aunt Gracie was standing near the pool, directing them where to put the furniture.

"Hi, handsome," she said, when she saw me. "You ready for tonight?"

"I think so," I said. "Rehearsal went okay, so I don't think I'll screw up anything."

She rapped me lightly on the head. "Knock on wood."

"What do you need for me to do?" I asked.

"Well, first of all, I want you to help me eat the tuna salad I made for us. I hope you're hungry."

"A little," I said.

"Good. I'll fix lunch as soon as the guys finish. And after we eat, we'll start by hanging those lights." She pointed to the boxes of outdoor string lights sitting on the poolside table. My father had bought the lights months ago to decorate our backyard, but hadn't gotten around to hanging them, and they'd been collecting dust in the garage.

When the delivery men left, we went to the kitchen. On the floor, next to the breakfast table, were several shopping bags of graduation stuff—banners, pennants, streamers, posters and signs—that Aunt Gracie and I would hang outside later.

"Serve us some tea, would you?" she said. "Pitcher's over there by the sink."

I took two glasses out of the cupboard, filled them with ice and poured the drinks. She made tuna sandwiches, which she served with slices of cantaloupe.

Aunt Gracie and I seldom spent time alone together because either Uncle Ryan or my mom were always around.

So when we sat down to eat, our initial conversation was a bit awkward.

"Today's your big day, huh?"

"Yeah."

"You nervous?"

"No."

"But you're excited, aren't you?"

"Of course."

Long pause. Then, "Molly told me that you're thinking about majoring in mechanical engineering when you go to UT."

"Yeah, I guess."

"You don't sound too sure about it."

"No, it's fine."

"Well, you could certainly do a lot worse than that," Aunt Gracie said. "I mean, look at me. I have a bachelor's in art history and can't do anything with it. Molly was smart. She got her degree in education and has always been able to find a teaching job. And if Mark hadn't gotten into that silly wrestling thing, he'd probably be in some high position with the FBI right now."

"I don't think my father's career is silly," I retorted. My mom's family had always looked down on his profession, despite his enormous success in it.

"Sorry, I didn't mean it that way," Aunt Gracie said. "I'm glad it worked out for him. It's just that Molly never expected Mark to do that for a living. You know, I still remember how excited she was when he was drafted by the Dallas Cowboys. Then when they released him during training camp, she thought he was going to sign with another team. But he gave up football to become a . . . *wrestler*." Aunt Gracie spat out the word as if it had a sour taste. "Honestly, Jesse, I don't know how Molly stood by all those years, watching Mark chase after what I used to call his pipe dream. If it had been me, I would've made him give it up and find a regular job, or I would've left him."

"My mom did," I said.

Aunt Gracie caught herself. "Yeah, but that's water under the bridge, right? What I'm saying is that you'll be getting a degree you can actually do something with."

She went on about how smart I was, and that not just anyone had the brains to be a mechanical engineer. And as I listened to her, I decided that getting a degree in that field might not be so bad. I'd always done well in math and science, and I figured I could handle the college courses without too much trouble. But I still wanted to give pro wrestling a shot at some point. I owed it to myself to at least try it. Anyway, if for whatever reason things didn't work out, I'd always have a solid career to fall back on.

CHAPTER THIRTEEN

The commencement ceremony was scheduled to begin at seven o'clock, but so many people arrived late to the Freeman Coliseum, that Dr. Ríos waited another twenty minutes before starting.

In the meantime, my fellow graduates and I stood in the back, dressed in our navy-blue caps and gowns, talking and laughing. Ms. Delaney kept telling us to lower our voices, but the arena was so noisy, I doubted if anyone could hear us.

Finally, the band began playing "Pomp and Circumstance," and on Ms. Delaney's cue, we walked out, amid the cheers of encouragement from thousands of friends and relatives.

During rehearsal, I hadn't felt emotional about graduating. But seeing my parents, my grandparents, my uncles and aunts, and Wally and her mom, waving and yelling my name, made my heart flutter. I don't mind admitting that I teared up a little, too.

The ROTC Color Guard marched behind us, carrying the American and Texas flags. They presented the colors, and José Escamilla, the Color Guard leader, asked the audience to rise for the Pledge of Allegiance and the "Star-Spangled Banner."

Next, Dr. Ríos welcomed everyone. He introduced some school board members and city officials, who offered congratulatory messages.

Erin Brown, the Student Body President, and Víctor Jasso, the Senior Class President, made tribute statements (Erin in English, Víctor in Spanish) in which they recognized our teachers, parents, grandparents and other family members, who had supported us throughout our school years.

Then, Hanna Ling, the salutatorian, and Brenda Mercado, the valedictorian, delivered their commencement addresses.

What stood out for me about Brenda's speech was a quote she read by the writer, Francois de la Rochefoucauld, that said: "Nothing is impossible. There are ways that lead to everything, and if we have sufficient will, we should always have sufficient means. It is often merely for an excuse that we say things are impossible." I felt as if the author was speaking directly to me about my plans after graduation.

Following Brenda's speech, Ana Peña sang "Homeward Bound."

At last, the moment everyone had been waiting for, arrived. As each graduate's name was called, they went onstage to receive their diploma. The crowd was loud but civil—until my name was announced. The second they heard, "Jesse Alfonso Baron," my friends began chanting, "Death! Death! Death! Death!"

People who knew who my father was laughed, but many others, who didn't follow professional wrestling, were appalled by my classmates' behavior.

An hour-and-a-half later, the last diploma was handed out, and we stood for the singing of our school song, "All Hail to Thee, Erastus Smith High." On the last note, we cheered and tossed our mortarboards in the air. Then, as the band played a recessional piece, we exited the coliseum floor, waving to our friends and families on our way out.

In the back, my fellow graduates and I experienced what I'd call a communal sense of joy. What I mean is that we hugged and celebrated one other, even classmates we weren't close to, because we'd been on a long, sometimes arduous journey together, and had made it to the end.

I was relieved that school was finally over. But at the same time, I felt a certain sadness, knowing that after tomorrow, I wouldn't see most of my friends again. We'd be going our separate ways to shape our own worlds and lead new lives.

During her speech, Hanna posed an interesting question: "When we have our ten-year high school reunion, and people ask you what you do for a living, what do you think you'll say?"

I hoped that I could answer, "I'm the American Championship Wrestling heavyweight champion."

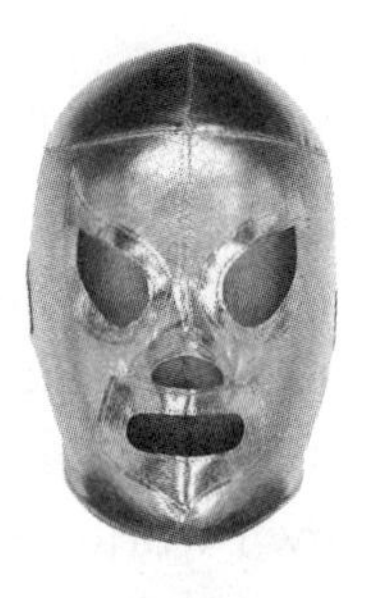

CHAPTER FOURTEEN

There must be some truth to the saying, what goes around, comes around, because just like I'd tried to steal the spotlight from Riley King at the prom by wearing a wrestling mask, my friends basically ignored me during my graduation party, after my father and some of his ACW buddies showed up.

My father wasn't home when the party started. He'd been at the Factory, meeting with Travis McKeon, whom he'd put in charge of the wrestling event scheduled for that evening. But the minute he got to the house and went to the backyard, my friends swarmed around him. They took tons of photos and bombarded him with questions about his career.

"What made you decide to become a wrestler?"

"How long have you been wrestling?"

"Of all your matches, which are your favorites?

"How long does it take for you to put on your makeup?"

"Can you really hypnotize people?"

Their excitement rose as other wrestlers began arriving.

"Oh, my god, is that Jason Cage?" Amanda Birch asked Claudia Gutiérrez.

"I think it is. Girl, he's even hotter in person than he is on TV."

Amanda giggled. "I almost didn't recognize him with his clothes on. C'mon, let's go say hi to him."

"Look!" Sam Morales cried. "There's Red Lassiter. And Tashira Nagasaki."

"And that's Solomon Grimm behind them," Wendell said. They jumped out of the pool and ran to meet them.

Wally was no exception. She geeked out, too. "Holy cats, Jessup! I think I saw Prince Romulus. I'm going to see if I can get my picture taken with him."

Goose cornered Frank Collins and his wife Terri, whose onscreen persona was backstage interviewer, Penelope Precious. He told them he was going to be a wrestler and wanted to know how to get a job with the ACW. Mr. Collins was polite, but evasive, only advising Goose to work hard at learning his craft.

Bucky almost made me laugh when he pulled me aside and asked, "What's Butcher Murdock doing here? I thought he and your dad hated each other."

"Seriously?" I said. "Don't be such a mark, Bucky. That was just part of an old storyline."

Don "Butcher" Murdock and my father were former tag-team partners, and later, "sworn enemies." But outside the ring, they were as close as brothers.

"Is it okay if I talk to him?" Bucky asked.

"Suit yourself," I said, and he took off.

My father had invited his long-time friends from American Championship Wrestling to my party when *Monday Night Mayhem* was in town. I felt honored that they'd taken time from their busy schedules to come to it. Some of them even brought their spouses and girlfriends.

Altogether, I estimated we had close to two-hundred guests, including classmates, relatives and older friends who weren't part of the wrestling industry.

My mom had planned the party for at least that many people. But being a high school teacher, and understanding the teenage mind, instead of using traditional caterers to provide the food, she hired a hamburger truck from a company called Roll 'Em Out Burgers. The owner parked his vehicle at the bottom of our driveway, and he and his assistants grilled burgers on a griddle inside the truck. They also cooked hot dogs and chicken patties, which they served with a choice of french fries, onion rings, potato salad and ranch-style beans.

In addition to the hamburger truck, my mom rented a cart from a *paletería.* She filled it with assorted flavors of *paletas,* enough for everyone to have as many of the frozen treats as they wanted. As for the music, she brought in Rick Dunham, a local radio personality, and he played songs similar to the ones I'd heard at my prom.

All evening, my friends kept telling me what a great party it was and how much fun they were having. And while I may not have been the center of attention, I was glad they were enjoying themselves, swimming and dancing, visiting and eating.

However, one person who didn't seem happy to be there was Carlos Montoya's wife, Melba. She and my mom were sitting together, and as I walked by their table on my way to throw my trash, I happened to catch part of their conversation.

"We could go to the movies or out to eat without anybody bothering us," Melba lamented. "Then one day, Frank tells Carlos that he's changing his Azteca Dorado gimmick to Brother Jeremiah, and that he has to wrestle without his mask, which he'd worn for years. Ever since then, I've had to deal with . . . *that.*" She glared at my friends, who were crowding around her husband. "It happens every time we're out in public."

"Believe me, Melba," my mom said. "I know exactly what you're going through. You'd think that Mark wouldn't be recognized without his face paint. But when you're six-foot-seven and weigh over three hundred pounds, people are going to notice you. And it doesn't take wrestling fans long to figure out who he is. I can't begin to tell you how many times our plans were ruined . . ." She stopped talking when she saw me staring at them, and I moved on. But listening to them gave me a brilliant idea.

I dumped my trash in one of the large plastic containers, then returned to my table, where Wally and I had been eating with my cousin Monty.

I leaned into her and whispered, "I want to talk to you about something, but in private, okay?"

"Sure," she said, and got up.

"Where are you guys going?" Monty asked.

"Jessup's going to show me his etchings," Wally said playfully.

"His etchings? Hey, *primo*, I didn't know you were artistic."

She laughed at him for not getting what I supposed was a joke. I didn't say anything because I didn't get it, either. I took her hand and led her to a far corner of the backyard, away from everyone.

Wally searched my face for clues as to what I might tell her that I didn't want anyone to hear. Then she said, "Well, you're either going to try to break up with me again, or you're going to ask me to marry you. Which is it?"

I glanced around to make sure no one was within earshot. "Neither. I've decided that after I get settled at UT, I'm going to look for an indie promotion to wrestle for. They have them all over the state. A lot of companies hold their shows on Saturdays or Sundays, which won't interfere with my classes. I can get up early and drive to wherever they have them. Then I'll go over my match with whoever I'm wrestling that night. After that, I'll just hang around and do some studying until the show starts. And as soon as my match is over, I'll drive back to Austin."

"Holy cats, you're serious, aren't you?" Wally said. "So what happened to graduating from college first before thinking about a wrestling career?"

"I would, except that right now I'm in the best shape of my life," I said. "And I really believe that if I dedicate my time and energy to my father's training, I can be ready to wrestle in less than three months. But if I wait until after college, I'll be at a minimum, four years older, and who knows what condition I'll be in?"

"I see. And what about your dad? How do you think he'll feel about it?" Wally knew what my father thought of my desire to pursue a wrestling career.

"He won't know because I'm not going to tell him. If I sign with a company, my plan is to wear a mask and use the gimmick of a *luchador*."

Wally covered her mouth to stifle a laugh.

"What's so funny?" I asked.

"Nothing. It's just that . . . well, how are you going to pass yourself off as a *luchador* when you can't speak Spanish?"

"*Yo sé hablar español*," I said defensively. "At least enough to get by."

I hated whenever she brought up my limited Spanish-speaking skills. Maybe I wasn't fluent like her, but I could generally make myself understood.

"I'm sorry, love, I know you can. I wasn't trying to make fun of you. But it seems to me that you'd be better off wrestling as an American with a mask, like your dad did, when he was the Annihilator. That way, you can conduct your promos in English without worrying about making a mistake that could give you away."

Wally was being tactful, but I could tell she didn't have confidence in my Spanish.

"I thought about that," I said. "The thing is, my father knows a lot of Texas promoters, and sometimes he goes to their shows to watch his former students wrestle. If by some chance he happens to pop up at an event where I'm wrestling, and they introduce me as a *luchador* from, let's say . . . Oaxaca . . . hopefully he'll think I'm just another Mexican wrestler trying to make it in the US and won't realize it's me."

I was pretty sure I could pull off the gimmick. I'd been around pro wrestling long enough to know that the trick to winning over an audience is to make them believe you really are the character you're portraying, even if you're an enigmatic figure like the Angel of Death.

Wally, though, wasn't sold. "Don't you think your dad will still recognize you? I know I would."

"I doubt it," I said. "He and I have always been kind of distant, mainly because when he was wrestling, he was gone a lot. We hardly ever spent time together until he retired. So I don't think he'll know it's me."

"What about his promoter friends?" she asked. "How are you going to keep them from telling your dad that you're wrestling for them? Or are you going to give them a fake name?"

"I don't think that'll be a problem either," I said. "Not if I let them know from the start who my father is, and that I want to make it on my own without his help. They'll probably respect me for not trying to capitalize on his name and keep quiet about it."

As we spoke, I noticed a look of consternation growing on Wally's face. It didn't hit me until later that she may have been thinking that if I spent my weekends wrestling, I'd never come home. But at that moment, I was too focused on my goal to worry about it.

"Well, you're a big boy now and old enough to make your own decisions," she said. "If that's what you want to do, then I say go for it."

"Thanks. Anyway, I'm going to need a mask. Something original. Do you think you might be able to design one for me?"

"Maybe. What did you have in mind?"

"I don't know. I'll leave it up to your imagination."

"All right. Do you have a ring name I can use as a guide?"

"Not yet," I said.

"Oka-a-ay. Then how about some paper and a pencil?"

"Yeah, I've got them in my room."

"Ah, now we're getting somewhere," she kidded.

We went inside the house through the patio doors, where we found Goose and Wendell in the den, giving my friends a tour of my father's wrestling memorabilia: his championship belts, his plaques and trophies, magazine covers on which he'd been featured, photos of some of his most unforgettable matches, his community service awards, various Angel of Death action figures, plus gobs of other souvenirs.

When Goose saw Wally and me climbing the stairs, he shouted, "Hey, you'd better not be doing *cochinadas* up there!"

Wally tittered in amusement.

"What does that mean?" I asked her.

"Google it," she said.

Wally sat at my desk, and I pulled a book from my bookcase titled *Mundo de la Lucha Libre*. It was a collection of photos of *luchadores*, most of them wearing masks. I'd borrowed the book from my father but hadn't returned it.

"Take a look through this," I said. "It might give you some ideas."

I stood over Wally and watched, as she turned the pages, skimming through each photo. I was familiar with some of the legendary wrestlers, like El Santo, Blue Demon, Rayo de Jalisco, and Mil Máscaras, but I didn't know who many of the others were.

"I like this one," she said, staring at a photo of Tiger Mask. She flipped the page. "Oh, and these, too." She pointed to Psicosis and Dos Caras.

She continued going through the book, studying each mask, until she reached the end.

"So what do you think?" I asked.

She sighed. "I wish I could help you, Jessup, but it's hard for me to come up with a design, not until you decide on a character. I mean, these masks go with the wrestlers' names in one way or another. Are you sure you don't have any idea as to what you want to call yourself?"

I shook my head.

"Nothing?"

"Well, I had thought about using the name Jesse The Red Baron."

She burst out laughing. "Geez and crackers, my three-year-old sister can come up with a better name, and I don't have a sister."

"Come on, Wally. That's why I asked for your help. I'm not creative like you."

"All right. What else have you got?"

"Now I'm embarrassed to tell you."

"Well, it can't be any worse than Jesse The Red Baron."

"The Angel of Death, Jr.," I muttered.

"Ah, excellent choice," she said. "Your dad will *never* suspect it's you."

"You know what?" I said, scowling. "Let's forget it."

"Oh, don't be mad, love. I'm messing with you. I really want to help, but you've got to give me something to work with. Maybe if you were to . . ." Wally slapped her forehead. "That's it! I've got it. It's perfect."

"Look, Wally, if this is another joke . . ."

"No, I'm serious. How about this?" She ran her hand across the air as if she were reading the name in lights. "Máscara de la Muerte."

"The Mask of Death?" I said.

"Yes. Don't you see? It's a combination of your dad's ring name, plus the fact that you'll be wearing a mask. Yet it's different enough that he won't make the connection."

"Máscara de la Muerte," I said slowly, letting it sink in. "I like it. I like it a lot!"

Wally blew on her fingernails, then rubbed them on her shoulder. "I'm good, huh?"

"The best," I said. "Thanks."

"And I just got a great idea for the mask," she said. "You know how your dad paints his face like a skull? I'll design a mask that looks like one."

"You mean like the kind La Parka wore?" I asked, then opened the book to show her a photo of the famed *luchador*.

"Sort of," she said. "But with a lot more details. And without the hood. Give me something to draw on."

I took a spiral notebook from my desk hutch and flipped through it until I found a fresh page. Wally grabbed a pencil from my pen-and-pencil holder and began sketching a skull.

"Do you have someone who can sew the mask for you?" she asked.

"Yeah, Shirley Washington. She's the ACW's seamstress. Shirley sews all the wrestlers' tights and jackets and stuff.

She's the one who designed my father's Angel of Death gear. I'm sure that if I ask her, she'll do it."

"Good. Well, when you talk to her, you might suggest that she use black mesh for the eye sockets and the nostrils and around the teeth. That way, you'll be able to see and breathe out of it. And if she can, have her pad the cheekbones and the area around the brows, and maybe give the jaw a squarish look."

"I'll do that," I said, making a mental note to also tell Shirley to keep my mask a secret from my father.

"There," Wally said, when she was done.

"Whoa, this is great," I said.

"It's just a rough sketch. I'll draw a better one later. Maybe on a body. And I'll add white tights and white boots to it. And a cape. Definitely a cape."

While Wally was describing her idea, my phone chimed.

"It's my mom," I said. "She's wondering where I am. We'd better get back to the party."

We hurried down the stairs and out the patio doors.

My mom had been looking for me because she wanted me to open my presents. She set the gifts on the patio table, then called our guests to watch as I went through each one.

Most of what I got were graduation cards with gift cards and cash inside them. But I also received some items for my dorm: towels, bedding, a mini fridge, a microwave, a coffee maker and a hand-held steamer.

For my final present, my parents announced that they were taking me to London at the end of July. I'd known about the trip for a while, so the news wasn't a surprise to me. But I was glad that they'd let everyone know. My friends raved about how lucky I was, which got me even more pumped up about going.

The other thing I was excited about was my wrestling training. At first, I hadn't been particularly interested in it. I'd even considered turning down my father's offer. But now that I had an end goal, I couldn't wait to get started.

CHAPTER FIFTEEN

The following Saturday morning, thirty-eight potential students, including Goose, attended the tryouts. Three of them were girls around my age—athletic types—who likely either participated in sports or spent a lot of time in the gym. Some of the men were muscular, others were heavyset or had average builds. One guy looked like he might weigh a hundred and fifty pounds after a full meal. Regardless, they were there because they shared a common dream—to become professional wrestlers.

Each of them followed the instructions on the announcement posted on the PWF website, and came dressed in appropriate workout clothes—shorts, T-shirts, sneakers and such—except for one guy. He wore a baggy Hawaiian shirt, khaki pants and black dress shoes. What did he think he was going to do at a wrestling tryout?

They paid their fees to María Núñez, my father's accountant. She then handed them accidental-waiver-and-release-of-liability forms and other paperwork to fill out.

Because I wasn't officially going to be enrolled in the course, I didn't need to be at the tryouts. And since my father owned the company, I wasn't required to sign anything. But Goose begged me to go with him for support, so I sat with him at ringside and waited, along with everyone else.

"Man, I can't believe I'm gonna be a wrestler," he said.

I didn't want to burst his bubble, but the fact was that as many as half of the candidates quit on the first day, before the rigorous tryouts were over.

"We'll see how you feel later," I told him.

At first, the group was mostly quiet, no doubt feeling jittery, perhaps having second thoughts about being there. Then after a while, they relaxed and began talking to one another about their favorite wrestlers and matches.

In time, my father came out of his office. When the group saw him heading toward the ring, they applauded for the larger-than-life figure they'd watched on television and were about to get the opportunity to be trained by him.

He climbed through the ropes and gazed at his new crop of candidates. "Good morning, everyone. My name is Mark Baron. Professionally, I'm known as the Angel of Death."

"Death! Death! Death! Death!" the group chanted.

"Please don't do that," he said. "You're not here today as fans. You're here to see if you've got what it takes to be part of one of the most exciting but also one of the most misunderstood professions in the world."

My father had spent his career defending what he did for a living, not only to my mom's family, but to strangers he met, who asked what type of work he did.

"I'm sure you've heard people say that pro wrestling is fake, and therefore it isn't a real sport," he said. "Sometimes they refer to it as live-action cartoons. Or low-brow theater. Or even soap operas for men. And you know, they're right, because in one way or another, pro wrestling encompasses those things. But it's also a unique form of entertainment that transcends all cultures and socioeconomic statuses, and can be performed only by powerful, highly skilled athletes."

The group bobbed their heads and murmured sounds of approval.

"Now before I tell you about this course and what you'll be doing today, let me ask you something, and I want you to be honest with me. Knowing what the general public thinks of professional wrestling, why do you want to get into it?"

Goose shot his hand in the air and began waving it like a little kid in school.

"Yes, stand up and tell us your name," my father said. He knew Goose, but he wanted everyone to introduce themselves.

With his face beaming, Goose replied, "My name is Abel Guzmán, and the reason I wanna be a wrestler is 'cause I wanna be rich and famous, like you."

His response got some laughs from the group.

Goose gave them a goofy smile. "Well, he told us to be honest, and I'm being honest."

"Thank you," my father said, without commenting. "All right, who else?"

A guy with a chiseled body got up. "I'm Lightning LaBelle, sir, and . . ."

"Hold on," my father interrupted. "Is Lightning Labelle your actual name?"

"No, sir. It's Matt. Matt Perryman. Lightning LaBelle's a ring name I'm thinking about using."

"Well, for now, why don't we call you Matt, okay?"

The guy blushed. "Yes, sir. Anyway, I just got out of the Army, and I've been thinking about what I want to do. I've been a wrestling fan all my life, and I've always wondered what it'd be like to be a wrestler. So I googled wrestling schools in Texas and found yours."

"Thanks, Matt. I appreciate it," my father said. "Who else?"

One of the girls lifted her hand and stood. "Hi, my name is Misty Raines. And *yes*, that is my real name. My parents were trying to be cute when I was born. Me and my friends, Valen Durán and Noreen Tipton, are from San Marcos." She motioned for the other girls to stand with her. "We played volleyball and soccer when we were in high school, so we're used to performing in front of a crowd. Anyway, we thought we'd try wrestling next."

"We've also done some modeling, and we're hoping that if we ever get to be on TV, somebody'll notice us, and maybe it'll lead to better modeling jobs," Valen said, who like Goose, took my father at his word about being honest.

"Or even an acting career," Noreen said excitedly.

My father thanked the girls without making any remarks about their reasons for being there.

Another guy introduced himself as Larry Beasley. He told my father that he used to be the class clown. "I was known as Hilarious Beasley. Get it? Hi-*Larry*-ous."

The group didn't seem to think Larry Beasley was "Hi-Larry-ous" because they stared at him with vacant expressions.

"I've always been a showoff," he said. "So I think I'd be real entertaining in the ring. Plus, I'm in pretty good shape, if I do say so myself." He flexed his less-than-impressive biceps.

The hundred and fifty pounder went next. His name was Juan Serrano. He said he got bullied a lot when he was in school and wanted to become a wrestler to learn how to defend himself. He also hoped that if he made it big in wrestling, he could shove his success in the faces of the people who used to pick on him.

A heavily tattooed man named Bobby Lee Taylor admitted he'd served time in prison for armed robbery. He claimed that while he was there, he found God and had turned his life around.

"I wanna be a role model for little kids. Somebody they can look up to, know what I'm saying? I wanna go to the schools and talk to them about making good grades and staying out of trouble, so they don't end up like me."

On and on, each of the candidates rose, stated their name, and explained why they'd come. Their reasons varied, but overall, they wanted a chance to perform in front of an audience and to make a name for themselves.

Finally, my father introduced me. "This is my son, Jesse. He'll be training with you until he leaves for college in August."

He didn't ask me why I wanted to get into pro wrestling. As far as he was concerned, that conversation was over. But if he had, I would've boldly proclaimed, "Because I was born to do this, and one of these days, I'm going to be the best wrestler in the world!"

Okay, maybe I wouldn't have said that, but I thought it.

My father stepped out of the ring and sat on the apron to get closer to the group. "Each one of you has lofty goals," he said. "That's good. I hope you reach them. But if you want to make it in this business, first and foremost, you've got to have a passion for it. You've got to be willing to put your bodies on the line and risk serious injuries for the sake of entertaining a crowd that might sometimes be as few as fifty people in a bingo hall. You've got to want it bad enough that you'll drive three hundred miles somewhere, just to get beaten up for maybe twenty bucks. And you've got to be prepared to live with pain every day and learn to block it out, so you can wrestle your next match."

Goose looked at me, worried. "Is that true?"

"We'll talk about it later," I told him.

"Don't get me wrong," my father said. "I want you to follow your dreams. But I also want you to understand the reality of this profession. To be perfectly frank, the odds of you making it to a major-league company like American Championship Wrestling are almost as slim as winning the lottery. That's not to say it can't be done. The PWF has had a number of students who have gone on to wrestle for the ACW and other top promotions. Just know that you'll have to make a lot of sacrifices to get there. You'll have to prioritize this business over your family, your friends and your other interests. In other words, you'll need to devote your entire life to it. And even then, there's no guarantee that you'll ever make it past the indie circuit. Like legendary NBA coach Pat Riley once said, 'Hard work, commitment and dedication don't guarantee you a thing. But without them, you don't stand a chance.'"

My father's words brought back unpleasant memories of him being absent for most of my childhood. Still, I'd made up my mind about what I wanted to do, and nothing he said was going to change it.

Not everyone felt the same way, though. The guy in the Hawaiian shirt whose name was Arthur Bennett and said he wanted to be a wrestler because he'd always dreamed of appearing on television, raised his hand. "Uh, excuse me, Mr. Baron. I've decided that I don't want to do this. Can . . . can I get my money back?"

"No problem. Go see María. She'll take care of you."

When Arthur Bennett stood up, two other guys did, too, and followed him out the door.

My father wasn't surprised or disappointed to see them leave. It happened at every tryout. A lot of people pictured only the flashy side of pro wrestling. They didn't realize what being a wrestler actually entailed.

"For those of you I haven't scared off yet," he said, giving us a crooked smile, "let me tell you about this course. We meet

Mondays through Thursdays, from six-thirty until nine. In the beginner's class, we'll teach you basic holds and moves and how to perform them without hurting yourselves or somebody else, and we'll show you how to put them together in simple sequences. You'll learn about ring awareness and stage presence. We'll advise you on proper nutrition and diet, which foods to eat and which to avoid. In addition to that, we'll run you through lots of strength training and cardio exercises to help you build your stamina." He looked at Matt Perryman and Bobby Lee Taylor. "I can tell that some of you lift weights, and that's great for your appearance. But you don't need a body builder's physique to be a wrestler. Great wrestlers come in all shapes and sizes. Just look at Jumbo Jefferson, for instance. He won't ever be confused with Mr. Universe, and yet, he can probably outlast any of you in the ring."

Larry Beasley let out a horse laugh, but my father quickly shut him up with his piercing dark eyes.

"Then depending on how much progress you're making," he continued, "we'll switch you to an advanced group, where you'll learn more intricate holds and moves, complex sequences and match development. Plus we'll teach you how to use ring psychology to tell stories. We'll give you tips on how to make an entrance and how to cut promos. And we'll help you create a character and a stage name. Then after four or five months, if we feel you're ready, we'll use you in our shows. Your matches will be recorded, and we'll critique them with you."

A guy named Andy Robinson raised his hand. "I have a question, sir. Will we get paid when we wrestle? And if so, how much?"

"Yes, you will, but I wouldn't plan on taking a trip to Bermuda with it," my father said dryly. "The amount of money you earn will depend on the type of performer you turn out to be, and whether people come, specifically, to watch you wrestle. I will tell you, though, that scouts from larger promotions attend our events from time to time, and if they're impressed by your performance, hopefully they'll offer you a heftier contract."

Next, my father introduced his trainers, Travis McKeon and Joe Ellis. "These gentlemen will be assisting me throughout the course. They have years of ring experience, and their expertise will be invaluable to you." He went on to explain that if the candidates chose to participate in the program, their thirty-five-dollar tryout fee would count as part of their tuition. He also pointed out that their tuition included a lifetime membership to the Factory, and that they'd be able to use the facilities anytime they wanted.

"In just a moment, Coach McKeon and Coach Ellis are going to have you do some exercises to test your endurance and to determine whether you're in condition to start our program," he said. "If you discover that you're not quite ready for it, don't get discouraged. I suggest you get yourself in shape and come back another time. Anyway, I want to thank you for choosing the Ox Mulligan Pro Wrestling Factory, and I wish you well."

Travis and Joe didn't teach us any holds or moves that day. We didn't even step inside the ring. Instead, they led us through an intense series of push-ups, pull-ups, sit-ups, crunches, squats, jumping jacks, box jumps and burpees.

There's a well-known phrase: dropping like flies. I know what it means, but I don't understand why people say it. I've never seen flies dropping, unless I've swatted them with a magazine. But that's how I would describe what happened to the candidates once the tryouts got underway.

The first one to quit was the not-so-hilarious, Larry Beasley. He gave up thirty minutes into it. Stuart Jennings, an insurance adjuster, who wanted to do something besides work in an office, was the next to go. Fred Chambers, an orderly at a nursing home, who like Goose, had visions of wealth and fame, soon followed.

"Your dad's wrestling school's a scam," Fred complained to me. "I thought we were gonna do dropkicks and suplexes and stuff like that. I coulda saved myself thirty-five bucks and done these exercises at home."

Noreen Tipton lasted almost an hour before deciding that pro wrestling wasn't the best way to further her modeling or acting career. Her friends tried to convince her to stay, but as they were talking to her, she threw up.

"You still hanging in there?" I asked Goose, while we were doing box jumps.

Gasping for breath, he answered, "I . . . I think I'll . . . make . . . make it."

By the end of the tryouts, only twenty-four people remained. They were dragging their feet, sweating like pigs. Sweating like pigs is another expression I've never understood. I didn't realize pigs sweated that much.

"Go home and get plenty of rest," Travis told us. "Then, if you're ready to do this again, we'll see you on Monday."

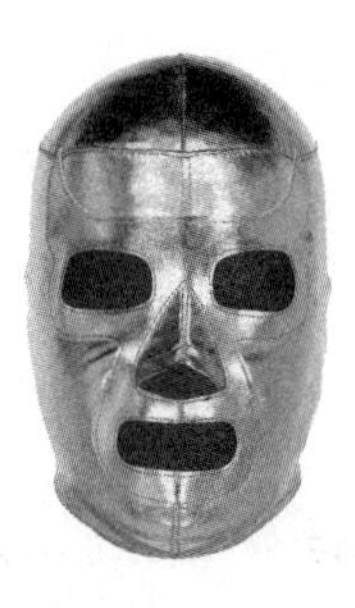

CHAPTER SIXTEEN

I was used to exercising regularly—but at my own pace—not the grueling one I'd been put through. My arms and legs felt as if they were about to fall off.

The workout also left me hungry. My mom was spending the day with Aunt Gracie, and wasn't home to fix me lunch, so I slapped together a ham and cheese sandwich that I ate with the leftover tortilla chips I found in the pantry, then washed everything down with a long drink of milk straight out of the plastic container. My mom would've pitched a fit if she saw me doing it. "*Use a glass!*" I could hear her say. But I was alone, so the rules didn't apply.

To soothe my aching muscles, I changed into a pair of swimming trunks and soaked in the hot tub. The warm jet sprays were just what my body needed. I could've stayed in there all day, but I knew better than to sit in the hot tub for too long.

After a while, I climbed out, showered, got dressed, then lay on my bed and turned on the TV. I came across *The Lion King*, which I used to love when I was little, so I started watching it. Then sometime after Mufasa explained the circle of life to young Simba, I dozed off.

Four hours later, I woke up. I listened for sounds inside the house but didn't hear any. I walked down the hallway and leaned against the banister. "Hello?" No answer. My mom was probably still with Aunt Gracie, and my father was either at the Factory or hanging out with his buddies.

I didn't have anything to do, so I texted Wally to see if she wanted to catch a movie, but she didn't write back. I waited awhile, then texted her again. No response. I tried calling her. She didn't answer. I was about to head to her house, when it dawned on me that she might be at work. She told me she'd gotten a job waiting tables at Ernie Lou's, but I didn't know her schedule.

Ernie Lou's Texas Classics was a well-known restaurant chain that specialized in home-style cooking. I'd eaten there on a number of occasions with my parents, and the food was really good. I especially liked their pecan-crusted catfish.

I decided to drive out there. If Wally was working, I'd ask for a table at her station and kiddingly give her a hard time about having to wait on me.

When I got to the restaurant, I saw a line of people snaked outside it, which I should've expected on a Saturday night for such a popular place. As packed as it was, I thought I'd go in, say hi to Wally, and then leave.

At the entrance, a hostess whose name badge identified her as NAOMI welcomed me with a friendly smile. "How many in your party?" she asked.

"I'm not eating," I said. "I'm looking for Wally."

"Who?"

"Wally Morúa. She's new here. I was wondering if she's working tonight."

"She?" Naomi turned to another hostess, a woman named Jada. "Do we have a girl on our staff named . . . Wally?"

Jada grinned. "He means Turquoise. That's what we call her," she told me. "You know, 'cause of her hair."

"Is she here?" I asked, tickled by Wally's new nickname.

"Yeah, I'll see if I can find her." Jada picked up the microphone attached to the hostess stand. "Turquoise to the front! Turquoise to the front!"

"You can wait over there," Naomi said, motioning me aside, so she could tend to the customers behind me.

I stood near the corner and studied at the photos of Texas landmarks hanging on the walls. Among them were the Alamo, the Fort Worth Stockyards, the State Fair of Texas, the San Jacinto Monument and the Johnson Space Center.

A few minutes later, Wally showed up, looking frazzled.

"Turquoise?" I said jokingly.

"What are you doing here, Jessup?" she asked, unamused. "Do you need something?"

"No, I just came by to say hi," I said, surprised by her harsh tone. "Actually, I was going to invite you out. If you check your phone, you'll see that I've been trying to reach you."

She pointed irately to the crowded room. "Take a look around you, Jessup! Do you honestly believe I have time to go out?"

"Hey, don't yell at me!"

"Sorry, I'm just real exhausted right now. This place is running me ragged."

"You're exhausted?" I said. "Try doing push-ups and sit-ups and box jumps for two hours straight, like I did this morning. My body's so sore right now, I can barely move."

"And you don't think this job is tiring? Listen, I've worked a split shift every day this week. My legs are about to go out from under me, and I still have to be here till eleven."

"Turquoise!" growled a guy wearing a red, Ernie Lou's polo shirt. "C'mon, you ain't got time to visit. Table seven's waiting for their food, and table five wants their check."

"I've gotta go," Wally said.

"Wait. When can I see you?"

"I . . . I don't know."

"Well, what days are you off?"

"I don't know."

"You don't know when you're off?"

"Geez and crackers, Jessup! Stop asking me so many damn questions!"

"Fine then, forget it!" I said and stormed out of the restaurant.

I sat in my car, seething. If Wally couldn't handle waiting tables, that was her problem. She didn't have to take her frustrations out on me.

Rather than going home, I texted the guys, offering to treat them to pizza at Romo's if they weren't doing anything, but only Goose was available. Wendell was in Dallas with his mom, visiting the Southern Methodist University campus, and Bucky was with Ramona at the movies, watching *The Quadrangle*, the action flick I'd wanted to take Wally to see.

Dinner with Goose on a Saturday night wasn't exactly my idea of an exciting evening, but it was better than sitting in my bedroom, stewing over my fight with Wally.

When I picked him up at his apartment complex, the first words out of his mouth were, "Man, I've never worked so hard like I did this morning. I've got pain on top of my pain."

"You'll get used to it once your body develops muscle memory," I said. "Assuming you decide to stay with the program."

"I am. I'm just glad you're gonna do it with me. Otherwise, I might've quit, like a lot of those guys. And that poor chick, the one who threw up, I kinda felt sorry for her."

"That's why my father has the tryouts," I said. "To weed out anybody who's not ready to take the course."

I drove past Erastus Deaf Smith High School and made a right turn on Hanson Road. A short time later, I pulled into Romo's parking lot.

Mona welcomed us at the door, but Bonnie was our server. I told her to bring us an extra-large meat lover's pizza, plus two glasses of iced tea.

With our training coming up, I probably shouldn't have ordered something so heavy, but after the way I'd been treated by Wally, I felt that a pizza might comfort my bruised ego.

"*Qué gacho*, man," Goose said, when I told him about it. "And in front of everybody, too. Like I told you before, I've always thought you could do better than her."

"She was just tired," I said. "We both were. I'll call her tomorrow and apologize."

"For what?" Goose said, making a face. "You didn't do nothing wrong. Look, Jesse, I know you like her, but it's time for you to find somebody else. I mean, Wally was fine when you were in high school, but you're moving on. You're going to college. UT's full of hot chicks, and you're gonna meet a bunch of them. So there ain't no reason for you to hang on to her, especially not after how she dissed you."

"It wasn't that big a deal," I said. "We've had disagreements before. We'll put this one behind us, like we always do."

"It's up to you, man. But if Yolanda had talked to me that way in public, I would've dumped her, just like that," Goose said, with a snap of his fingers. "I'm thinking about doing it, anyway. You know, I asked her out tonight, and she turned me down to go to her six-year-old *prima's* birthday party. What was she gonna do there? It's a party for little kids."

"I'll see what happens," I said, which was my way of ending the conversation.

My anger toward Wally had subsided, but it bothered me that she'd gotten a job at Ernie Lou's, knowing this would be our last summer together before I moved to Austin. She should've realized that if she was working a split shift every day, we'd barely get to see each other in the little time I had left.

Bonnie brought our drinks, and when it was ready, our pizza. "Y'all enjoy," she said.

While we were eating, Goose asked me about our wrestling training, wanting to know what to expect when we reported to the Factory on Monday.

"They'll probably have us warm up by doing the same exercises we did this morning, but to a lesser extent," I said. "They might also take us to the park behind the shopping center to do hill runs."

Goose's shoulders slumped like a deflated balloon. "Aw, man. I thought your dad said we were gonna learn holds and moves and stuff."

"We are. But conditioning's a big part of the training. You've got to have a lot of strength and stamina to wrestle safely."

"Oh, well. If that's what it takes to get rich, I guess I can do it," he said. "I'm not sure about some of the other guys, though. That skinny kid, Serrano, for example, I'll bet you he doesn't last long."

"I don't know," I said. "He seems to have a lot of heart. He reminds me of Alonzo Barclay, one of my father's wrestlers. Alonzo was Serrano's size when he started at the Factory. I didn't think he had a chance, but now he's on the roster and wrestles regularly."

Goose nodded thoughtfully. "And what about the chicks? That Misty Waters and the other one that didn't puke. You think they'll make it?"

"Hey, don't talk about puking when we're eating pizza," I said. "And Misty's last name is Raines, not Waters. The other girl's name is Valen. Valen Durán."

"Well, I hope they do make it," Goose said, grinning. "Maybe we'll get to practice some holds on them."

I didn't say anything, but the same thought had crossed my mind. The females trained with the men, and inevitably, we'd have lots of physical contact.

"Hey, I got an idea," Goose said. "Now I'm just talking here, all right? But let's say that you decide to dump Wally, and I dump Yolanda. Maybe we could hook up with those chicks."

"Yeah, right," I scoffed.

"Why not?"

"First of all, what makes you think they'd be interested in us? And second, they probably already have boyfriends. Girls like them usually do. And third, if they don't like us hitting on them, they might complain to my father, and he'll kick us out of the program."

"Aw, you're no fun," Goose said.

It wasn't that I didn't find the girls attractive. They were both super good looking. If they hadn't said they were models, I might've guessed it, anyway.

Misty was fair-skinned, with bright blue eyes and shoulder-length, blond hair. Valen's brown complexion matched mine. She had hazel eyes and long black hair pulled back in a ponytail. I could easily go for either one. But I was already dating Wally. Besides, I was too chicken to make a move on them.

I'd had two girlfriends—Sara and Wally—and I met both by accident. Sara, back in middle school, when I stopped some bullies from mugging her, and Wally, when I wrongly accused her of stealing my dog.

Samson was originally mine, a birthday present from my grandma. When I got him, I thought his puppy bark sounded like a duck's honk, so I named him Duck. Unfortunately, my mom didn't want him in the house. Duck had a doghouse and lots of backyard space to run around in. But he must've not been happy with the living arrangements because he kept digging under the fence and getting out.

On his final escape, he went missing for about two years. Meanwhile, Wally found him. Since he didn't have tags, and she didn't know if he belonged to anyone, she kept him and named him Samson. One day, I saw her walking Duck near my house, and I learned that she'd had him the whole time. In the end, I let her keep the dog, and from there, our friendship grew.

All the same, Goose had gotten me questioning my relationship with Wally. We had agreed not to break up until we both felt the time was right. I wondered if I was starting to see the signs.

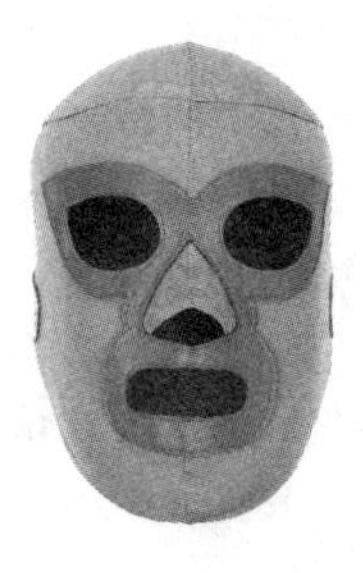

CHAPTER SEVENTEEN

After I dropped Goose off, I went directly home. My parents were back, and we chatted for a while. They wanted to know where I'd been. Not in an accusatory way, just to make polite conversation. I told them I'd had dinner with Goose at Romo's, omitting the part about why we'd gotten together. My father asked me how I was feeling after the morning workout. I told him I was a little achy but that I'd be ready to start training on Monday. Then I excused myself, saying I was tired and wanted to go to bed.

I'm a heavy sleeper, and once I zonk out, loud noises seldom bother me. Not my parents visiting with late-night guests downstairs, not the TV or music blaring, not even thunderstorms rumbling outside my window. My mom claims that a tornado could hit our house, and I'd sleep right through it. Yet, for some reason, the alerts on my phone always wake me.

At around eleven-thirty, I was having a weird dream in which Mufasa and Simba were sitting by my bedroom window, looking out. Almost as weird was that it was daytime, and the sun was shining on me. Sometimes, when I eat a big meal before I go to bed, I tend to have nightmares. But this wasn't a nightmare—just two Disney animated characters staring out my window like house cats.

Mufasa had just told Simba that everything the light touched was their kingdom, when my phone chimed a text alert, rousing me from my sleep. I reached across the bed and grabbed it from the nightstand. The message was from Wally.

Please forgive me for being rude to you tonight. I am so sorry. I have to work tomorrow, but I'll be free between 2 and 5. Can I see you then?

For a second, I couldn't think of what day tomorrow was. Then slowly, it came to me. Sunday. Church. Lunch. Home.

I was glad Wally had apologized, and I wanted to see her, but I decided to wait until morning to reply to her text. I didn't want her to think I'd been up all night, waiting to hear from her.

I placed my phone on the nightstand and went back to sleep. Soon, Mufasa and Simba reappeared in my room. Except now, they were perched on top of my bookcase, gazing down at me. I didn't know how they could fit in such a tiny space, but then, things don't always make sense in dreams.

In his melodious, baritone voice, Mufasa spoke to me, saying, "It's time to move on, Jesse. It's time to move on."

Simba smiled and nodded in agreement.

"Move on? From what?" I asked.

Mufasa threw back his head and laughed. "As if you need me to tell you that."

* * *

Sunday afternoon, Wally was waiting for me in front of Ernie Lou's. I had texted her earlier, offering to pick her up at the restaurant, but after our embarrassing scene, I didn't want to go inside.

I pulled my car along the curb, and she climbed in. Her black pants and red Ernie Lou's polo shirt were smudged with food stains and gave off a scent of brown gravy and yeast rolls. I hadn't noticed it last night, but her name badge said TURQUOISE. We greeted one other with a kiss, as if nothing had happened between us.

"You hungry?" I asked her. I'd already had lunch with my parents, but I didn't know if she'd eaten.

"No, I had a bowl of tortilla soup during my break," she said. "They let us have soups and salads and certain kinds of sandwiches for free. Everything else, we have to pay for. But I would like a *raspa*."

"Good idea," I said.

I exited the parking lot and headed to the Ice Cup-Ades, a snow cone shop housed in a strip mall. From noon, when the place opened for business, until nine, when it closed for the day, the Ice Cup-Ades was almost always crowded. Wally and I didn't mind standing in the long lines, though. In our opinion, the Ice Cup-Ades served the best snow cones in San Antonio.

Wally slouched in her seat and shut her eyes. She took slow, labored breaths, as if she were snoring.

"How was work?" I asked.

"Exhausting."

"I'll bet. So what are you doing, waiting tables?"

"I need the money."

"For what?"

"To buy a car."

"Whoa, you never told me you were interested in getting one," I said.

"I didn't want to say anything until I knew for sure that I could find a job to help me pay for it."

I could see why Wally would want a car. I'd always driven her around, but she may have been thinking about what she was going to do after I left for college.

"Still, is it worth killing yourself over it?" I asked.

She sat up and glowered at me. "Well, I'm not lucky enough to have a dad who's loaded and can buy me a brand-new Dodge Challenger whenever I want one."

"Seriously?" I said. "Now you sound like Goose, talking about how rich we are."

"Don't compare me to that troglodyte!"

"Then don't rip my father. Besides, I didn't ask for this car. It was a surprise birthday present. You were there when he gave it to me."

She leaned back in her seat. "Sorry, Jessup. I'm not trying to argue with you. All I'm saying is that my mom can't afford to buy me a car. She doesn't have any money."

"Huh, I thought you guys were well off," I said. "I mean, with her working as an exec for that pharmaceutical company and you living in a castle and everything."

"A castle?" Wally snorted a laugh. "You and I have different ideas of what a castle is."

"Well, it looks like one to me."

Wally's house was a two-story, stone building that sat on a hill. It had round towers on each side of the front, a spiraling staircase that led to the entrance and arched windows all around.

"The only way we've been able to stay in our house is because the insurance company paid off the mortgage when my dad died," she said. "But my mom's completely broke. My dear old stepdad made sure of it. Not only did he blow her life savings, he ran up a ridiculous amount of credit card debt before speeding off in a cloud of dust and a hearty hi-yo Silver. My mom's been struggling to pay the bills ever since. That dress I wore to the prom set her back a small fortune. I told her I didn't want it, but she insisted on getting it for me. And the sad thing is, I'll probably never wear it again."

Wally had shared portions of this story with me before, but I didn't realize they were in such bad shape financially.

"I'm sorry you're going through all that," I said. "But couldn't you at least have found a job that isn't such a beat-down?"

"Not one that pays nearly as much. Waiting tables may be a royal pain in the posterior, but the tips are great."

"Well, I'm sure you'll get used to the work once your body develops muscle memory," I said. "That's what I told Goose about our training."

"Oh, yeah. How did the tryouts go?"

I told Wally about our backbreaking exercises, which I explained was the reason I was so tired the night before. And about the strange people who showed up, including the Hawaiian-shirt guy, the ex-convict, Bobby Lee Taylor and the wanna-be comedian, Larry Beasley.

I didn't mention that three girls had also tried out, and it wasn't because I thought Wally would be jealous. The PWF had a number of females on its roster. They were all very attractive, but she'd never insinuated that I might be interested in any of them. I think it might've been because I was going to be putting my hands on Misty and Valen during our training, and I felt self-conscious about it.

The Ice Cup-Ades was as busy as we had expected it to be. The line around the metal railing went all the way out the front door. While we waited our turn, I glanced at the menu board and read the names of the different flavors. I did it every time we went in there, even though I almost always stuck to my favorites: strawberry, pineapple, banana, lemon and grape. Sometimes I ordered a snow cone with a combination of syrups. Wally preferred flavors like mangonada, horchata and chamoyada.

"Get whatever size you want, Jessup," she said. "I'm buying today."

"That's okay. I'll take care of it."

"Nuh-uh, your money's no good here, mister. You always pay when we go out. Now that I'm working, it's my turn."

"Don't worry about it. Save your money for your car."

Wally's face flushed with indignation. "Hey, I'm not exactly the Poor Little Match Girl! I can certainly afford to pay for a couple of raspas."

"I didn't say you couldn't."

"But you implied it."

"No, I didn't."

"Of course, you did."

"What's your problem, Wally?" I said, starting to grow irritated. "You've never complained about me paying for you before."

"That's because I hadn't told you about our money situation," she said. "And now that you know, I feel like you're treating me as if I'm a charity case."

Some people in line were watching us, making me uncomfortable.

"Fine, then, have it your way! Buy the raspas. Do whatever you want."

"You know what?" she said. "I've changed my mind. I don't want one anymore. I want to go home."

"It's up to you," I said, and reached inside my pocket for my keys.

"But I don't want you to take me. I'm upset, and I'd rather be upset alone. I'll call an Uber to pick me up."

"Oh, come on, Wally. Don't do that. You'll just be wasting your money for nothing."

"See? This is what I'm talking about, Jessup! You think that just because your family's wealthy, you're the only one who can afford anything."

"All right, that's it!" I said. "I'm done here. You can go to hell for all I care!"

I stalked out of the Ice Cup-Ades, wondering how long Wally had harbored these feelings toward me. Was it because my father had made millions throughout his wrestling career and could afford to buy me a muscle car without blinking? That we lived in what some people might perceive to be a mansion? That my parents had thrown a huge graduation party for me and were taking me to London?

I'd never said or done anything to make Wally feel as if she were beneath me. On the contrary, I'm the one who thought of myself as intellectually inferior to her. Maybe she resented the fact that she had to get a job to pay for what she wanted, and I didn't. If that was the case, then the rift between us was on her.

As I drove home, Wally somehow seemed less important to me. Great things were happening in my life. Tomorrow would be the first day of my training. Next month, I'd be vacationing in Europe with my parents. In August, I was going to start school at UT, and soon after that, I planned to begin my pro wrestling career.

The things Wally was mad about were beyond my control. I couldn't help how we lived. She could either accept me for who I was or not. I wasn't going to lose any sleep over her.

Hakuna matata.

CHAPTER EIGHTEEN

On Monday, I arrived at the Factory shortly after five o'clock, wanting to get a feel for the ring before everyone showed up. Not that I was a stranger to it. Sometimes, when I went to the Factory to work out, if the place was empty, I'd practice taking bumps and running the ropes, which weren't ropes at all. They were steel cables covered with a thin foam padding and rubber tubing, meaning they hurt when you bounced against them, until your body grew accustomed to it.

Falling on the mat could be painful, too. It was made of canvas, with a two-inch thick cushion and sheets of plywood underneath. The bottom of the ring had a suspension system that reduced the impact, but wrestlers still had to learn how to bump properly to avoid breaking their necks.

Based on what I'd seen my father do in the past, I figured one of the first lessons he was going to teach was how to run the ropes, and I wanted to brush up on the skill, hoping to impress him.

When I walked in, I was surprised to see Misty and Valen sitting at the merchandise table, doing what appeared to be homework. They had a stack of textbooks next to them and were typing on their laptops.

I debated whether I should introduce myself or act as if they weren't there. On the one hand, I didn't want the girls to think

I was trying to flirt with them. On the other, I didn't want to seem rude or standoffish.

Come on, Baron, your father's the Angel of Death. He's going to be their trainer. They'll be thrilled that you gave them the time of day.

I made my way toward them casually and said, "Hi, I'm Jesse."

The girls looked up from their laptops and smiled. A good sign.

"Nice to meet you," Misty said. "I don't know if you remember our names, but I'm Misty and this is Valen."

"Actually, my name's Valentina," she said. "I was born on Valentine's Day, which is where the name comes from. But I had a teacher who called me Valen for short. Anyway, I loved it 'cause it was different, and I've been going by it ever since."

"You sound like my girlfriend," I said. "Her name's Wally Ann, but she prefers to be called Wally for the same reason."

"Oh, so you have a girlfriend?" Valen asked.

"Well, she's not really my girlfriend," I said. "I mean, we go out sometimes, but it's nothing serious."

I don't know what made me say that. Wally and I had dated exclusively for a long time, and despite our recent spats, we hadn't broken up. At least not yet. Was I trying to leave the door open for Valen or Misty in case things went sour between Wally and me?

Switching the subject, I asked, "So what are you guys doing here so early?"

"We're taking summer classes at San Antonio College," Misty said. "We live in San Marcos, and it's too far to go home and come back, so we're just hanging out here doing our work until the training starts. Coach Ellis told us it'd be okay."

"That makes sense," I said, thinking their plan was similar to mine. "Are you working toward a degree, or are you just getting your basics out of the way?"

"Both," Valen said. "I'm taking English and history right now, but I'm going to major in kinesiology. I'd like to be an elementary school P.E. coach someday."

"Cool." I turned to Misty. "And you?"

"Computer science, but I'm not sure what I'm going to do with it."

"You might want to talk to Steve Dalton, one of my father's wrestlers," I said. "He's a software engineer. He may be able to give you some ideas."

"Thanks. I'll keep it in mind."

"Your dad mentioned that you'll be leaving for school in the fall," Valen said. "Where will you be going?"

"Not too far. UT Austin."

"Wow, that's awesome. Me and Misty and Noreen, the girl who was with us on Saturday, applied there, but none of us got accepted."

"I just lucked out, I guess," I said. "Listen, I'd better let you get back to your studying."

The girls were a lot friendlier than I had expected. I was afraid they'd be like some of the ones at my school who automatically set up their invisible shields whenever certain guys tried to talk to them.

I went behind the curtains to work out in one of the practice rings. The moment I set my duffel bag on a chair, I heard my phone chime. I took it out of the bag and saw that Wally had texted me two drawings—a detailed Máscara de la Muerte mask, and a full body image of a wrestler with a mask like it. The wrestler had white tights, white boots with skulls on the sides, and a long, white cape lined in black and silver, with an upturned collar.

The picture Wally had drawn at my house was great, but these looked professionally done. If Shirley Washington could design my wrestling gear to match them, I'd be one classy-looking *luchador.*

I started to answer Wally when it struck me that the drawings may have been her way of breaking up with me. Why else would she have sent them with no message? If she was just upset with me, she would've waited until we made up before giving them to me. And she would've handed them to me in person.

I didn't have Wally's witticism, but I could imagine her thinking: *I'm submitting a final payment and closing my account. Adiós, Jessup. Au revoir. Auf Wiedersehen. Goodbye.*

Strange, but I didn't feel hurt or bothered by it. Nor did I feel happy or relieved. It was as if my brain had gone numb, incapable of processing the fact that in all probability, Wally had just dumped me.

I thought about calling her to make sure I hadn't misinterpreted her text. But if it turned out I was right about what she meant, I didn't want to end up getting into another argument. Regardless, I felt I should let her know that I'd received the pictures, so I replied with a single word.

Thanks.

I climbed inside one of the rings and worked on my drills. Before long, I heard male voices coming through the curtains. I glanced at the wall clock. It was six-fifteen. The other trainees were beginning to arrive.

I toweled myself off, then went out to mingle with them. It was important to me that they saw me as a fellow trainee, not as Mark Baron's kid, who was simply killing time at the Factory until he left for college.

One of the guys I met was Joaquín Luna. He told me he used to play basketball in high school and had hoped to go to college on a basketball scholarship but didn't get any offers.

"They used to call me 'Wild King' Luna," he said. "You know, 'cause it sounds like my name."

"Oh, great," a trainee named Pete Vogel said. "We've got another Hilarious Beasley in our group." Pete was a barrel-chested guy with tree-trunk arms and legs. He wasn't ripped like some of the other trainees, but my guess was that he had the strength of at least two ordinary men.

"Make fun all you want, bro," Joaquín told him. "But when I start wrestling, I'm gonna call myself Wild King Luna. And one of these days, I'm gonna be a household name."

I also met George Galloway, a former NFL tight end, who'd played for a number of teams, including the Houston Texans. Now he worked as a real estate agent.

"I'm doing this to stay active and to enjoy the limelight again," he said. "But you never know. I may turn out to be even more famous than your old man."

One of the trainees who initially creeped me out was Bobby Lee Taylor. I was leery of him, knowing he'd been in prison for holding up convenience stores at gunpoint. Plus he was scary looking. Bobby Lee was almost as tall as my father. He had a shaved head, dark-brown caterpillar eyebrows and a Viking beard. Along with his jacked, tattooed body, I thought he'd make a perfect heel once he turned pro.

"Your name's Jesse, right?" he said. "I remember you from the tryouts. I'm Bobby Lee." His voice was low and raspy, like the one my father used as the Angel of Death, except his was natural.

"Good to meet you, sir," I said, and shook his hand, which was twice the size as mine.

"Sir? Ain't no need to be so formal with me, friend. I'm just plain old Bobby Lee."

I responded with a weak, "Okay."

"I got a good feeling about being here, know what I'm saying? I think pro wrestling's gonna give me a new direction in my life."

"My father's a great trainer," I said. "You'll learn a lot from him."

Bobby Lee Taylor may have looked like a psycho killer, but he seemed like a nice guy. I decided to give him the benefit of the doubt.

At promptly six-thirty, Travis and Joe gathered us in the fitness room for calisthenics. Then as I predicted, they took us to Henley Park behind the Starlight Shopping Center for hill runs. They started us with power walks, then short runs, long runs, slow ones and fast ones, up and down the park's hilly terrain. The warmups were tiring, but not exhausting, like the ones on Saturday.

When we were done, we were given a dinner break. We had been told that the concession stand would be closed, and we'd have to bring our own food. I took my lunch sack out of my duffel bag and ate with Goose in the back row of chairs

"Hey, take a look at these," I said, and showed him Wally's drawings. "This is what I'm going to look like when I wrestle as Máscara de la Muerte. Wally designed it for me."

"Man, that's awesome," he said.

"The thing is, she and I had a huge fight yesterday."

"Another one?"

"Yeah. Then today she sent me these pictures, but you'll notice that she didn't write anything. What do you think that means?"

Goose studied the drawings again. "I don't know. Maybe she's still mad at you and didn't feel like adding a message."

"No, I think it's more than that," I said. "I think this is Wally's way of breaking up with me."

"Oh, yeah? Hey, you know what? You may be right. She's kinda weird like that." Goose looked across the room at Misty and Valen, who were eating together. "Maybe now we can try to hook up with those chicks."

"I told you, I'm not interested in them," I said, although I wasn't ruling out the possibility. "Besides, I don't know for sure where I stand with Wally."

"Well, even if she didn't dump you, you need to get rid of her, man. She's old news."

Goose had never cared for Wally. She was too offbeat and brainy for his taste. And she only tolerated him because of me. She described him as being "half ignoramus and half cretin."

I knew my feelings for Wally were genuine, but I also realized that school had been part of what kept us together. Until this past weekend, I hadn't seen her since my graduation party. And after our last fight, I didn't know if I'd ever see her again. If our relationship had reached its end, this was probably the least painful way to go about it, by letting it wither away, with neither of us making an effort to mend it.

After the break, my father rang the time keeper's bell, calling everyone to the ring to begin our first lesson of the evening.

CHAPTER NINETEEN

"I want you to walk across the mat," he told the group. "You'll see that it isn't as springy as a trampoline. Nor is it soft, like a mattress. It's a rough sheet of canvas on a foam pad with three-quarter inch plywood underneath. It's got some give, but not as much as you may have thought from watching wrestling on television."

My father gave everyone a couple of minutes to familiarize themselves with the ring. Then he had us climb off it while he went over what we'd be doing.

"Today, I'm going to show you how to take a back bump," he said. "A bump is a wrestling term for falling down."

Some of the trainees murmured that they already knew what a bump was.

"You may have noticed that the middle of the ring is softer than the edges. It won't always be possible, but when you bump, that's where you want to land, because it's the safest spot."

He bounced on it to show the group what he meant.

"In order to take a back bump, you need to thrust your body forward, then spring back and drop. But right before you hit the mat, tuck in your chin to avoid hurting your head or your neck. Spread your arms out, palms down, with your feet in the air.

Make sure to land on the upper part of your back, near the shoulder area. Watch."

My father demonstrated the move. He repeated the instructions, then bumped three more times. Next, he asked Travis and Joe to model it.

"All right, now it's your turn," he said. "Who wants to go first?"

Everyone looked at each other, waiting for someone to volunteer. As much as I wanted to, I resisted the urge to raise my hand. I thought the group would expect me to know how to take a back bump already, and I didn't want them to think I was showing off.

"I will," the hulking Pete Vogel said, and stepped through the ropes.

My father stood him in the center of the ring. "Take a deep breath and exhale," he said. "You always want to exhale before you bump, so you don't get the wind knocked out of you. Now remember, thrust forward, then jump back. Hit the mat with the upper part of your back, chin tucked in, arms spread out, palms down and your feet in the air. You got that?"

"I think so," Pete said uneasily.

"C'mon, Pete! You can do it," Andy Robinson urged.

"Show us how it's done," George Galloway said.

"Do it, bro!" Joaquín Luna shouted.

Pete hesitated for a moment, then sprang back and crashed on the mat, full force. I couldn't help but picture a hippo being flipped backwards.

"Yeow, that hurt!" he cried, arching his back.

"That's because you landed on the lower part of your back," my father said. "Try it again."

Pete took another bump. This time he hit the mat with his shoulder area.

"Good, but lift your feet a little higher," my father told him. "You don't want to risk breaking an ankle. Pretend you're a baby getting ready for a diaper change."

The group laughed.

Pete took four successive back bumps. After the last one, he stood and bowed, and we clapped for him.

"Great job, Vogel," my father said. "All right, who's next?"

To my surprise, Valen climbed through the ropes. Without waiting for my father to give her the go-ahead, she took a fast bump. She winced a little, then got up and did it again. And again. And again. Each time she did, we cheered her on. When she was done, Misty, encouraged by Valen's bravery, went next.

After that, my father divided us into three groups. He kept one, and Travis and Joe took the other two. Goose was assigned to my father and wanted me to join him, but I didn't feel confident that my father would give me his full attention, so I went with Travis. I was tempted to work with Joe's group because Valen and Misty were part of it, but I didn't want the girls to suspect that I was attracted to them.

Some of the guys in my group, like Matt Perryman and Juan Serrano, were able to perform the back bump correctly on their first try. Others botched it a few times before getting it right. When I took my turn, Travis praised me, saying, "You're a natural at this, Jess. But then, why wouldn't you be?"

Once everyone was done, my father brought us together. "How many of you can play a musical instrument?" he asked.

Several hands went up, but not mine, even though I could play the guitar, and to a certain extent, the drums, because the question wasn't meant for me.

One trainee said he used to play the tenor sax in his high school band. Another said he played the trombone in his. Juan

Serrano told my father he played the piano, which caught his interest.

"Me, too," he said. "I took lessons from a sweet old lady name Miss Lavender. You any good at it?"

"I think so," Juan said. "I'm our church's pianist."

"Excellent. Well, the reason I asked if you played an instrument is because if you're like me, you didn't become an accomplished musician overnight. You had to practice over and over and over. I used to go to Miss Lavender's house for an hour each week. But if I only practiced the piano during the time I was there, I wouldn't have learned anything. What I'm saying is that we'll teach you the skills, but it'll be up to you to practice them on your own. The Factory is open every day, except Sundays, and you're welcome to come anytime to work out. Either Coach McKeon or Coach Ellis or I will be here to assist you. I don't hold classes on Fridays or Saturdays, so the four rings will be available to you all day. I suggest you make good use of them."

With the limited amount of time I had left before I started school, I knew I'd have to spend tons of hours at the Factory. Goose mowed lawns with his uncle, but maybe he could ask for some time off, and we could practice together.

For our next lesson, my father said, "One of the most basic moves in professional wrestling is running the ropes. In a moment, I'm going to show you how to do it. But first, let me explain that this is an eighteen-by-eighteen-foot ring, which is the standard size for most wrestling rings, although some may be smaller, others a little larger. Whenever you climb inside any ring, you want to get an idea of how many steps you need to take to get from one side to the other in order to know how to pace your speed."

My father crossed the ring in four long steps to illustrate what he meant.

"Now, there's a certain technique to running the ropes, so listen closely. As you run toward them, right before you hit the ropes, turn your body and lean against them with your back. Grab the top rope with one hand and the middle rope with the other. The reason for this is that it's always possible that the ropes could break, and you want to have something to hold onto. Also, if the ropes are loose, it'll keep you from falling through them. Watch."

Back and forth, my father went, taking long strides across the ring. As he did, he hit the ropes with his back, while grabbing them for just a second, before releasing them and springing forward.

Travis and Joe followed up his demonstration by performing the maneuver, too.

"It's only fair to warn you that when you hit the ropes, it's going to sting, and it might leave you with some bruises," my father said. "After all, these are steel cables you're running into. But you need to hit them hard to give the illusion that your opponent has flung you forcefully against them. It'll also help you with momentum during your sequences." He looked around for someone to try it. "All right, Guzmán, come up here. Let's see what you can do."

Goose gawked at me, surprised that he'd been chosen.

"It's okay," I told him. "You'll do fine."

He climbed inside the ring and walked across it to measure the distance. Then he took a running start. When he neared the ropes, he spun around and leaned gently against them.

"Don't slow down, Guzmán!" my father shouted. "Come on, hit those ropes! Hard!"

Goose ran the ropes again and again, grimacing each time he hit them, until he looked as if he might pass out.

"All right, you can stop now," my father told him. "Good job, Guzmán."

Goose staggered out of the ring and was about to rejoin me, when his eyes suddenly widened. He hurried to the restroom, but before he could make it, he vomited on the floor. I jumped out of my seat and escorted him to the restroom, while Travis grabbed a bucket and a mop to clean the mess.

Goose rinsed his mouth, then blew his nose on a strip of toilet paper. "I don't know if I can do this, man," he moaned.

"Sure, you can," I said. "This happens all the time. That's why Travis had the bucket and mop ready."

I gave Goose some time to compose himself. Then we returned to our seats.

The trainees and I practiced running the ropes with our respective groups. Again, Travis praised me when I breezed through my drills. If my father noticed how well I was doing, he didn't say anything.

The last lesson of the evening was on how to perform rolls. We tried our best, but by that time, we were worn out, and we flopped more than we rolled.

My father concluded the session by showing us clips of ACW matches on the jumbo screen of wrestlers executing the moves we'd learned.

"These guys and gals started out just like you," he said. "The thing is, they wanted to wrestle for the ACW bad enough, so they found a way to get there. Now some of you may decide that this is as far as you want to go, and that's fine. I'll be happy to use you in our shows. But if you want to make it to the big leagues, you're going to have to work harder at this than anything you've ever done."

As my father was addressing the group, he didn't realize he was also speaking to me, and I was taking his words more seriously than anyone in the room.

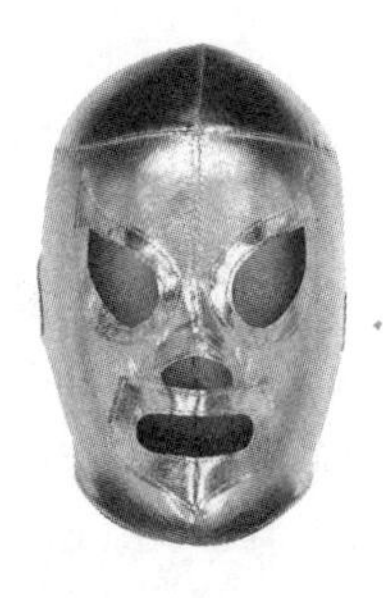

CHAPTER TWENTY

I wrote to Shirley Washington and attached Wally's drawings to the email. I knew Shirley was going to ask why I wanted the wrestling gear, so I explained that I was training with my father, and that I planned to wear it when I turned pro, but not to say anything to him about it, because I wanted it to be a surprise when I debuted my gimmick. I left out some details but everything I told her was true.

Shirley wrote back, saying she was swamped with work at the moment, and it'd be awhile before she could start on my outfit. I told her to take her time, that I wouldn't need it until September. By then, I'd be living in Austin, and she could have it delivered to my dorm without arousing curiosity from my parents if a large package arrived at the house for me. Shirley said she'd sew my gear for free but would have to charge me for the material. I told her to send me the bill, and I'd take care of it. I had plenty of graduation money to pay her.

I would love for Wally to see me wearing my *luchador* outfit once I got it, but our relationship was definitely over. I hadn't heard from her since the day she sent me the drawings, well over a month ago. Neither had I tried to call or text her. Goose had been telling me that I needed to move on from Wally. It hadn't occurred to me that she may have been thinking the same thing about me.

In the meantime, I continued to train at the Factory. I also kept up my exercise regimen—jogging, swimming and lifting weights.

Goose and I got together as much as we could to go over the skills we'd been learning in class. What I found interesting was how close he and I had grown during these past couple of months. Although I'd known Goose since middle school, I didn't think much of him. He was crude and obnoxious and not very bright. I used to hang out with him out of habit, same as I did with Wendell and Bucky. I didn't expect to see any of them after graduation. Yet, Goose had become my best training partner, and I was grateful that he'd decided to enroll in my father's wrestling school.

One afternoon, I arrived at the Factory early. Valen and Misty were inside the main ring, practicing their moves. Valen had Misty wrapped in a waist lock, and Misty was struggling to break free. Valen picked her up and slammed her on the mat.

"Good job," I said, clapping.

Startled, they turned around and looked at me, embarrassed. "How long have you been standing there?" Misty asked.

"I just walked in. But from what I saw, you guys are doing great."

"Thanks. We're trying."

"Why don't you join us?" Valen said. "I'm sure you can give us some pointers."

The girls had practiced with a lot of the guys in our class, but I wasn't one of them. I stepped inside the ring, fighting off the butterflies in my stomach. "What do you want me to help you with?"

Valen giggled. "Everything. We still aren't very good at this."

"All right, let's start with a basic, collar-and-elbow tie up," I said.

I grabbed Valen, one hand on her collar bone, the other on her elbow, she did the same to me, and we grappled for a few seconds.

"Now let's switch to a headlock."

"Who's going to do it? Me or you?" she asked.

"You."

"I thought so, but I wanted to make sure."

Valen wrapped her arm around my neck and pretended to squeeze it tightly, while I sold my pain.

"Swing me against the ropes," I said. "When I bounce back, knock me down with a shoulder block. Then as I start to get up, hit me with a dropkick. And if you can, lift me in a belly-to-back suplex and throw me down again."

Valen followed my instructions, and other than missing me completely with her dropkick, I thought she did a fair job.

"Oh, my god! I feel like a real wrestler!" she cried.

"Let's do it again," I said, feeling more comfortable about putting my hands on her. "This time I'll be the aggressor."

I tried to be gentle as I followed the sequence and took Valen down. Next, I went through the same set of moves with Misty.

We practiced hammerlocks, arm bars, arm drags and drop toeholds. We ran the ropes, worked on our front rolls, back rolls and quarter rolls.

After a while, I said, "I think we'd better stop. We want to be rested for tonight."

"Thank you so much, Jesse," Valen said. "No offense to your dad, but I think we've learned more from you today than we have in all the time we've been here."

Misty asked, "Do you think you might be able to work with us for a little bit each day before class starts?"

Sorry, Goose, but you've just been replaced.

"Sure, no problem. I can be here any time you want."

It seemed I had developed a pattern of meeting girls by accident. I couldn't tell if they were attracted to me, or if they just wanted to know how to wrestle, but I figured my odds of ending up with one of them were pretty good.

"Hey, listen, I'm going out for an early dinner," I said. "Would you guys like to join me?"

"I would," Valen said. "I'm starving."

She was a definite maybe.

"Me, too," Misty said.

"Have you guys ever eaten at O'Dell's?"

The girls looked at each other, then shook their heads.

"It's a deli, not too far from here. Come on, I'll drive." We walked out of the Factory to the parking lot.

When Misty saw my car, she squealed, "Oh, my god, Jesse! Is this yours?"

"Yeah," I said coolly.

She yanked the front passenger door open. "Shotgun!"

Valen gave her a dirty look, then got in the back seat.

The moment I slid into the driver's side, Misty squeezed my hand and said, "I'm so glad we met you, Jesse. At first, me and Val were kind of scared of signing up for your dad's wrestling school. We didn't know what to expect. But now that we've gotten to know you, and you're going to be helping us, we feel a lot better about it."

Valen instantly dropped down a notch. I had a feeling Misty was going to be my next girlfriend.

O'Dell's used to be a favorite hangout for Wally and me, but I hadn't eaten there in a long time. I told the girls I was treating, and they could have whatever they wanted. They ordered the salad bar, so I did, too.

"You guys mentioned that you've done some modeling," I said, while we were eating. "What kind?"

"We did a photo shoot for a swimwear company called The Blue Oyster," Misty said. "Ever hear of it?"

"No."

She chuckled. "That's okay. Nobody else has either. But at least we were able to add the photos to our portfolios."

"We've also done a few auto shows and boat shows," Valen said.

I couldn't believe I was having dinner with two gorgeous babes. I wished the guys from school could see me. Wally was attractive enough, but she was nowhere near as hot as Valen and Misty. We talked and laughed, and I couldn't remember when I'd had a better time.

As we were finishing our meal, I looked at my watch. "We need to get back," I said. "My father doesn't like it when people show up late to class."

We left the restaurant and got in my car. This time, Valen claimed the front passenger seat.

On the way to the Factory, I noticed her taking a tiny baggie from her purse with a white powdery substance inside it. She dug her fingernail into it and scooped some out.

"What are you doing?" I said, aghast.

She snorted the powder. "It's just an energy booster. Here, try it." She put her fingernail under my nose, but I pushed it away.

"Are you crazy? I don't do drugs! And you shouldn't, either."

"Oh, grow up, Jesse! How do you think we're able to handle the pain?" Valen passed the baggie to Misty, who also sampled the powder.

Drugs were a big problem in professional wrestling, which was why the ACW had a wellness policy, and wrestlers were tested randomly. If the girls were serious about entering the profession, they were starting off on the wrong foot.

My mind flashed back to the time I was driving TJ's car, and he and the girls who were riding with us were drunk. We got pulled over by a cop, and they ended up getting arrested for public intoxication. I was the only one who hadn't been drinking, so the officer let me go.

But if I were to get stopped now, and the police found drugs in my car, my whole future could fall apart—my school, my potential wrestling career—everything.

I pulled into a nearby gas station. "I'm going to drop you guys off here," I said. "You can call an Uber to pick you up. Or you can walk the rest of the way."

"Are you kidding us?" Valen shrieked.

"No, I'm not. Now go on."

She cussed me out, in English and in Spanish, which I thought sounded weird coming from such a beautiful girl. Then she and Misty climbed out.

"You're not going to tell your dad about this, are you?" Misty asked.

I drove off, without answering her.

CHAPTER TWENTY-ONE

I didn't return to the Factory that evening. Nor did I report Valen and Misty to my father. If they wanted to screw up their lives, that was their problem. The only person I told was Goose. He'd been flirting with the girls, and I thought he should know what they were doing before he got involved with them.

"Aw, man," he said. "One of the reasons I broke up with Yolanda is 'cause I thought I had a chance with Valen. But if she's a cokehead, I don't wanna have nothing to do with her."

I'd seen Goose do a lot of stupid things over the years, but drugs wasn't one of them. In fact, when I was planning to go to Mexico with TJ to buy steroids, he jumped all over me, warning me that I shouldn't be using them.

The girls must've thought I snitched them out because they didn't go back to the Factory, either, and the next day, they quit the program. It was just as well. The thought of having to train with them made my stomach turn.

In the days that followed, my father taught us how to apply submission holds, such as the Boston Crab, the Sharpshooter and the Figure-Four Leglock, as well as how to counter them.

"In boxing, fighters try not to let their opponents see how hurt they are," he said. "But because pro wrestling is more about entertainment, you want to show the audience that the holds are causing you excruciating pain. So you need to sell your agony. Scream and moan, but don't oversell it. Otherwise, it'll look comical, not painful."

One evening, the lesson was on how to throw punches.

"When you used to watch wrestling as a kid, did you ever wonder why, with all the punches wrestlers threw at each other, no one ever got black eyes, bruised cheeks, broken noses or busted lips?" my father asked.

The trainees laughed.

"The biggest illusion in professional wrestling is the punch," he said. "To most people, it looks and sounds real, but it's not. The trick to making a punch appear believable is to sell it properly. You sell it when you throw it, and you sell it when you get hit by it. Here's how it works. First, you want the audience to see that your fist is tight and ready to go. But just as you throw it, loosen your fingers."

My father smiled at me. For a second, I thought he was going to ask me to assist him with his demonstration, but he had something else in mind.

"When my son Jesse was little, his teachers used to complain to my wife and me that he had a hard time paying attention in class. They said he'd make binoculars with his hands and look around the room through them while they were teaching."

Bobby Lee Taylor leaned into me and whispered, "I used to do that, too."

"Let's all put our hands to our eyes and pretend we're looking through binoculars," my father said. As silly as his request sounded, everyone did as they were told, even me.

"When you throw punches, think of your fists as your binoculars. You want your hands to be that open, but don't let the audience see it. And they won't if you do it fast enough. Rear your arm back, hand closed, then swing. Turn your fist up, fingers loose and brush your fingertips against your opponent's face. That is, if you touch him at all. Continue your movement so it looks like you put a lot of power behind it."

He called Matt Perryman to the ring and positioned him against a turnbuckle. "I'm going to throw a punch at you, Perryman, and I want you to snap your head back, as if I hit you, but don't oversell it."

My father swung his fist at him.

Matt jerked his head and groaned an *ungh*, even though my father didn't touch him.

"Good job, Perryman," my father said. "Now the icing on the punch is the sound effect. Not only do you want the audience to see the punch, you want them to hear it, too. There are several ways to accomplish this. The old-school method is to stomp the mat with your foot every time you throw a punch. Watch."

My father swung at Matt, but this time, he stomped his foot simultaneously. He demonstrated the process again and again, with Matt selling each punch.

"Another method is to slap your bicep, your chest or your thigh, each time you throw a punch or a kick." My father performed the move so fast that even after he told us what he was going to do, it sounded as if he had punched Matt on the jaw. "There's a third way. Here, you actually hit each other to add realism to your move, but it's more of a slap punch. When you strike your opponent, do it with the back of your hand, not the knuckle area, and hit him on the neck or the shoulder. By then, your bodies will be sweaty, and the slap will sound loud." He looked at Matt. "You okay if I do it to you?"

"Go ahead," he said. "That's why I'm here."

My father slap punched him on the neck, but Matt reacted as if he'd been hit in the face.

"Some wrestlers like to wrestle stiff, and they'll hit each other much harder than that," my father said. "And that includes attacking each other with folding chairs and other objects, but that's something they agree on ahead of time."

My father broke us up into groups and had us practice throwing punches at each other.

"Hey, bro, that hurt!" Joaquín Luna complained when Bobby Lee hit him on the jaw.

"Sorry, friend, I ain't used to throwing fake punches," he said.

My father checked on Joaquín to make sure he was all right. Then he told everyone, "This is one of the hazards of the business. In the heat of the action, your opponent might accidently hit you with a potato. If that happens, there's a tradition that a lot of wrestlers follow. If your opponent connects with a stiff punch you hadn't planned for, you have the right to send him a receipt. By that, I mean that you can hit him just as hard as he hit you, to remind him to watch what he's doing."

Bobby Lee Taylor sighed. He patted Joaquín on the back and said, "Okay, friend. Go ahead. Tag me."

Joaquín looked at my father, unsure of what to do. Then he stared at the other guys, who had stopped to watch. Finally, he popped Bobby Lee lightly on the cheek.

"God bless you, friend," Bobby Lee said. "We good now?"

Throughout my training, I had built a strong rapport with the guys, and I really enjoyed working with them. I almost wished I didn't have to go to London, but my parents and I flew out the following week.

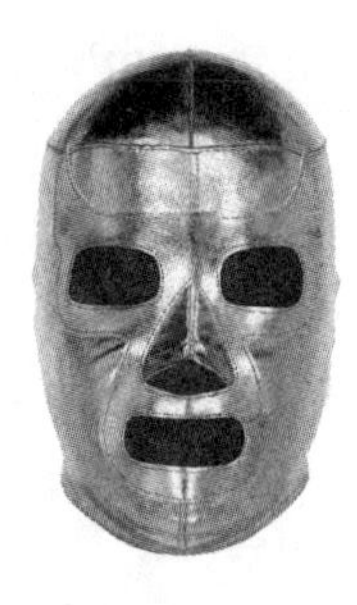

CHAPTER TWENTY-TWO

Being out in public with my father has always been a problem for my mom and me. No matter where we go, wrestling fans recognize him. He can tie his hair back, tuck it under a gimme cap and put on a pair of sunglasses. Yet, even without his skeleton-face makeup, they still know it's him.

Some fans will politely ask for an autograph and to have their picture taken with him. Others will interrupt us while we're having dinner at a restaurant, or when we're at the movies, or at the mall, and start taking photos, without first asking for permission. What irritates my mom more than anything is when women shamelessly throw themselves at my father, right in front of her.

I thought things would be different in London. They weren't.

When we checked into the Knightsbridge Hotel, the clerk read my father's name on the registration information and matched it to his face.

"Oh, my days!" she cried. "You're the Angel of Death, aren't you!"

"Some people call me that," he said, with a slight smile.

The instant the clerk identified my father, my mom, knowing what was coming next, walked away from the registration desk and wandered around the lobby, while he finished checking us in.

"I know you've heard this before, Mr. Baron, but I truly am one of your biggest fans," the clerk said. "As a matter of fact, I have a poster of you hanging in my flat that I bought a few years ago when my boyfriend and I went to see you wrestle at the O2."

"Thank you. It's always nice to meet a fan," he said.

"If I bring my poster tomorrow, do you think you might autograph it for me?" she asked.

"I'd be glad to."

The clerk was a cute, short-haired brunette, not much older than me. According to the brass-plated name badge on her black blazer, her name was Bronwyn.

"My boyfriend's not going to believe it when I tell him who's staying at our hotel," she said. "Would you mind if I take a selfie with you so I can show him?"

"No, not at all."

Bronwyn came around the registration desk. "How about if we take it over here?"

She led my father to a table with a large floral arrangement on it, and he put his arm around her, like she was his girlfriend. Then she held up her phone and took a photo.

"Why don't we let my son take the next one?" he said. "This is Jesse."

"Oh, wow, I can see the resemblance," Bronwyn said.

"And that's my wife over . . ." My father looked across the lobby, but my mom had disappeared into the next room.

Any other time, it would've bothered me if my father had asked me to take a picture of him with a fan, but now I could see myself in his place. Bronwyn handed me her phone, and I took several shots.

After we'd gotten our key cards and had taken our luggage to our rooms, my parents and I went out for lunch at a restaurant called the Mayfair Chippy. I had suggested eating fish and chips for our first meal because I wanted to sample typical British food.

The day was pleasant, and the Mayfair Chippy wasn't too far from our hotel, so we walked to it. Along the way, people stared at my father. I couldn't tell if it was because they recognized him, or because a six-foot-seven inch, three-hundred-twenty pound giant was walking among them.

London was just as I'd seen it in movies and TV shows. Red double-decker buses and black taxi cabs rode down the busy streets, and crowds of people filled the sidewalks. The city's architecture was a breathtaking mixture of gothic and modern design. It reminded me of Dorothy's line in *The Wizard of Oz*: "Toto, I've a feeling we're not in Kansas anymore."

At the restaurant, no one recognized my father, and we were able to enjoy our lunch quietly. My fish and chips were great, but the dish came with mushy peas. My mom explained that in England, mushy peas are traditionally served with fish and chips. I can't stand the taste of green peas, so I passed on them, even if they were a British food.

During our ten-day stay, we visited well-known sites, such as the Tower Bridge, Trafalgar Square, Piccadilly Circus, the British Museum, Buckingham Palace, St. Paul's Cathedral, Westminster Abbey and the Houses of Parliament, including Big Ben. We also took excursions to Stonehenge and Canterbury Cathedral. And everywhere we went, my father stopped to sign autographs and pose for photos.

Each day, I got up early and jogged through Hyde Park, which was near our hotel. The Knightsbridge didn't have a fitness room, and I wanted to stay in shape.

One morning, while I was jogging, I heard someone shout, "Stop him! He stole my wallet!"

A guy was racing toward me, with an old man chasing after him. It made me mad to see a senior citizen getting robbed, so I stuck my foot out and tripped the guy, sending him tumbling to the ground. As he got up, I grabbed his arm in a wristlock, then twisted it into an arm lock and applied a rear chokehold on him. The guy squirmed and wriggled, but he was smaller and skinnier than me. There was no way he was going to break free.

The old man caught up to him, gasping for breath. "Where's my wallet?" he demanded.

"Give it to him!" I told the guy, tightening my grip.

"Aaah, lemme go!" he bawled. "You're hurting me!"

"It's going to hurt a lot more if you don't do what he says."

The guy reached inside his pocket with his free hand and pulled out a brown leather wallet. The old man snatched it from him and checked its contents to make sure everything was in there.

A woman who was watching the confrontation, said, "I called the bobbies. They're on their way."

It took me a moment to remember that a *bobby* is what Brits call a police officer. The woman wasn't alone. A crowd was gathering around us, and people were taking pictures.

"I'd just gotten off the Tube when this scoundrel bumped into me," the old man said. "All of a sudden, my pocket felt lighter and I realized he'd filched my wallet."

The guy looked up at me and whimpered, "C'mon, mate. I'm just a poor bloke trying to feed my family. Honest to god. How 'bout setting me loose?"

"Don't you let him go," the old man said. "I'm pressing charges against this lowlife. Pickpockets like him think they can do whatever they want in this city."

I wished the bobbies would hurry because I didn't know what to do with the guy. He'd already given the old man his wallet, so for all intents and purposes, the matter was resolved.

As luck would have it, a bobby must've been in the area because he appeared a moment later.

"What's going on here?" he asked.

"He stole my wallet," the old man said. "And this young man helped me get it back."

The bobby pulled out a pair of handcuffs, and I turned the pickpocket over to him. He cuffed the guy and sat him on the ground.

"And who might you be?" he asked me.

"My name's Jesse Baron. I was jogging out here when I saw what was happening, so I decided to try to stop him."

"Not a very clever thing to do, if you ask me," the bobby said curtly. "I know you meant well, but pickpockets can be dangerous."

"Good Lord!" the old man exclaimed. "Is that all you can say to him for doing *your* job? Where were you when I was yelling for help?"

The bobby didn't reply.

"My name is Charles Davies," the old man told me. "I want you to know how indebted I am to you. Most people would've looked the other way and done nothing." He opened his wallet and pulled out a bill. "I don't have much money, but let me give you this twenty-pound note."

"That's okay," I said, waving it off. "I'm glad I could help."

"You sound American. Are you from the States?"

"Yes, sir. I'm from Texas. My parents and I are here on vacation."

"Well, God bless you, son, and God bless America."

The bobby radioed for a police car to take the pickpocket away. When he ended his call, I asked him if I could phone my parents.

"Go ahead," he said. "But after that, I'm going to need for you to give me a statement for my report."

I called my mom and explained what happened. I tried to sound calm, but she went off on me, ranting about how I could've gotten hurt. "We'll be right there!" she said.

Mr. Davies and I gave our statements. Then he left, but not before thanking me once more for what I'd done.

My parents arrived almost at the same time as the police car.

"How are you doing, Jesse?" my father asked. "You okay?"

I told him and my mom that I was fine. Then I filled them in on the details of the incident.

The bobby was sliding the pickpocket in the back seat of the police car when he noticed my father. After the car drove off, he approached him and said, "Pardon me, sir, but would you by any chance happen to be the Angel of Death from American Championship Wrestling?"

"I am," my father mumbled, not in the mood to chat with a fan.

"I saw you a couple of months ago on *Monday Night Mayhem*," he said. "Are you planning on making a comeback?"

My mom sighed in annoyance. "Officer, if you're done here, can we take our son back to our hotel?"

"Yes, of course. But before you leave, Mr. Baron, do you mind if I take a selfie with you?"

Reluctantly, my father posed for a quick photo.

After that, we returned to our hotel. I showered and got dressed. From there, we headed to the Tower of London, which was on our schedule for the day.

The Tower of London is a huge stone fortress built almost a thousand years ago. A Yeoman Warder, also known as a Beefeater, met us at the entrance and gave us a guided tour. He told us stories of the many people who'd been imprisoned and executed there, including Anne Boleyn and the Princes of the Tower, the two young sons of King Edward the IV. He took us to the White Tower, where we saw exhibits of historical suits of armor. Among them were some of the ones worn by Henry the VIII. I also got to see the Crown Jewels collection. I couldn't believe I was walking through rooms filled with so much gold, diamonds and other precious stones.

Our visit to the Tower of London was fascinating, but tiring, and I was glad when we got back to our hotel.

A woman was sitting in the lobby, waiting for us. I thought she was another wrestling fan wanting to meet my father, but she moved past him and came up to me. "Jesse Baron? My name is Dana Murphy. I'm from *The Times.* If you don't mind, I'd like to ask you a few questions about what happened at Hyde Park this morning."

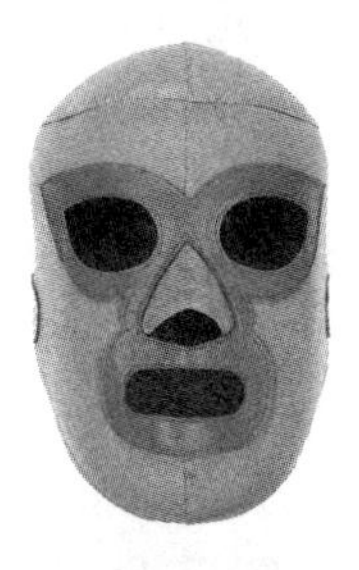

CHAPTER TWENTY-THREE

I was getting ready for the day when my hotel phone rang. I couldn't imagine who it might be. If my parents wanted to talk to me, they would've called me on my cell or come to my room.

"Hello?"

"Jesse, have you seen today's paper?" Bronwyn asked. "There's an article about you in it."

"Oh, yeah. I knew there was going to be a story about me, but I didn't know when. What does it say?"

"Come downstairs and look at it."

I laced up my sneakers, then hurried to the lobby, curious to read what the reporter had written. She hadn't asked me a lot of questions, other than to verify what she knew already—that I'd nabbed a pickpocket who'd stolen an old man's wallet. At most, I expected to see a tiny article buried in the back of the newspaper.

When Bronwyn showed it to me, I was totally blown away. On the front page of *The Times of London* was a photo of me with the pickpocket in my grasp. Next to it was a photo of my father as the Angel of Death.

Son of the Angel of Death Outwrestles Pickpocket at Hyde Park by Dana Murphy

For centuries, this city has been a hunting ground for pickpockets. But when an alleged thief lifted a wallet from a senior citizen, Jesse Baron decided to take action.

Baron, 18, son of retired American Championship Wrestling performer, Mark Baron, who wrestled under the name of the Angel of Death, was jogging yesterday morning at Hyde Park when he heard a cry for help.

Seeing the suspect, Harry Weems, 36, fleeing, Baron used the wrestling skills he learned from his father and took Weems to the ground. He picked him up by the arm, turned it into a wristlock, then bent it into an armlock and held him until a bobby arrived.

The victim, Charles Davies, 72, told police, "I generally don't carry much cash, but my credit cards, my identification and other important documents were inside my wallet. If it hadn't been for Jesse's bravery, I would have lost everything."

Baron and his parents are here on vacation from San Antonio, Texas, in the United States. The trip is part of Baron's high school graduation gift.

When asked if he intends to pursue a career in professional wrestling like his father, Baron's only comment was, "You never know."

Although police discourage the public from interfering with a crime in progress, Davies says he owes a great debt of gratitude to Baron. "As far as I'm concerned, Jesse's a hero. We Londoners should learn from him and do more to help keep our city safe."

"This is unbelievable!" I said.

"Shame on you for keeping it a secret from me," Bronwyn teased. "Here, I've made a friend who's a hero, and he doesn't mention a word of it to me."

"Well, I couldn't exactly come up to you and say, 'Hey, guess what, Bronwyn? I caught a pickpocket today.' Not without sounding like I was bragging."

"Ah, so in addition to being a hero, you're also modest," she said. "A good quality to have. I'm sure your mum and dad are very proud of you."

"Thanks. Hey, listen, is it okay if I borrow your paper? I'd like to show it to them."

"By all means," she said. "But under one condition."

"What's that?"

"After you're done with it, I want you to autograph it for me."

I chuckled. "Seriously?"

"I'm going to frame it and hang it in my flat next to your dad's poster," she said.

My first autograph hound, I thought. Hopefully, the first of many.

I went upstairs and knocked on my parents' door. When my mom opened it, I held the newspaper to her face. "Tada-a-a!"

"Oh, no," she moaned.

"What's the matter?" I asked.

"Jesse, the last thing this family needs is more publicity. I really wish you hadn't spoken to that reporter yesterday."

"What did you expect me to do? Tell her to get lost?" I said, disheartened by her reaction.

Without answering, she took the newspaper from me and read the article. As she did, she curled her lips and shook her head.

"I thought you'd be excited about it," I said. "I don't know why you're mad."

"Like I told you yesterday, that pickpocket could've had a knife. He might've hurt you. And for what? Just so you could get a stranger's wallet back?"

"Mom, it happened so fast, I didn't have time to think about it."

"Well, you *should have!* I mean, we're in a foreign country, and you decide to get involved in something that isn't any of your business."

Hearing the commotion, my father came out of the bedroom. "What's going on?"

"Mark, look at this."

"Oh, nice," he said, grinning. "We'll have to buy copies to give to our friends and relatives."

My mom stared at him, dumbfounded. "I don't know why you're so happy about it. Jesse could've gotten himself killed."

"Honey, I'm not saying that what he did was right, but everything turned out okay. And now he's on the front page of *The Times of London*. Imagine that." My father pulled out his phone. "Let me see if the article is online." He made a quick search. "Here it is. I'm going to call my parents and send them the link."

While he was on his phone, my mom read the article again. Although she was upset by what I'd done, the proud mama in her couldn't help but brag about me. She picked up her phone and began sharing the link with her friends and family, too.

I posted it on social media, and within seconds, people started commenting.

That's awesome, dude!

I didn't know you were such a badass!

Don't mess with Texas!

The pickpocket was lucky you didn't give him the Death Drop Piledriver!

I'm calling it right now. Jesse Baron vs. The Pickpocket in a Steel Cage Match!

In the end, my mom accepted that however dangerous my actions may have been, I'd brought pride to our family, and she spent all morning on the phone talking about me.

My trip to London was an incredible experience, one I'd never forget. But what made it even more memorable was that I'd gotten my first real taste of fame.

CHAPTER TWENTY-FOUR

Early Friday morning, we flew out of Heathrow Airport. The long flight back to San Antonio wiped me out, and the minute we got home, I went straight to bed without bothering to unpack my suitcases.

The next day, I was suffering from jetlag. I didn't feel like doing anything, but my father was putting on a show that evening, and he expected me to run the ticket counter. I couldn't say no to him, not after the amazing graduation present he and my mom had given me. Besides, it'd be my last time working the events. In two weeks, I'd be moving to Austin.

My father had been at the Factory all day, catching up on work he'd put aside while we were on vacation, and making sure everything was set for the night's show. I didn't have to be there until six, when the doors opened.

At five-thirty, I left the house. I drove down Oakwood Road, past Erastus Deaf Smith High School, and turned the corner at Salazar Park. When I did, I was taken aback when I spotted, of all people, Wally. She was walking Samson by the park's clubhouse. I didn't know whether to honk, or stop and talk to her, or pretend I hadn't noticed her and keep going.

Then she saw me. She offered a timid wave, so I pulled my car along the curb and got out. As an ex-boyfriend, I wasn't sure how to greet her. With a kiss? A hug? A handshake?

Unable to decide, I shoved my hands in my pockets and ambled up to her. "Hi, Wally," I said softly. "It's good to see you."

Like me, she didn't display any affection. Maintaining her distance, she said, "Hola, Jessup. You must've made it back from London yesterday."

"How'd you guess?" I couldn't remember if I'd told her which days we'd be gone on our trip.

"I saw the *Times of London* article you posted. I didn't realize you were so brave."

"I'm not. I just happened to be in the right place at the right time."

"Well, for what it's worth, I'm very proud of you for what you did."

"Thanks." I licked my lips and cleared my throat. "Listen, Wally . . . I . . . I want to apologize to you for what happened between us. I acted like such a jerk. I shouldn't have talked to you the way I did. You didn't deserve that."

"Hey, don't hog all the credit," she said. "I was a bit of a horse's patootie myself. I don't know what came over me. I'm sorry, too."

"You know, looking back, I think that there were so many changes going on in my life that I wasn't quite ready for," I said.

"Ditto."

I stretched out my hand. "Friends?"

"Oh, we can do much better than that." I thought Wally was going to give me a hug or a kiss. Instead, she reached inside her messenger bag, took out two pieces of peppermint candy, and handed me one. "This'll help bring back our friendship."

Wally was a firm "believer" in what she called the "magical healing properties" of peppermint candy.

I unwrapped mine and popped it in my mouth. "So how have you been doing? Did you ever buy a car?"

"I did. A Chevy Malibu that's getting up in years. But I'm not sure how much longer I'll get to keep it."

"Why?"

She laughed nervously. "I got fired from Ernie Lou's."

"Wow, that's too bad."

"It's all right. I was going to quit anyway. My mom didn't want me working there, and I hated the place. I have enough money in the bank to make the next few car payments, but I need to find a job in order to hold onto it." She glanced at a nearby picnic table. "Let's sit down. I want to hear about your trip."

"I'd like to, but I'm on my way to the Factory," I said. "My father's putting on a show tonight, and I have to work it."

"Oh. Some other time, then," she said, sounding disappointed.

Whatever the reasons were that we broke up, I was grateful to reconnect with Wally. Now that I had, I was afraid that if I let her go, there wouldn't be *some other time*.

"I have an idea," I said. "Why don't you go to the Factory with me? You can help me sell tickets."

Wally looked down at Samson and brushed his head but didn't say anything.

You're such an idiot, Baron. You haven't seen her in forever, and instead of inviting her somewhere nice, you want to put her to work.

"If you can't, that's all right," I said, giving her an out.

"No, no. It's just that I promised Samson I'd take him to the movies tonight. He's been dying to see that new doggie flick, *Barking Up the Wrong Tree*." Wally took him by his snout. "I'll take you to see it tomorrow, boy. Okey doke?"

It was great to see her back to her cheerful, quirky self.

We climbed into my car, and I drove them to her house. She took Samson inside. Then we headed to the Factory.

Wally had been to the PWF events before, but this was the first time I'd asked her to work one with me. She greeted the customers as if she owned the company. She asked them if it was their first time there, who their favorite wrestlers were, and she told them to have a good time. Little kids and senior citizens, especially, were drawn to her, which wasn't unusual. She'd always had a way with people in those age groups.

By contrast, I kept my conversations to a minimum. I quoted the customers the price of admission and took their money. If they paid with a credit card, I said, "Sign here." That was about it. I didn't like making chit-chat with strangers.

The show opened with a match between Klondike Katie and Oona the Enchantress.

Klondike Katie came out first. Her real name was Katherine Crawford, and she lived in The Woodlands, a city outside of Houston. Her character, though, was from the Yukon Territory in northwest Canada. Katie had on a fur parka and wrestling boots made to look like mukluks. Underneath, she wore a red plaid spandex tank top and tights. She played a baby face, so the audience welcomed her with cheers and applause.

Next, Oona the Enchantress' music sounded. Knowing she was the heel in the match, the fans booed the moment she stepped through the curtains.

In real life, Oona Sifuentes was happily married, had two kids and lived in Georgetown, a city near Austin. But as Oona the Enchantress, she hailed from the "Island of Men's Dreams." Oona wore a white toga with a gold-colored mesh belt around her waist, and white leather boots. Her dark hair was tied back in a french braid and was decorated with gold, star-shaped hair clips.

With a microphone in her hand, she taunted the crowd, saying, "I look around this arena and all I see is a bunch of fat, ugly, out of shape women. Admit it, ladies. I am everything you wish you could be. Beautiful. Alluring. Sexy. And men, I am the goddess of your dreams and desires. But you will *never, ever*, possess me!" She laughed wickedly as the crowd showered her with boos. Oona was terrific at drawing heat.

Pointing to Klondike Katie, she said, "The only thing I find more disgusting than having to wrestle in front of you people is having to get inside the ring with that filthy, smelly, Canadian moose!"

Wally giggled. "I could totally do that," she said.

"What? Wrestle?" I asked.

"No, antagonize a crowd. Playing a heel looks like a lot more fun than playing a baby face."

"That's what my father used to say. He understood that he needed to reinvent his character from time to time, but he never liked working as a face."

Clyde Conner made the proper introductions. At the sound of the bell, Oona began shoving Katie, telling her, "Who do you think you are, honey? Do you actually believe you have a chance against me? Face it. No matter how hard you work, no matter how much you try, you will never be as good or as beautiful as me."

Katie answered Oona's insults with a slap to the face. Then she flung her against a corner and stomped her repeatedly with her boot. Doug Fletcher started a five count, threatening to disqualify her if she didn't stop. Katie stepped back, allowing Oona to get to her feet. As she did, Katie charged at her with an Avalanche and knocked her back down.

"Boo!" Wally yelled.

"Hey, you're working here," I said. "You're not supposed to show favoritism toward the wrestlers."

"Sorry, I got carried away."

Katie grabbed Oona by the hair, but Oona caught her with a forearm to the face, then swung her against the ropes. When Katie sprang back, Oona took her down with a drop toehold.

"Yay!" Wally shouted. "Oops."

For the next ten minutes or so, the women battled back and forth, until Oona hit Katie with a double knee drop. Next, she climbed on a top turnbuckle and leaped off it with a moonsault, which she dubbed, "The Broken Dreams." She landed on Katie and pinned her shoulders. Doug Fletcher slapped the mat three times, then raised her arm in victory. Clyde Conner announced Oona the Enchantress as the winner of the bout, amid a roar of boos and jeers.

"She's fantastic," Wally said. "Except for the wrestling part, I'd love to play Oona the Enchantress."

"Well, you sort of need to do both," I said. "You can't have one without the other."

She sighed. "*Qué lástima.*"

After the matches, I invited Wally out to dinner, but she declined my offer, without giving me a reason, so I took her home.

She undid her seatbelt and slid out of the car. "Thanks for letting me work the show with you, Jessup," she said. "I had a great time." Then she went inside her house. No kiss. No hug. No handshake.

Wally may have thought that with me leaving for college in a couple of weeks, there was no point in trying to restart our relationship. She was probably right. I drove away, wondering if I'd see her again.

CHAPTER TWENTY-FIVE

By the end of my training, I had added twelve pounds of muscle to my body. I'd also wrestled lots of practice matches, with Travis coaching me on how to improve my techniques, until I felt confident that I was ready to turn pro.

When Travis first asked me why I was so gung-ho about my training, I brushed him off with an excuse about simply wanting to stay in shape. I wasn't sure if I could trust him. Travis had been a fan of my father's for years. The black shirt with the white skull he wore when he wrestled was a tribute to him. Travis now worked as an inspection manager for the Merriday Trucking Company, but he spent his time off at the Factory, because he considered it an honor to help my father.

He was the only coach I'd trained with, and we became friends, close enough that before I left, I decided to reveal my plans to him.

He told me, "When I was your age, I tried to enroll at a wrestling school in Dallas. The owner was an old toot named Amos Brown, who wrestled back in the day as Stackhouse Brown. He took one look at me, then cussed me out, saying I had no business trying to be a wrestler, so I left. Later, I found out that he did that to everybody, to see how badly they wanted to wrestle. Anyway, I kept thinking about what might've been, and eventually, I signed with another wrestling school. The owner there was a lot like your dad, who encouraged and motivated his students, instead of trying to put them down."

Until Travis retired as a full-time performer, he had enjoyed a successful wrestling career. He never wrestled for the ACW, but he worked for promotions all over the country, as well as in Japan, Canada and Mexico.

"Believe me, Jess, I know exactly what you're going through," he said. "Stackhouse Brown almost made me give up my dream, but something inside me refused to let it go. So my advice to you is this. Do what you think will make you happy. You'll find out, sooner or later, whether you made the right decision."

In addition to my training, I watched tons of wrestling videos. I made mental notes of how the heels used bad-guy tactics, such as poking their opponent's eyes, choking, punching, kicking and hiding behind the referee, to rile the audience. And at what point the baby faces made a comeback from the beating the heels were giving them to build the story they were telling.

I also googled wrestling promotions in Texas. San Antonio had four of them, including the Ox Mulligan Pro Wrestling Factory. Austin had two. They'd be the first ones I'd check out. Corpus Christi had three. Houston had six. College Station and Waco had one each. There were seven in the Dallas/Ft. Worth area, and five in El Paso. As soon as my *luchador* outfit came in, I was going to start writing to some of those promoters.

I know this sounds stupid, but the one worry I had about making it as a pro wrestler was that I didn't have an outgoing personality. I'd never been a people person, and I was afraid that I wouldn't be able to connect with an audience. I wasn't any good at cutting promos, either. I wrote some down and practiced them in my room, but they sounded like essays. My father often invited guest coaches to offer his trainees tips on how to develop their mic skills, but I'd be gone by the time he got to that part of the course.

Then one day, I was standing in front of my mirror, wearing a pair of running shorts and my father's Annihilator mask, practicing poses for my Máscara de la Muerte photos, when without thinking, I pointed to my reflection, and in a low, guttural voice, said, *"Listen to me, Grimm! You can run your mouth all you want, but you can't run from me! Next Monday night, I'm gonna take your ACW heavyweight championship, and there won't be a damn thing you can do about it!"* I paced back and forth in my room, snarling like a wild animal, then returned to my mirror. *"I'm telling you right now! There ain't no one in the world who can beat me 'cause I was born and bred to win!"*

It was amazing how with the mask on, I became a different person, like Dr. Jekyll and Mr. Hyde. Without it, I was shy, quiet, Jesse Baron. Masked, I was brash and bold.

As Máscara de la Muerte, I planned to use that same gravelly voice. And I'd do my promos in English so the audience could understand me, but I'd sprinkle a few Spanish words here and there to let people think I was fluent in both languages. I might even speak with a thick Mexican accent.

I am so ready for this.

On my last day of training, Travis surprised me with a burnt-orange cake with the University of Texas longhorn logo in white on top, and white lettering that said: Hook 'em Horns, Jesse! The guys raised their fingers in a "Hook 'em Horns" salute and sang "The Eyes of Texas."

Then, as if that wasn't enough, Matt Perryman handed me an envelope with a card that said: NEVER GIVE UP ON YOUR DREAMS, NO MATTER HOW HARD IT GETS! It was signed by everyone. Inside it was a cash card.

"We thought you might need a little spending money when you're in school, so we all chipped in to get this for you," Matt said.

When I looked at the back of the cash card to see how much it was worth, my eyes nearly popped out of their sockets. "Wow, thanks!" I said. "This really means a lot to me, guys. Listen, I've enjoyed getting to know all of you, and I'm going to miss training with you, but I know you're going to be awesome wrestlers."

My father put an arm around me and told the group, "I'm very proud of Jesse for choosing a career where he'll be using his mind instead of his muscles. Now as much as I love this business, I'm going to tell you what I told him. Go to college. Get a degree. Pro wrestling is like any other form of art, whether it's acting or writing or playing a musical instrument or painting landscapes. If you have a passion for it, by all means, do it. But have something else lined up in case this profession doesn't work out for you."

After the celebration, no one was in the mood to train, so my father ended the session early. I stood by the door and said goodbye to everyone as they left.

"We're gonna miss you, bro," Joaquín Luna told me.

"*Te felicito, mi amigo*," said Juan Serrano, who was looking less skinny. "*Qué te vaya bien*."

Pete Vogel swallowed me up in his tree-trunk arms, almost squeezing me to death. "Best of luck to you, Jesse. It was a pleasure training with you."

"I'm gonna keep you in my prayers, my friend," Bobby Lee Taylor said.

Goose gave me a big hug. As he did, his eyes teared up. "Thanks for everything you've done for me, man. You're the best friend I've ever had."

"Let me know when you have your first match, so I can come watch you," I said.

"You got it. And maybe someday the world will see a match between Cyclone Suárez and Máscara de la Muerte."

The thought made my heart swell. "You never know, Goose. It just might."

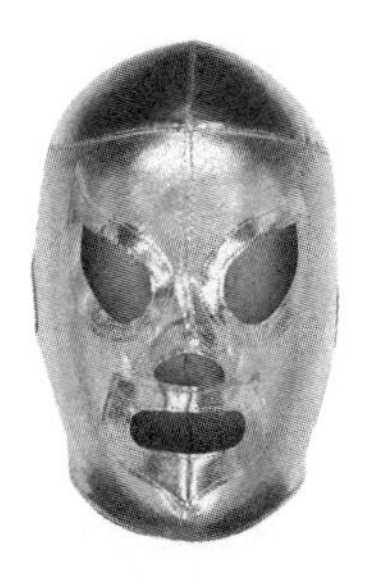

CHAPTER TWENTY-SIX

Before our trip to London, my parents and I attended freshman orientation at UT. While I was there, I visited the Cockrell School of Engineering, where I met with an academic advisor named Ms. Lowry. She discussed a degree plan with me and helped me register for my fall classes. I was also assigned to a dorm at Beeker Residence Hall and was given the name and contact info of my roommate, a guy named Templeton Sadler, which made me think of the rat from *Charlotte's Web*. After that, I had an ID card made.

On moving day, my parents helped me pack my stuff and load it in my car. From time to time, my mom wept softly, but for the most part, she kept her composure. It wasn't until I was about to leave that she fell apart.

"Jesse, I feel like I'm losing you all over again!" she wailed.

"Come on, Mom. You never lost me," I said. "We were always a phone call or a text away."

When my parents divorced, my mom moved to Dallas, and she expected me to go with her. But after years of moving around, I decided to stay in San Antonio with my father, and she felt that I'd abandoned her.

"Promise you'll always stay in touch with us," she said.

"I will. And I'll try to come home whenever I can."

My father said, "I'm not going to give you any advice, Jesse, because I know we've raised a fine son who's learned right from wrong. All I ask is that you make us proud."

As we said our goodbyes, I kept my cool and didn't shed any tears—until I drove off. I hadn't realized how much I loved my parents until it sank in that I wouldn't live with them anymore. The weird thing is that I hardly ever spent time with them, other than when I was at the Factory with my father. Even then, I didn't talk to him much, because he was always working with his trainees. If I was home, I holed myself up in my room, except for when we had dinner. But I think that just knowing they were around gave me comfort, and I was going to miss them.

To top it off, I was feeling nervous about living on my own. I didn't know if I was ready to start a new life in an environment that was completely different from what I was used to. What was Templeton Sadler like? Would we get along as roommates? Would I be able to handle university-level courses? What if I flunked and got kicked out? I kept thinking I should've waited a year or two before starting college, like I had originally planned.

Late that afternoon, I pulled into the parking garage nearest Beeker Residence Hall. There was no turning back. I grabbed my suitcases from my car and walked into the building.

At the front desk, I introduced myself to the resident assistant. I presented my ID card, and he gave me a key to my dorm.

The door was open, and I found Templeton hanging his clothes in one of the closets.

When he heard me, he turned around and gaped, wide-eyed. "Dang, dude! Are you like a superhero or something?"

"What do you mean?" I asked.

"Well, with the muscle thing you've got going, I thought you might be one of the Avengers."

"I work out a lot," I said. "Hi, I'm Jesse. You must be Templeton."

"Temp," he said. "I go by Temp. And you can spare me the Templeton the rat jokes because I've heard them all."

"I hadn't made the connection," I lied. In a way, Temp did remind me of the rat. He was short and thin, but had a bulbous belly. He had a long pointy nose and Chiclet teeth, and his dark hair was slicked back with gel.

"I wish I'd had you around when I was getting picked on in high school," he said.

"Trust me, Temp. I've dealt with my share of bullies, too, guys who wanted to prove how tough they were."

"Oh, these weren't guys," he said. "We had some real mean girls at Madison High, back in Marsville, where I'm from."

He has Wally's wry sense of humor.

I sat my suitcases on the bed across from his. At home, I slept in a king-size bed. This one was a twin. Something else I'd have to get used to.

"I've got more stuff in my car. I'll be right back."

"I'll help you bring it in," Temp said, and followed me out the door.

As we were unloading my things, he noticed my guitar. "Dude, are you in a band?"

"Nah, I brought it to give me something to do in case I get bored," I said. "I'm not very good at it, though. Mostly I play chords."

"Well, I play the flute," he said. "And I *am* good at it. I'm going to be in the Longhorn band."

"Cool. Maybe I'll get to hear you play sometime."

"You will, if you go to the games."

"I'll see. But I'm planning to be pretty busy on the weekends," I said, without explaining what I intended to do.

We made two trips. After the second one, Temp helped me make my bed and arrange my things. His half was already set up.

"Are you into comic books?" I asked, staring at the posters of superheroes hanging by his bed.

"Yeah, I brought a whole collection with me. They're in one of my boxes. How about you?"

"Not much, although I've read some of Neil Gaiman's stuff."

"I brought his graphic novels, too," he said. "You're welcome to read them anytime you want."

Temp and I chatted for a while. Then we walked around outside to acquaint ourselves with our surroundings. He pointed out the Butler School of Music building where the Longhorn band practiced. I found the Gregory Gym, which had state-of-the-art fitness equipment. I planned to spend a lot of time in there.

Afterwards, we had dinner at one of the dining centers. When we returned to our dorm, Temp took his flute out of its case and asked me to accompany him on my guitar. We played a few tunes, just jamming out. He was an amazing flutist, and somehow, he made me sound like a better guitarist.

I have to confess that when I first saw his photo, I was a little disappointed. I had hoped to get a roommate who was athletic, someone I could work out with. But I liked Temp right away, and I knew we were going to get along fine.

CHAPTER TWENTY-SEVEN

I overcame my anxieties about college in no time at all. I felt so grown up doing things on my own without having to be reminded by my parents. And I took part in so many meet-and-greet social activities that I didn't have time to be homesick. I was invited to join several fraternities, but I decided to hold off on them, until I knew what my weekends would look like. My courses were challenging but not overly difficult.

Temp turned out to be a terrific roommate, although we didn't see each other much. When he wasn't in class, he was practicing with the Longhorn band. I spent my free time studying or working out at the gym.

Shortly after school started, Shirley Washington wrote to me, saying that she had my wrestling gear ready. I gave her my new address and paid her for the material. She said she'd send it out that day.

Meanwhile, I scouted out the two wrestling promotions in Austin. One was Capital City Wrestling. They put on weekly shows at a strip mall called T-Town Plaza. Their building was flanked by a Metro PCS on the left and a Subway on the right. Above the entrance was a white metal sign with CAPITAL CITY WRESTLING in blue lettering, and an image of the state's capitol building outlined in red.

I tried the doors, but the place was locked. The windows were covered with black plastic sheets, so I couldn't see inside. A sticker on one of the glass door panels listed their opening time at seven o'clock on Saturdays.

Texas Roundup Rasslin' was the other promotion. Their shows were held once a month in a seedy-looking wooden building called the Chaparral Bar & Grill. I decided to pass on that one. All I could picture was a bunch of drunks throwing beer bottles at the wrestlers.

Friday afternoon, my gear arrived. I took the package to my dorm, anxious to see what it looked like. When I opened the box, my jaw dropped. I knew Shirley was an exceptional seamstress, but I couldn't believe how well she'd captured Wally's drawings. I put on the tights. They fit perfect. So did the leather boots. The mask, which was made of Lycra, didn't have laces, and it looked more like an actual skull than a wrestling mask. I slipped it over my head. Then I hooked the cape around my neck and stood in front of my dresser mirror with my fists on my hips.

At that moment, Temp walked in. "Dang, dude!" he exclaimed. "You *are* a superhero!"

I spun around, embarrassed, and pulled off my mask. "I was going to tell you about this when the time came," I said. "I'm going to look for a job as a professional wrestler."

"So that's why you're such a fitness freak," he said. "A wrestler. Dang. How'd you ever decide to do that?"

"Do you watch *Monday Night Mayhem*?" I asked.

"Not really. I mean, I catch it now and then when I'm flipping channels, but I wouldn't call myself a fan."

"Well, do you know who the Angel of Death is?"

"Isn't he the dude who wrestles as a grim reaper-type character?"

"He used to," I said. "He's retired now. Anyway, he's my father."

"Get out! No fooling?"

"That's where I got the idea."

Temp circled me, eyeing my outfit. "Dude, I feel like I've just discovered that Bruce Wayne is Batman. So what do you call yourself? The Skull?"

"Máscara de la Muerte," I said.

"That means mask of death in Spanish, right?"

"Yeah. I've been waiting for my gear to arrive so I can start contacting promoters. Listen, do me a favor, would you? Take my picture." I handed Temp my phone and put my mask back on.

He aimed the phone at me, then brought it down. "This isn't going to work," he said. "You need a backdrop that doesn't look like a dorm." He yanked his blue bedsheet off his bed. "Let's hang this up somewhere."

Temp and I pinned the bedsheet on a wall. Then I stood against it and struck several poses while Temp clicked away. After a half dozen shots or so, we reviewed each one.

"I like this one the best," I said, stopping at a photo of me with my arms crossed and my head lifted and turned slightly to the side.

"When you have your first match, I'll invite a bunch of people to it," Temp said.

"You'd better wait until after I've wrestled a few times," I told him. "I don't want to be worried about botching my moves. But yeah, I think that if I get booked at Capital City Wrestling, the promoter will like it that I have a fan base."

After I got dressed, I sent Wally the photo and told her about my plan.

She wrote back.

Now I know what Dr. Frankenstein felt like when he saw his creation. You look phenomenal, Jessup! Good luck with Capital City.

I was overwhelmed with excitement. At long last, my dream was about to come true.

Or so I thought.

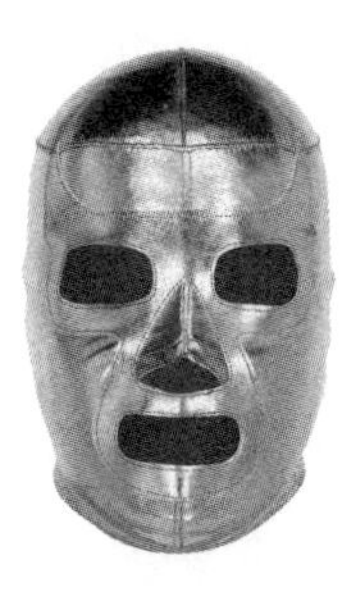

CHAPTER TWENTY-EIGHT

The Capital City Wrestling website listed the promoter as Mitch Green. It had an email address where he could be reached, but rather than writing to him, I decided to go to his show. I figured I'd have a better chance of getting booked if I spoke to him in person.

The walls inside the building were painted black. Along with the covered windows, the place looked like it was halfway to being a Halloween Fun House.

The ring stood in the middle of the darkened room, with a lighting truss above it. It had a black apron, but no logo. The front-row seats were old wooden pews that may have come from a church that had gotten rid of them to buy new ones. Metal folding chairs made up the back rows.

An old woman with a gray, beehive hairdo, was sitting at a table by the entrance, selling tickets. I found out later that she was Mitch Green's mom. The pews were sold out, so I bought a ticket in the general admission section, which was still close to the ring. A quick head count told me that there were roughly seventy-five people in attendance.

I had hoped to make my wrestling debut somewhere fancier, but if Mitch Green were to offer me a contract, I wouldn't complain. What mattered was getting the experience of wrestling in front of an audience, regardless of its size. My father had gotten his start in similar venues and didn't feel any shame over it. He often brought it up when he talked to his trainees about how they needed to pay their dues to make it in the business.

At eight o'clock, the timekeeper rang the bell to signal the start of the show. The announcer climbed inside the ring, microphone in hand. He wore a burgundy and gold, paisley tuxedo jacket, with a white shirt, a black bowtie and black pants.

"Ladies and gentlemen, welcome to Capital City Wrestling, where you can see the superstars of today and tomorrow!" he thundered.

The small crowd responded with boisterous cheers and applause.

"The following contest is scheduled for one fall, with a fifteen-minute time limit. Introducing first, weighing in at two hundred, thirty-seven pounds, from Round Rock, Texas . . . John Sha-na-ha-a-a-n!"

I had no idea who John Shanahan was, but the crowd did, and they popped loudly when he stepped through the curtains.

"And his opponent, weighing in at two hundred, sixty-eight pounds, from Missouri City, Texas . . . The Ruffian, Garland Wo-o-o-olfe!"

By the reception he got, Garland Wolfe was the heel.

The match got off to a fast start, with both men trading punches. Shanahan gained the upper hand when he hit Wolfe with a dropkick, followed by two German suplexes. With Wolfe down, Shanahan raised his arms in victory. As he was celebrating, Wolfe connected with a blow to Shanahan's kidney area, then a forearm to his face, then a neck breaker.

Capital City Wrestling may have been a low-budget operation, but the wrestlers were putting on an intense performance.

During the match, I asked the security guard where I could find Mitch Green.

"That's him over there," he said, pointing to the ring announcer.

"Do you think I might be able to talk to him?" I asked.

"I ain't gonna stop you," he said. "But you should wait till the match is over."

Minutes later, John Shanahan defeated Garland Wolfe with a Shooting Star Press off the top turnbuckle.

After the wrestlers had cleared the ring, I waited for Mitch Green to introduce the next bout. When he returned to the announcer and timekeeper's table, I hurried up to him.

"Mr. Green, may I speak with you for a moment?" I asked.

"What's up?"

"My name's Jesse Baron, and I'd like to talk to you about possibly wrestling for your promotion."

He checked his watch. "I can give you ten minutes. That's how long this match is supposed to last. Let's go to the back where it's quiet."

He led me through a maze of black curtains hanging on PVC pipe frames.

I wasn't expecting the backstage area to be the size of the Factory's training facility, but my dorm was bigger. There were no showers or exercise equipment. Not even lockers. What also surprised me was that the room was empty.

"Where are the wrestlers?" I asked.

"They wait in their cars till my mom calls them," he said. "As soon as they finish their match, she pays them and they leave."

Okay, so this isn't the PWF, but it's better than nothing.

I showed Mr. Green the photo Temp had taken of me. "My ring name is Máscara de la Muerte," I said.

He nodded an approval. "I could use a *luchador* on my roster. Where have you wrestled?"

"Actually, I haven't wrestled anywhere yet. I'm hoping. . . ."

"Sorry," he said, cutting me off. "You've gotta have a minimum of three years of experience before you can work here."

I stared at him in disbelief. "Please, Mr. Green, just give me a chance. Let me prove to you how good I am."

"Look, son. I deal with kids like you all the time, wannabe wrestlers who are dying to get in the ring. You probably think that because we're a tiny promotion, we'll accept anybody. Well, let me tell you something. We may be small, but I take a lot of pride in our product. I don't put amateurs in our shows. It's too risky. Sorry, but that's the way it is."

He started to walk off when I blurted out, "Wait! My father's the Angel of Death!"

He looked at me curiously. "You're Mark Baron's kid?"

"Yes, sir," I said, now feeling hopeful. "I just finished training with him at the Ox Mulligan Pro Wrestling Factory."

"You did? Then how come you're not wrestling for him?"

His question caught me off guard, and instead of explaining the situation, I said simply, "Because he won't let me."

"Hmph. Well, I guess that must say something about your talent, if your own father won't use you."

"No, sir, it's not like that at all. It's that . . ."

"Listen, I've gotta go," he said. "The match is almost over. Thanks for considering us, but I can't help you." He left and returned to his table.

I stood there, momentarily paralyzed, my mind refusing to accept what had just happened. Then I trudged out of the building and drove back to my dorm.

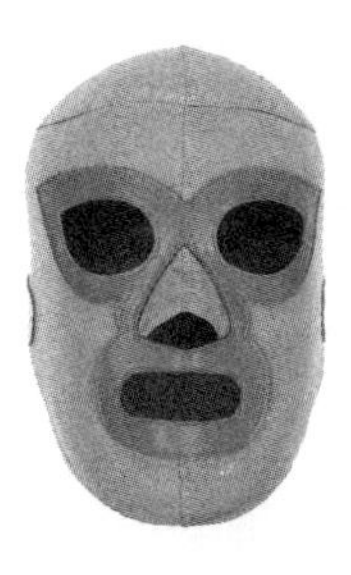

CHAPTER TWENTY-NINE

After I got over my hurt feelings, I decided to try other promotions. I started with Star-Spangled Wrestling in Houston. TJ used to wrestle there, and he'd always spoken highly of the company, and of the promoter, Hank Hewitt. In spite of that, I resisted the temptation of texting TJ to put in a good word for me.

Not that it would've mattered. Mr. Hewitt wrote back, saying he'd need a résumé of my work and a demo video or a YouTube link of some of my matches. I had neither.

I tried another company in Houston, this one called Lone Star Wrestling Federation. Gordon Roberts, the promoter, asked for the same thing.

I reached out to the ones in Dallas and Fort Worth, as well as in Corpus Christi and Galveston. Most of them didn't respond. The few that did, weren't interested—not without a résumé and a video of one of my matches.

I could create a fake résumé and hope they wouldn't check it out, but I'd still need a video.

I wrote to Goose about my predicament and asked him if he could have a match with me at the Factory the following Saturday that I could record. He said he'd gotten a job at a Discount Tire store and had to work, but that he'd try to get the morning off. We set the time tentatively for ten o'clock. My feeling was that if Goose and I could put on an outstanding performance, promoters would be impressed enough by it that they'd bypass the résumé and give me a shot.

I also wrote to Wally. Now that we were on friendly terms again, I asked her if she'd be willing to record our match. She said she would.

Friday, after my last class, I drove home for the first time since I'd moved away. My parents and I texted regularly, but it was great to see them again. We visited awhile, then I took my duffel bag upstairs to my bedroom. I left my *luchador* outfit in the trunk of my car. I'd change into it at the Factory.

It was refreshing to be able to stretch out and walk around in my much larger room, after being cramped in my dorm for so long. I took off my sneakers and lay on my bed. As I did, I stared at the framed newspaper article from *The Times of London* hanging on my wall. Temp would get a kick out of seeing me catching the pickpocket. He'd say he'd known all along that I was a superhero. I'd have to remember to take the article with me when I went back to school.

For dinner, my parents and I ate at Ernie Lou's Texas Classics, where Wally used to work. I was a bit worried that the hostesses would recognize me, but as usual, all the attention went to my father.

While we were eating, I noticed the manager reaming out one of the busboys, and it bugged me to think that he'd treated Wally the same way. She was so chill and even tempered, it took jerks like him to bring out the worst in her. Then I realized that I was guilty of doing the same thing. I should've been more understanding and compassionate when she was stressing over her job. Wally wasn't my girlfriend anymore, but I hoped we'd always be friends.

The next morning, I picked up Goose at the Discount Tire store. He was waiting for me outside with a backpack strapped across his shoulders, presumably with his ring gear in it.

"My boss told me I could have an hour off," he said. "So I need you to bring me back as soon as we finish."

"No, problem," I said. "It shouldn't take that long."

Wally was waiting for us in the Factory parking lot, standing next to an old, dark-blue car. I wanted to hug her, but nothing in her body language indicated she'd be receptive to it, so I greeted her with a friendly hi.

Goose regarded her snootily and said, "Hey, man, long time no see."

"Not long enough," she muttered.

Obviously, the passage of time hadn't changed their mutual dislike for one another.

"So this is your car, huh?" I said.

Wally smiled proudly. "Yep. His name is Captain Midnight."

"Cool. You'll have to give me a ride in it sometime."

"Maybe after we're done," she said. "Let's go inside. I can't wait to see Máscara de la Muerte in action."

"Just keep your fingers crossed that this isn't Máscara de la Muerte's one and only appearance," I said.

"It won't be. I have faith in you, Jessup. You're going to have every promoter in Texas fighting over you."

My father didn't have a show scheduled that night, but the Factory was open for wrestlers to use the facilities. Travis had morning duty. The second we walked in, he came around his desk and shook my hand. "It's great to see you, Jess. How's school?"

"It's going well."

"Are you looking for your dad? 'Cause he's not in right now."

"I know. I just left him," I said, then told him why we were there.

"Well, generally speaking, when promoters ask for a video, they want to see you wrestling in front of an audience," he said. "But if we can make your match look official, it might work. There's a referee's shirt in the cabinet. I'll put it on and be your ref. María's in her office. I'll tell her to be the timekeeper."

Goose and I went to the locker room to change. He put on a pair of silver trunks and black boots he bought on eBay, and a black vest with CYCLONE stitched on the back in silver lettering that his grandma had sewn for him.

Goose was making his wrestling debut as Cyclone Suárez the following Saturday. He was going up against Juan Serrano, who was also taking part in his first match. Juan's character would be a wealthy, Spanish aristocrat named Fernando Octavio Montemayor.

When I finished dressing, I strutted into the arena with my cape flowing behind me.

"Holy cats!" Wally shrieked. "It's alive! It's alive!"

"Wow, you've really gone all out, haven't you?" Travis said. "Too bad your dad won't let you wrestle for us. I think you'd be an awesome addition to our roster."

"Maybe someday he'll wish he had," I said. My father liked to brag about PWF trainees who'd gone on to wrestle for the ACW. I wondered if he'd brag about me if I made it there, too.

"Have you guys decided how you want to handle your match?" Travis asked us.

"This is Jesse's show, so he definitely needs to go over," Goose said.

"I agree." Travis looked up at the wall clock. "Let's set this match for about eight minutes. That should be long enough.

Now Jess, you're going to need a strong finisher, something that'll catch a promoter's attention."

"I was thinking about a brain buster," I said. "I know it's dangerous, but Goose and I have practiced it a bunch of times."

The brain buster was a move I'd considered using for a while. With my strength, I could lift almost any opponent vertically, then drop him, head first, without botching it. And since my character was supposed to represent Death, I thought about calling it The Big Sleep.

Travis looked at Goose.

"I'm fine with it," he said.

"All right, then. You guys ready?"

We told him we were. Goose and I removed our accessories and draped them on a chair. The moment we climbed inside the ring, Wally began recording. Travis stood between us, and at his signal, María Núñez rang the bell. Goose and I began our match with a collar-and-elbow tie up. Then I shoved him into a corner and hit him with punches and kicks. He tried to fight his way out, but I swung him against the ropes with an Irish Whip. When he bounced back, I tagged him with a forearm to the face, knocking him down. I went for a cover, but he powered out, and our match continued.

Throughout it, we attacked each other with just about every move we'd learned in our training: missile dropkicks, crossbodies, hurricanrana takedowns, powerbombs and standing moonsaults.

Seven minutes into our match, María held up a finger to let Travis know how much time we had left. He leaned into us and said, "Okay, let's take it home."

I flung Goose against the ropes. When he sprang back, I hit him with a superkick. Then I picked him up by the hair, lifted him over my head and finished him off with a brain buster, The Big Sleep. Travis made the three count and María rang the bell.

"Holy cats!" Wally cried. "I knew you guys had been training, but I had no idea you were this good!"

"Let me see the video," I said anxiously.

I took off my mask, and the five of us sat down to watch the match. Goose and I knew each other so well that even after not being in the ring together for a while, we were able to execute our moves flawlessly.

"Do you think this'll be good enough to convince a promoter to book me?" I asked Travis.

"I can't see why not," he said. "I wasn't nearly as skilled as you are when I started. So yeah, I think you'll get signed easily."

I thanked him and María for their help. Then Goose and I went backstage to shower and change.

When we came out, I told Wally I needed to take Goose back to work and invited her to go with me.

"Sure, but let's go in my car," she said, which I thought was funny, given how she felt about Goose. But she wanted me to ride in Captain Midnight.

After we dropped him off at the Discount Tire store, I asked Wally if she'd like to have lunch with me at O'Dell's.

"Okey doke," she said. "But we'll each pay for ourselves."

She wasn't going to get an argument from me.

At the deli, I had a flashback of eating there with Misty Raines and Valen Durán. I wondered what had become of them. I shuddered to think of Valen working as an elementary P.E. coach, with her nasty drug habit.

Wally ordered the Mediterranean Wrap, and I had the Chicken Club Salad. While we were eating, she told me that her theater arts group was working on a musical about the Addams Family, and that she'd be playing Morticia.

"If you can, I'd like for you to come to it," she said.

"I will. I promise. Even if I'm supposed to wrestle that night, I'll cancel it to be there."

"Thanks. And when you have your first match, I want you to invite me to it," she said.

"I don't know where it might be. I mean, it could be as far away as Dallas, or even Marsville."

"It doesn't matter," she said. "Máscara de la Muerte was my creation, and I want to see him when he makes his debut."

I would've loved to have spent more time with Wally, but she said that Saturday was cleaning day at her house, and she had to help her mom.

Back at the Factory, I undid my seatbelt and stepped out of her car. She got out, too, and came around to say goodbye.

"I really hope the video helps you get a wrestling gig," she said.

"Me, too. Thanks for recording my match."

"Most welcome." She rummaged through her messenger bag, then brought out an empty hand. "Sorry, Jessup. I'm all out of peppermint candy. Here, maybe this'll bring you luck." She kissed me lightly on the lips. "Hasta Las Vegas," she chirped, and drove away.

I didn't know if the kiss meant anything romantic, or if it was simply a gesture of friendship, but it warmed my heart, nonetheless.

* * *

That afternoon, I wrote to the Houston promoters, Hank Hewitt and Gordon Roberts, and sent them the video but no fake résumé. I told them who my father was and explained why he wouldn't let me wrestle for him, so there wouldn't be any misunderstandings, like there'd been with Mitch Green.

I looked over the list of promoters I hadn't contacted yet and wrote to some of them, too. Surely one of them would make me an offer.

CHAPTER THIRTY

Monday morning, I was sitting in my Introduction to Engineering class, listening to my professor, Dr. Dobbins, discussing the relationship between engineering and economics, when my phone buzzed an alert. I pulled it out of my pocket and stole a peek at it. Hank Hewitt from Star-Spangled Wrestling had sent me an email.

With high anticipation, I hurried into the hallway and opened it. But as I read the message, I felt as if I'd been kicked in the gut.

Dear Jesse,

You seem to have a natural wrestling ability, and I would love to book you. However, I have a lot of respect for your dad, and if he doesn't want you to wrestle, I'm not going to go against him. He's right about school. I know he enjoyed a successful wrestling career, but not everyone does. I've had too many guys come through my doors who were once stars, but are now broken-down has-beens, who keep wrestling because they don't know how to do anything else. They still have name recognition, which is why I use them, but that's all they've got going for them. Don't make the same mistake. I'll honor your request and not say anything to your dad about you contacting me.

Best regards,
Hank Hewitt

His email left me dispirited, but I tried not to remain discouraged. Star-Spangled Wrestling was just one company. If Mr. Hewitt liked my video, other promoters would, too. It was just a matter of time before one of them booked me.

But as the day progressed, my hopes grew dimmer and dimmer. I kept receiving emails from promoters who basically echoed Hank Hewitt's message. They told me I was a good wrestler, but they didn't want to buck my father.

I had thought that by being honest about why I wasn't wrestling for the PWF, promoters would understand. Instead, it backfired on me, and my wrestling career appeared to be over before it started.

"I don't know what to tell you, dude," Temp said. "Maybe you should talk to your dad about letting you wrestle for him. I mean, you've done what he wanted, and your grades are good. I don't see why he wouldn't let you to do both. Besides, you'd only wrestle for him twice a month."

"I can't," I said. "Wrestling's a sore subject between us. If I'm going to make it, I'll have to do it on my own."

There was one company I hadn't tried yet—Texas Roundup Rasslin' at the Chaparral Bar & Grill. I'd been avoiding it because I was leery of wrestling in a bar. But I'd just about run out of options.

According to their website, the owner and promoter was Amir Safi, whose name didn't exactly bring to mind a good ol' Texas boy. I was pleasantly surprised to see that the place wasn't a total dump, like it looked from the outside. The

Chaparral Bar & Grill served burgers, nachos, chicken wings and fish and chips, among other comfort foods. Photos on their webpage showed people dancing and a band performing onstage—but no wrestling ring. I wondered if Texas Roundup Rasslin' had folded, as indie promotions often do. I called the number listed.

"Chaparral Bar & Grill," a woman answered. "This is Frances. What can I do you for?"

"Do you still hold wrestling events there?" I asked.

"Shore do. Got one coming up Friday. Starts at seven."

That was encouraging. "May I speak to Mr. Safi?"

"He's busy right now. You wanna leave a message?"

"Yes, ma'am. My name's Jesse Baron. Tell him I'm a wrestler, and that I'd like to talk to him about working in his promotion."

"Hold on a sec."

I could hear voices, but they were drowned out by country-and-western music playing in the background.

Moments later, Frances returned. "Amir says to come in tomorrow morning at eleven. He can talk to you then."

At least he didn't say no. Maybe this was the break I'd been waiting for.

The next day, I left my calculus class early and drove to the Chaparral Bar & Grill. The place had just opened, and there were no customers.

A dark-skinned man with close-cropped black hair and a close-cropped black beard walked over to me. "Jesse? Morning, I'm Amir Safi. I understand you're a rassler."

He may have been an Arab, but his accent was pure West Texan. Mr. Safi wore a black western shirt with mother-of-pearl buttons, blue jeans and brown cowboy boots. He pronounced his last name so it rhymed with taffy.

"Yes, sir." I showed him a photo of me as Máscara de la Muerte. He smiled at it, seemingly pleased with my gear.

"Where've you rassled?"

"At the Ox Mulligan Pro Wrestling Factory in San Antonio," I said, which wasn't a lie. I'd just had a match there with Goose on Saturday. "That's also where I did my training."

"Ain't that the place the Angel of Death operates?" he asked.

Immediately, I felt my stomach tighten. "Yes, sir. Do you know him?"

"I know *of* him. I mean, who doesn't? But I ain't never met him personally."

Thank God. "Well, I'm a student at UT, and with all the homework I have to do, I can't always make it to San Antonio. That's why I thought about your promotion."

"I getcha," he said. "Have a seat." We sat at the end of a long wooden table. "I ain't got nothing fancy here. I put on five matches once a month. Each man gets paid forty bucks, plus a free meal."

I nodded to show that I was satisfied with the compensation. "Where's the ring?" I asked.

"We take down the stage and set it up there," he said, staring at the raised platform. "Now here's the thing. I ain't looking to hire nobody at the moment. But one of my boys called me yesterday and told me he's got the flu. He says he thinks he can be ready by Friday when we have our next show, but I don't want him coming here and infecting my customers. I ain't been able to find a replacement for him yet, so the job's yours if you want it. You'll be rasslin' a fella by the name a Dale Mulder. Dangerous Dale, if you will. You interested?"

If I hadn't been sitting down, I think my knees would've buckled. "Yes, sir."

"Good. I got some paperwork that you'll need to fill out. You can bring it with you on Friday. Now the show starts at seven, but you need to be here no later than five. *Comprende?*"

"Yes, sir. Um . . . Mr. Safi? Is there a chance that I could wrestle here regularly?"

"Don't put the cart before the horse, son," he said. "Let's see what you can do first. But fellas come and go through these doors all the time, so you never know."

He went to his office behind the register and came out a few minutes later with a file folder. "Here you go," he said. "See you Friday at five o'clock."

Outside the bar, I let out a huge gust of pent-up breath. Finally, after months of training and hoping and praying, I was about to become a wrestler. *A rassler!*

CHAPTER THIRTY-ONE

I shared my good news with Wally and Goose. Wally said she'd be there. Goose said he had to work until six-thirty on Friday and didn't want to push his luck by asking his boss for permission to leave early, since he'd just asked for time off the other day. I told him not to worry about it, that I'd send him a video of my match.

Also, I told Temp to go ahead and bring our friends. I figured if Mr. Safi saw how well I could draw in a college crowd, I'd have a better chance of getting booked again.

My courses had gotten tougher, and they'd caused me to slack off on my exercise routine, but for the rest of the week, I devoted every free moment to getting into tip-top shape, jogging and working out at the Gregory Gym.

I threw my tights in the washer with my regular clothes, remembering what my mom had taught me about separating the whites from the darks. But I washed my mask by hand in the dorm sink to make sure I didn't ruin it. I polished my boots and used my hand-held steamer to smooth the wrinkles on my cape. Then I stored my outfit in the garment bag I bought for it.

Friday, I arrived at the Chaparral Bar & Grill at twenty minutes to five. My father preached punctuality. He'd tell his trainees, "If a promoter wants you at an event at one o'clock, and you get there at one o'clock, you're already late."

The ring was set up where the stage normally stood. It was smaller than the ones at the Factory. I'd have to get a feel for it before the show started.

Mr. Safi was sitting at the bar with several men, whom I assumed were wrestlers because of their size. I walked up to him, my garment bag in one hand and the file folder in the other. "Evening, sir. Here are the forms you asked me to fill out."

"Hey, good to see you, son," he said, taking the folder from me. "Boys, this is Jesse Baron. He's gonna be rasslin' Dale tonight."

"What happened to Cheyenne?" one of the guys asked.

"He's got the flu real bad. Can't seem to shake it."

"Ah geez. Seems to be a lot of that going around," the guy said. "Nice to meet ya, Jesse. I'm Hunter Riggs."

"And I'm Laramie Wilder," the guy next to him said.

I didn't know if those were their actual names or their ring names.

The third guy didn't introduce himself to me. He asked Mr. Safi, "Does Dale know that Cheyenne's not coming?"

"I left him several messages, but he didn't get back to me," he said.

I looked at Mr. Safi warily. "Is that going to be a problem?"

"Nah, he'll be fine. It's just that Dale doesn't particularly like working with new talent. But he's a professional. He'll take good care of you. Sit down. Lemme buy you a beer."

"I don't drink," I said. "I'll have a Diet Coke, though, if you've got it."

The guy who didn't introduce himself to me asked, "Whassa matter? You a Babdist or one of them Seventh Day Adventurers or something?"

"No. Actually I'm not old enough to drink," I said. "I'm only eighteen."

"This stuff'll rot your guts out, anyway," Laramie said. "Least Amir's will," he added with a wink.

As we were talking, Dale Mulder showed up. He was a burly guy, a little taller than me, with a bald head and a walrus mustache. He greeted everyone, then said, "So Cheyenne's sick, huh?"

"Yeah, but I gotcha another dancing partner," Mr. Safi said, pointing a thumb at me.

"Hi, I'm Jesse Baron."

Dale shook my hand, but I could tell he'd done it reluctantly. "You don't look like you've been wrestling too long. Where've you worked?"

"At the Ox Mulligan Pro Wrestling Factory in San Antonio," I said.

"Oh, then you must know Steve Dalton and Mando Villanueva and them."

"Yeah, I used to work at the Factory until I started school this semester at UT," I said, implying that I was a former PWF wrestler.

"Then we oughta have us a solid match."

By five o'clock, the rest of the wrestlers arrived. I found out that the guy who didn't introduce himself to me went by the name of "Nasty" Ned Thatcher. The others were Damien Grey, Jacob Storm, Nehemiah Blaze, Fabio Ortega and James Logan. The referee was Teddy Lane.

Mr. Safi ushered us to a storage room behind the ring. Inside it were rows of metal racks stocked with dry goods. There were cases of drinks on the floor, a large walk-in freezer against a wall, and an employees' restroom near it. Our names and the order of our matches were written on a marker board by the door. My match with Dale was third on the list.

"Excuse me, but would it be okay if Dale and I went first?" I asked Mr. Safi.

He gave me a lopsided grin. "What's the matter? You getting the willies?"

"No, sir. I've got friends coming in from San Antonio. They plan to head back home tonight, and I don't want it to get too late on them."

I *was* suffering from the willies. Big time. I'd been dealing with them all day. I wanted to be done with my match before I had a heart attack.

He turned to Dale.

"Don't matter to me. First, last, I don't care, so long as I get paid."

"Good," Mr. Safi said. "Damien, you and James will now be third." He erased our names from the marker board and made the switch.

"Actually, I go by Máscara de la Muerte," I said, when he wrote JESSE BARON.

Dale chortled. "That's gonna be a mouthful for you, Amir."

"How do you spell it?" he asked.

I told him, and he made the correction.

"And introduce me as coming from Oaxaca, Mexico," I said.

Mr. Safi regarded me quizzically. "You *are* here legally, ain't you?"

"Yes, sir. I was born in Dallas, but my character's from Mexico."

He pulled his phone from his pocket and typed the information on his notes app. "How much do you weigh?"

"Two forty-seven," I said.

He added the information. "All right, any other special requests?" he asked the group, in a way that suggested he was making fun of me.

No one answered.

"Y'all get yourselves ready then. I'll check back with you later."

After Mr. Safi left, I asked Dale what he wanted us to do in our match.

"Don't worry about it. I'll call it as we go along. But just to be clear, I'm going over."

"That's fine," I said. This was my first appearance at the Chaparral Bar & Grill, so I had expected to job to him.

"For my finisher, I use the Tornado DDT off the second rope," he said. "That all right with you?"

"Sure, no problem." Travis had taught me the move, which was a variation of his Spinning DDT.

"Then I guess we're all set," he said.

The employees' restroom was available for privacy, but the men stripped off their clothes in front of everybody and changed into their gear, with no sense of modesty. I was used to being around naked guys in the locker room at school when I played football, but it was weird seeing them in the Chaparral Bar & Grill's storage room. Most of the wrestlers wore trunks or tights with wrestling boots. Ned Thatcher's ring gear, however, was a pair of gray sweat pants, a white, stained tank top, and black sneakers, which I supposed was part of his "Nasty Ned" character.

I didn't want to change into my outfit until my friends showed up because I wanted to visit with them before my match. I texted Wally to find out where she was. She said she and her friends, Alyssa and Emily, were nearing Austin, and would be at the Chaparral Bar & Grill soon.

Seconds later, Temp texted, saying he and six other guys from our residence hall were standing by the entrance. I went out and chatted with them for a few minutes. Then I told them to get a table, but to save three seats for Wally and her friends.

"How will I know who they are?" Temp asked.

"You can't miss Wally," I said. "She'll be the one with the short, blue-green hair."

Time was approaching, and I needed to get back to the storage room. But first, I climbed inside the ring to test the ropes. They were strong and tight. Next, I measured the distance as my father had advised.

After that, I returned to the storage room, unhooked my garment bag from a metal rack, and went to the restroom to change. While I was getting dressed, Wally texted to let me know that she and her friends had arrived. I couldn't wait for her to see me wrestle.

When I walked out of the restroom, Nasty Ned hee-hawed loudly. "Holy crap! What the hell have you got on?"

Suddenly, I felt terribly overdressed.

"Didn't nobody tell ya that Halloween ain't till next month? Wait'll Dale sees what he's getting in the ring with." Nasty Ned looked around. "Where *is* Dale?"

"He stepped out a little while ago," Hunter said. "But I ain't seen him lately."

At that moment, Dale showed up, and he seemed upset about something.

"Hey, Dale," Nasty Ned said. "Look at what you're gonna rassle tonight."

Dale ignored him and me. He took off his AC/DC T-shirt, left his jeans on and laced up a pair of black boots. Like Nasty Ned, he didn't wear standard ring attire.

"Good luck," I said, extending my hand, but he refused to shake it. My first thought was that he'd just had a fight with his wife. I'd witnessed plenty of them when my parents used to argue about my father's career. I hoped Dale's foul mood wouldn't be a problem when we got in the ring. My only assurance was what I'd been told about him being a professional.

Mr. Safi opened the door and poked his head inside. He goggled at me, then shouted, "All right, ladies! Let's give the rubes a good show!"

Teddy Lane followed him out.

Dale and I stood by the door, waiting for our introductions. He didn't say anything to me or even look my way.

Outside, I heard Mr. Safi roar in his West Texas accent, *"Ladies and gentlemen! Welcome to Texas Roundup Rasslin' at the Chaparral Bar & Grill, where we serve the finest adult beverages in the state! My name is Amir Safi, and I am your host for the evening. We got a outstanding lineup for you tonight, so sit back and enjoy! The first contest is scheduled for one fall, with a twenty-minute time limit. Introducing first, weighing in at two hundred, seventy-five pounds, from Enid, Oklahoma . . . Dangerous Dale Mul-l-lder!"*

Dale walked out to a loud pop from the crowd.

"And his opponent, weighing in at two hundred, forty-seven pounds, all the way from south of the border in Oaxaca, Mexico . . . Mascara de la Mue-e-erte!" He pronounced *Máscara* like the word for women's eye makeup.

I was welcomed with a clamoring of whistles, cheers and applause. A lot of the noise came from my friends, but I think the crowd was excited to see someone dressed like me. I could almost guarantee that after tonight, Mr. Safi would want to book me again.

Teddy Lane called Dale and me to the center of the ring to go over the rules. Then I went to my corner, removed my cape and handed it to Mr. Safi.

At the sound of the bell, I thought Dale was going to lock up with me in a collar-and-elbow. From there, he'd tell me what to do. But to my shock, he kicked me in the ribs. Hard! As I doubled over in pain, he began pounding me on my back with sledgehammer punches, each one knocking the wind out of me.

What was wrong with him? Was this supposed to be some type of initiation Mr. Safi hadn't warned me about?

Dale lifted me off the mat and hit me with vicious chops to my chest that burned like fire. Then he flung me against the ropes. When I bounced back, he picked me up and dropped me with a Sidewalk Slam. I started to get to my feet, but he hopped on the second rope and took me down with his finishing maneuver, the Tornado DDT. He hooked my leg, and Teddy made the three count.

Mr. Safi scowled at us, evidently unhappy with our match. Then he climbed inside the ring, microphone in his hand. "*The winner of the bout, in one minute, sixteen seconds . . . Dangerous Dale Mul-l-lder!*"

The crowd booed and made thumbs-down gestures. I'm sure they'd been expecting to see a better performance from me. I couldn't tell them that I'd been beaten up for real.

Dale stormed out of the ring without waiting for his hand to be raised.

After he left, I stood on rubbery legs, my body throbbing, and tottered to the storage room, confused as to why Dale had gone rogue on me. Mr. Safi followed us, no doubt, wondering the same thing.

In the back, Dale shoved a finger in my face. With spit flying out of his mouth, he yelled at Mr. Safi, "Do you know who this punk is? He's the Angel of Death's kid! I talked to Steve Dalton at the PWF. He told me that, yeah, this scumbag used to work there . . . *selling tickets for his old man!* He ain't a wrestler. He ain't never even had a match in his life!"

Mr. Safi's eyes bulged from their sockets. "So you lied to me! You went out and got yourself a fancy costume and thought you could pass yourself off as a Mexican *luchador*! I want you outta here now! And don't expect to get paid, neither!"

I grabbed my stuff and walked out of the storage room, still masked, which was a blessing, because that way, no one could see the tears in my eyes. My friends came up to congratulate me, but I ignored them and hurried out of the building, afraid I'd start blubbering.

I jumped in my car and drove off. Nowhere in particular, only to get as far away as possible from the Chaparral Bar & Grill and the most humiliating experience of my life.

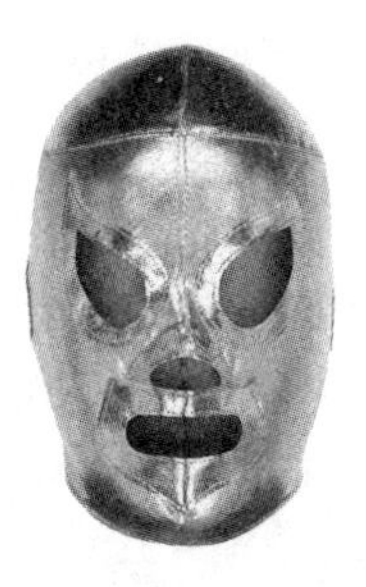

CHAPTER THIRTY-TWO

I didn't know what in the world had possessed me to believe that I could ever be a wrestler. First of all, I had zero charisma. I wasn't witty or outgoing like Wally. People weren't naturally drawn to me, unless they found out who my father was. Plus I didn't like being around crowds that much. Not that I was anti-social. I had manners, of course, and tried to be polite to everyone, but after a while, I grew tired of them and wanted to be by myself. My nomadic childhood might've made me an introvert. Or maybe I was born that way.

Whatever the reason, if I were an ACW wrestler, I'd be expected to make public appearances, where I'd have to pretend to enjoy meeting a bunch of nerdy fans, who'd ask me all sorts of stupid questions about pro wrestling. I'd have to sit there and listen to them blather on and on about what they'd do if they were running a promotion. They'd drive me nuts. And did I really want to put on a gaudy costume to entertain *those* people?

Second, I'd never have my family's support. My parents would go ballistic if they found out what I'd been doing. Aunt Gracie would ridicule me for getting into that "silly wrestling thing," and my grandparents on my mom's side would tell me how disappointed they were that, like my father, I'd chosen to pursue a disreputable profession.

Even if I could look past all that, no promoter was willing to book me unless I had experience. But how was I supposed to get experience if nobody would book me?

After the fiasco at the Chaparral Bar & Grill, I came to terms with a harsh reality—that my dream had reached its end. It was over. Finished. Kaput. It simply wasn't meant to be. For all the time and effort I'd put into my training, for all the pain I'd endured, I realized I wasn't cut out to be a wrestler. I didn't have what it took and I'd have to accept it. As Clint Eastwood said in one of those *Dirty Harry* movies, "A man's got to know his limitations."

When I returned to my dorm that night, Temp wanted to know why I'd left the Chaparral Bar & Grill so abruptly. All I said was that things didn't work out. I was still upset over what had happened and didn't feel like talking about it. I took a quick shower, then went to bed.

Wally, though, deserved a better answer. She had texted me, asking the same thing. I told her it was a long story, and that I'd explain everything tomorrow when I drove to San Antonio to watch Goose wrestle.

I considered offering him my outfit. I didn't have any use for it. Maybe he could wrestle as both Cyclone Suárez and Máscara de la Muerte. But I decided against it. Wally would be hurt if I gave Goose the gear she had designed for me.

Saturday morning, I invited her to an early dinner at Casa Guanajuato and to the PWF matches afterwards. She said yes and wanted to know if she was going to get to sell tickets with me. I told her the job had been given to one of the trainees. She replied with a sad face emoji.

Since Wally enjoyed working the ticket counter, I wondered if my father would hire her to do it on a regular basis. I asked him about it when I went home.

"It isn't much of anything," he said. "You know that. The most she'd work would be a couple of hours. But sure, it's hers, if she wants it."

"Great. I know she'll love it," I said. Then I had another thought. "Would it be possible to hire her part-time doing something else? Wally's been looking for a job to pay for her car, and she's got graduation expenses coming up. She could really use the money."

My parents were friends with Wally's mom, but I didn't know if they were aware of her financial situation.

"I suppose," he said. "She can come to the Factory in the evenings to do some chores. I can't pay her a lot, but it should help her with what she needs."

"Thanks, Dad. I'll tell her."

My father had a soft spot for people down on their luck. I was sure he'd find something for Wally to do that wouldn't be such a beatdown.

CHAPTER THIRTY-THREE

"Holy cats! For real?" Wally cried, when I told her about my father's job offer on the way to the restaurant.

"Yeah. All I said was that you wanted to know if you were going to be selling tickets with me tonight, and he started coming up with all these jobs for you. He told me he was short-handed and needed the help."

I had to be careful what I said. Otherwise, Wally might accuse me of treating her like a charity case again.

"Tell him I'll take it! I'll be the announcer or the timekeeper or the referee, if he wants."

"You can discuss the details with him when you see him tonight," I said. "But I think he's mostly going to want you to clean the restrooms and sweep and mop the floors."

Before long, I pulled into the Casa Guanajuato parking lot, dodging potholes as I looked for a place to park.

The restaurant was as ratty as I remembered. Crowded and noisy, with little kids running around unattended, mariachi music blaring, and Christmas tree lights, faded piñatas and *papel picado* banners hanging from the ceiling. But I couldn't wait to try their Tacos de Cochinita Pibil again.

Wally insisted we pay for ourselves. I knew she was low on money, so that kind of bothered me. Just the same, I kept my mouth shut.

She ordered a dish called Huachinango Entero al Mojo de Ajo, which according to the English translation on the menu, was whole red snapper, sautéed in garlic and butter. I stuck with what I was familiar with and asked, in English, for the tacos. The server didn't have trouble understanding me. I didn't think she would. I figured Casa Guanajuato had customers who didn't speak Spanish. That's why they translated their menu items to English.

While we waited for our food, I told Wally about my match at the Chaparral Bar & Grill.

"Geez and crackers," she said. "You need to press charges against him. If Mulder had done that to you in the street, he'd be arrested and locked up for assault."

"I'm not going to do that," I said. "I just want to put it behind me. Besides, I've decided to give up on the whole wrestling thing."

"Why? Because of that knuckle dragger?"

"Nah, I just don't have it in me anymore."

"I don't believe that for one second," she said. "You're discouraged because Plan A didn't turn out the way you expected. And Plan B didn't work too well, either. But there are twenty-six letters in the alphabet, Jessup. You just have to keep trying."

"How am I supposed to do that if nobody will give me a chance?" I griped.

"Your dad doesn't know every promoter in Texas," she said. "He didn't know the one at the Chaparral Bar & Grill. Look, whether you realize it or not, you're an artist, and the ring is your studio. When you wrestled Goose the other day, you created a beautiful work of art. Your match was as good as anything I've seen in all my years of watching pro wrestling."

I didn't feel that Wally was showering me with false praise because I believed it, too. Goose and I had wrestled lots of practice matches, but never in full gear and with a referee and timekeeper present. The match we had last week was by far our finest performance. While we were wrestling, I wasn't thinking about the promoters or the fans or about being famous. I was doing what I was most skilled at. What I was born to do. With every perfectly timed move and hold, a surge of elation rushed through me. I'd never felt more alive than I did during those eight minutes.

I was crying sour grapes when I said I was ready to give up wrestling. What I really wanted was an opportunity to prove myself.

My Tacos de Cochinita Pibil were even more delicious than I remembered. Wally's seafood dish looked mouthwatering, too. I'd have to try it some time.

I asked Wally how her musical was coming along. She said it was going well, and that if I was planning to attend it, I'd need to buy tickets soon, because they were expecting the show to sell out. Now that I'd put my potential wrestling career on hold, I wouldn't be doing anything on the weekends, except studying, so I promised her I'd be there, and if Temp was available, I'd invite him to come with me.

When we finished our dinner, the server brought us our bill, and we paid at the register.

"Hey, look, Jessup," Wally said. She was pointing to a flyer pinned to a corkboard by the counter. On it were photos of masked wrestlers, and the words:

¡EXTRAVAGANZA DE LUCHA LIBRE!
CADA DOMINGO A LAS DOS DE LA TARDE
SEGUIN, TEXAS

"You ought to check them out," she said.

"Nah, I don't think so. *Lucha libre*'s not my thing."

"It's professional wrestling, so I would argue that yes, it *is* your thing," Wally said. "They're putting on a show tomorrow at two o'clock. Why don't we go to it? Seguin's only a thirty-five, forty-minute drive from here."

"I can't," I said. "I've got a ton of homework to do. In fact, I'm heading back to Austin first thing in the morning. I only came to watch Goose wrestle."

"Well, at least write to them. Find out who the promoter is and send him your video."

"I'll see," I said, but I didn't want to deal with another rejection, and certainly not from a promotion that featured a type of wrestling that didn't interest me.

We made it to the Factory minutes before seven-thirty. Carla Betancourt, one of my father's new trainees, was running the ticket counter. I introduced myself to her, and she let us in.

Unlike my family, Goose's relatives came in droves to support him. His parents, his siblings, his grandparents, his uncles and aunts, his cousins, the entire clan was there. I went over to say hi to them, then took my seat.

Joe Ellis rang the bell to signal the start of the show. The arena grew dark, and a vignette aired on the jumbo screen of Goose working out in the fitness room—on the weight machines, the dumbbells and on a body bag. All the while, a lively tune played in the background. Goose threw a final punch at the body bag, then faced the camera as it zoomed in on him.

"You don't need a weatherman to tell you that a storm's coming!" he said in a deep voice. "Cyclone Suárez has arrived in the PWF, and he's gonna blow away the competition! Tonight's forecast . . . cloudy, with strong, heavy winds and lots of damage and destruction! Count on it!"

His family rooted wildly for him.

The image on the jumbo screen switched to Juan Serrano. He was sitting at the grand piano in our living room, playing a Rachmaninoff piece. He wore a black tuxedo with tails, a white shirt and a white bowtie.

He stopped playing and turned to the camera. In a haughty, Spanish accent, he said, "My name is Fernando Octavio Montemayor. I attended the finest schools in Europe, where I received the best education in the world. My superior intellect has given me wealth. Talent. Power. And most important, a humble heart. So I have decided to leave my beautiful home here in Madrid to come to your city, to serve as your role model. To be a shining example for you." He affected a caring smile. "I know you people will never achieve my level of greatness. That is all right. I understand. But at least you will have someone you can look up to, someone you can admire and say, 'Oh, how I wish I had what he has. If only I could be like . . . Fernando. Octavio. Montemayor.'"

His vignette drew incredible heat. Juan hadn't made an appearance yet, but already, he'd established himself as a heel. When he stepped through the curtains he was met with a chorus of boos, even as he waved to the crowd, grinning like the Cheshire Cat. He wore the same coattail jacket, this time with a white tear-away shirt, black tights and black boots.

Goose appeared next. Along with his family, the crowd greeted him with cheers and applause.

Clyde Conner made the introductions. Doug Fletcher patted down the wrestlers and went over the rules with them. Then he sent them to their corners, where they removed their accessories and handed them to Clyde.

At the sound of the bell, they squared off with a collar-and-elbow tie up. Juan spun Goose around in a waist lock, took him down, then hit him with two elbow drops. He rose, winked at the audience and gave them a "thumbs up," as if they were on his side. They weren't, of course. It was Juan's way of drawing more heat.

I didn't ask Goose who was going to win the match, and he didn't tell me. But after watching Juan's longer vignette, and the fact that it had been filmed at our house, made me think that my father saw more potential in the Fernando Octavio Montemayor character than he did in Cyclone Suárez.

I was right. After twelve minutes or so, Juan hit Goose with a Front Facelock Cutter and pinned his shoulders for the win.

For Goose, the loss was insignificant. He'd have plenty of wins in the future. The match was about launching his wrestling career.

I wondered if I'd ever get my chance.

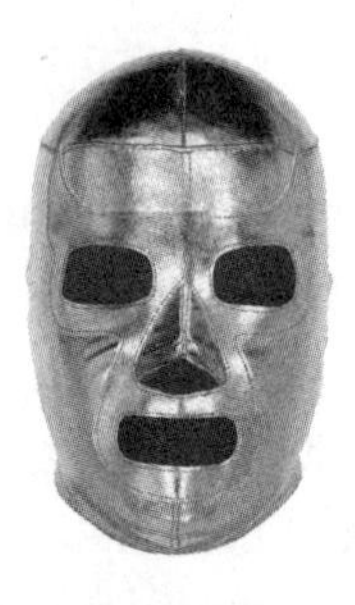

CHAPTER THIRTY-FOUR

Sunday morning, I was packing my duffel bag when Wally called.

"Jessup! I've got great news! I think I may have found a wrestling gig for you!"

I gasped. "You did? Where?"

"You know that *lucha libre* flyer we saw at Casa Guanajuato? Well, I checked out their website. The promoter's name is Santiago Reyes. Anyway, I wrote to him and sent him your video. He wants to know if you can meet with him today at one o'clock."

Wally's announcement was both a joy and a letdown. I was reminded of a writing activity my second-grade teacher gave us, called "Fortunately/Unfortunately." We had to write about a fortunate thing that happened to us, then counter it with something unfortunate.

Fortunately, I got a dog for my birthday. Unfortunately, it ran away. Fortunately, I found it. Unfortunately, it had been hit by a car. Fortunately, it was still alive. Unfortunately, our vet was out of town.

Fortunately, there's a promoter who may want to book you. Unfortunately, he runs a lucha libre promotion.

I didn't follow Mexican wrestling. For one thing, the shows were in Spanish. Also, the style was too acrobatic for my taste.

To me, the wrestlers were more interested in performing high-flying spots than in telling a story.

"I wish I could, Wally," I said. "But like I told you yesterday, I'm swamped with homework. I've got to get back to school. I'm just about to leave."

"Come on, Jessup, this could be a huge break for you," she said. "Extravaganza de Lucha Libre airs their shows on YouTube. Think of the exposure you'd get. You'd be seen by thousands of people from across the country, maybe even around the world."

After everything I'd been through, I didn't have any real hope that something like that could happen to me. But since Wally had gone to the trouble of contacting the promoter, I felt obligated to accept the invitation.

"All right, tell him I'll be there."

"You write to him," she said. "I'll text you his email address."

"No, it'd be better if you answered him," I said. "That way, the promoter will think you're my agent. And I'd like for you to go with me to be my spokesperson."

What I really meant was that I was afraid the promoter couldn't speak English, and I didn't want to make a fool of myself by stumbling through my limited Spanish.

"Okey doke," she said. "Chicken!"

Wally knew me too well to be fooled.

I told my parents I had decided to stay in San Antonio awhile longer, and that I'd go to church with them, but that I was having lunch with Wally.

At church, I prayed for God to help me with my wrestling career. I didn't know if He was listening, because in order to become a wrestler, I'd need to deceive my parents. But like they say, there's no harm in asking.

Lord, You gave me this body, these skills and this desire for a reason. I know You do things in Your own time, and I don't mean to rush You, but could You please reveal what You have planned for me real soon? And can You please help my parents be understanding, so they won't be mad at me when they find out? Amen.

After the service, I raced to Wally's house. She was waiting for me at the bottom of the steps.

My GPS took us to the Guadalupe County Center, a large metal structure in an open field, with a gravel road that led up to it. A yellow roadside sign with a flashing red arrow pointing toward the entrance, said in black lettering: ¡EXTRAVAGANZA DE LUCHA LIBRE! ¡HOY A LAS DOS!

The grassy parking lot was already beginning to fill with cars and pickups, and people were lined up outside the building, waiting to go in.

"I don't know about this place," I told Wally. "It looks kind of rank."

"You wrestled in a bar, so don't start acting bougie," she chided me.

We cut through the line and went inside. Two women were sitting by the door, selling tickets. Wally told them we had an appointment with Santiago Reyes, and they let us in.

The interior of the building was much more elaborate than I would've imagined. It was huge, much bigger than the Factory, and a far cry from Capital City Wrestling and the Chaparral Bar & Grill. LED flood lights with moving heads bathed the room with an array of colors, amid the blare of Latin techno music. The ring stood in the middle of the floor and was surrounded by rows of aluminum bleachers.

The place could easily seat three thousand people. Judging by the fans sitting down or walking about, and the line outside, at least half of the seats would be filled by the start of the show.

A concession stand was stationed along a wall where customers could buy hamburgers, french fries, nachos, elotes and different kinds of tacos, in addition to soft drinks and beer. A rolling cotton candy cart was parked next to it. A vendor at a table was selling *lucha* masks, T-shirts and wrestling action figures. At another table, two masked *luchadores* were peddling photos of themselves and autographing them. Wally asked one of them where we could find Santiago Reyes. He pointed to the wrestlers' framed entranceway across the room.

A heavyset security guard with a black Extravaganza de Lucha Libre T-shirt was standing in front of it, arms folded over his chest. Wally told him that Santiago Reyes was expecting us. He poked his head through the curtains and announced, "*Jefe, hay alguien aquí que quiere hablar con usted.*"

A moment later, Santiago Reyes stepped out. He appeared to be in his late sixties, but was fit for his age. His graying hair was combed back, and he had a nicely trimmed graying beard. He wore a black, short sleeve *guayabera* and black slacks.

"*Buenas tardes. ¿Cómo están*?" he greeted us and shook our hands.

We introduced ourselves. Then he said, "Morúa. That's an unusual name."

Good, he speaks English, I thought.

"Would you by any chance happen to be related to Dr. Wallace Morúa, who used to work at Southwest General Hospital in San Antonio?" he asked Wally.

"Yes, sir. He was my dad. But I never knew him. He died when my mom was pregnant with me."

Mr. Reyes nodded. "I remember when the accident happened. *Lo siento,* Wally. Your papi was a good man. He was my doctor. I used to tease him that I was funding his vacations because it seemed like I was going to him every year when I was wrestling. He did surgery on both my elbows, my shoulders, my knees and my hip. The only reason I was able to wrestle as long as I did was because of him. If you ask me, your papi was the best orthopedic surgeon in the country."

"Thank you. It's very kind of you to tell me that," Wally said.

This was unexpected. All of a sudden, I felt I had some clout. I added to it, saying, "By the way, my father is Mark Baron, the Angel of Death."

"*¿De veras?*" Mr. Reyes said, smiling. "That's right, you told me your last name's Baron. I haven't seen Mark in a long time. How's he doing?"

I had prepared an answer in case he knew my father. "Good," I said. "I did my training at the Factory with him, but I decided not to wrestle there because I didn't want the other wrestlers to think that my father was showing favoritism toward me."

"*Buena idea*," he said. "I admire that."

"But Jesse *has* worked at the Texas Roundup Rasslin' promotion in Austin," Wally said, without elaborating. "Now he wants to try *lucha libre* for a while."

I was so glad I'd brought her with me. I thought it was funny, though, that she referred to me as Jesse. As long as I'd known Wally, she'd always called me Jessup. I never asked why. I just accepted it as part of her quirkiness.

"Well, I must say that I was very impressed by your demo video, Jesse," Mr. Reyes said. "Your papi trained you well. I like your ring attire, too. Where did you get it?"

I told him about Shirley Washington and how Wally had designed it for me.

"You know, when I saw your match, I sensed that there was something special about you," he said. "And now that I've learned that the Angel of Death is your papi, and that Dr. Morúa's daughter came up with the idea for your wrestling name and gear, I'm beginning to believe that fate has brought us together. So if you're interested, I'd like to book you for next Sunday."

Wally squeezed my hand and smiled at me. I was too shocked to smile back.

"Okay," I said softly.

"The pay isn't much, only thirty dollars a show, to start. More, if you move up. Is that all right?"

That was the same amount of money my father paid his rookies. "Yes, sir, it's fine."

Mr. Reyes took a business card from his wallet. "Text me your email address. I'll send you some paperwork to fill out. Email them back to me as soon as you can."

While I was doing that, he told the security guard to call someone from the back named Gerónimo.

The security guard disappeared behind the curtains and returned with a muscular man with black hair tied in a bun. He wore a red, sleeveless, Gold's Gym T-shirt and white sweat pants.

"*Gerónimo Chávez, te presento a Jesse Baron y su amiga, Wally Morúa*," Mr. Reyes said. "*Jesse es luchador*."

Gerónimo shook our hands. "*Mucho gusto*."

"Nice to meet you, too," I said.

"*¿Háblas español?*" he asked me.

I made a side-to-side hand gesture. "*Más o menos*."

Mr. Reyes then said something else to him in Spanish. I didn't catch it all, but I understood enough to know that he was telling him I was going to be his opponent next week.

"*¿Eres rudo o técnico?*" Gerónimo asked me.

"I'm sorry, I . . . I don't understand," I said.

"*Es un rudo*," Wally interjected. She would explain to me later that a *rudo* is a heel, and a *técnico* is a baby face. She must've told him I was a rudo because of her preference for heel wrestlers.

"Well, on Sunday, I want you to wrestle as a *técnico,*" Mr. Reyes said. "Gerónimo's known in our show as a *rudo*."

I told him I'd be glad to do it. Gerónimo excused himself and returned behind the curtains.

"Does he speak English?" I asked Mr. Reyes.

"*Más o menos,*" he said, mimicking my side-to-side hand gesture. "Now, most of the time, when I hire a new talent, I like to put him in tag-team matches to cover up any weaknesses he might have. But I see star potential in you, Jesse. I want to push you as a singles wrestler."

The deal was getting sweeter by the minute.

"I know that you have some wrestling experience, and I've heard a lot of good things about the Ox Mulligan Pro Wrestling Factory," he said. "But *lucha libre* is different from American wrestling. I know because I've wrestled in both styles. So let me suggest that you join my *lucha* classes. They're not very expensive, only fifty dollars a month. We meet here every Tuesday and Thursday, from seven till nine."

"Thank you, sir, but I can't make it," I said. "I'm a full-time student at UT, and I'm bogged down with school work."

"Hmm. Well, it's not a requirement," he said, although his tone made me wonder if my push was tied to the training.

He went over some ideas for my match, including making it a best two out of three falls. Then he said, "As you know, in *lucha libre*, your mask is sacred. It's part of your mystique. Our fans must never see you without it. So have it on when you get here and when you leave."

I promised him I would.

"All right, enjoy the show, and I'll see you Sunday. Be here by twelve at the latest."

I thanked him, but said we couldn't stay because I needed to get back to Austin. I had a paper due the next day that I hadn't even started.

During the interview, I kept my emotions in check to avoid being crushed by another rejection. But outside, Wally and I happy-danced and laughed giddily.

Then out of the blue, I burst into tears. One second I was celebrating, the next, I was boohooing like a baby. I felt as if a gigantic burden had at long last been lifted off my shoulders.

Wally took me lovingly in her arms. "It's finally happening, Jessup," she said. "Next week at this time, the world is going to witness the birth of a new wrestling legend . . . Máscara de la Muerte!"

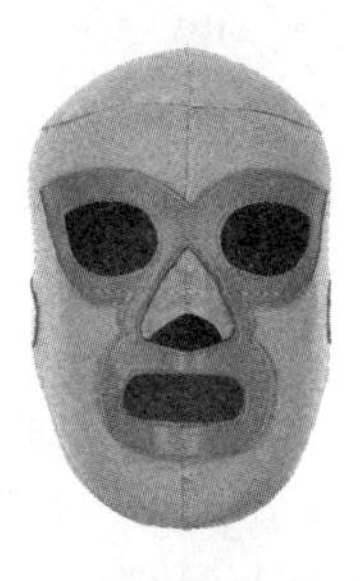

CHAPTER THIRTY-FIVE

I had essays due in American history and Rhetoric and Writing, plus chapters to read and questions to answer for my Introduction to Engineering class. As a result, I didn't get to hit the gym like I wanted, although I did squeeze in some time to jog.

During a break, I googled Santiago Reyes's name. I found out that he'd wrestled for almost forty years, in Mexico, as an *enmascarado* called Relámpago Blanco, and without his mask in the United States, as Jupiter Reyes.

I also spent a few minutes watching a YouTube video of Extravaganza de Lucha Libre. For a show that took place inside of what was essentially a giant shed on the outskirts of Seguin, the motion graphics made it look like a first-class operation, and the camera angles showed a crowd that appeared to be twice the size of the actual number.

Two ringside commentators welcomed viewers in Spanish, then turned the show over to Mr. Reyes, who served as the ring announcer.

A couple of *enmascarados* came out first. One was known as El Cartagenero. He wore a red, yellow and blue mask. The other, with a black and gold mask, went by the name of Anubis. They were the *rudos*. On the way to the ring, they stopped to argue with the fans, who in turn, yelled and cussed at them.

The *técnicos,* Elvis Trejo and Lorenzo Aragón, who weren't masked, followed.

Mr. Reyes introduced the tag-team match as a *dos de tres caídas*, two-out-of-three falls. I learned that most *lucha libre* matches are set up that way. By contrast, American matches are usually one fall. I only watched part of the first fall because I needed to get back to work, but at least I had an idea of what to expect.

I told Temp about my new job, but after my disastrous performance at the Chaparral Bar & Grill, I didn't encourage him to go. I didn't invite Goose, either. Wally, though, was a different matter. She said she'd definitely be there.

Sunday morning, I dressed in a black polo shirt, black pants and a black sports jacket. I thought I'd look cool in those clothes, wearing my skull mask. I took my garment bag out of the closet, grabbed my backpack with my books and laptop in it, and drove to Seguin.

On the way, I thought about how surreal it was that I'd be performing before a live audience and on YouTube, wrestling as a masked character Wally had created for me. I felt as if I was stepping out of one of Temp's comic books.

Mr. Reyes had booked me to win the match. "The way I see it," he said, "you'll take the first fall, Gerónimo, the second one, then you'll come back and win the third and final fall."

I told him about my finisher, The Big Sleep, to which he said, "That's a great name, but for our viewers, I think we'll call it *El sueño profundo*."

As I neared the Guadalupe County Center, I pulled my car along the shoulder of the road and slipped on my mask. Then I drove into the gravel entrance all the way around the back and parked where I'd been instructed.

The security guard who'd been guarding the wrestlers' entrance last week was standing by the rear door. He was talking to a group of teenage girls who had arrived early to take photos with the wrestlers and to get their autographs.

The second I stepped out of my car, the girls abandoned the security guard and rushed toward me, squealing with delight.

"*¿Cómo te llamas?*" one of them asked.

"*Máscara de la Muerte,*" I said.

The girls oohed.

"*¿De dónde eres?*" asked another one.

"*Oaxaca.*"

Then they started asking a bunch of other questions I didn't understand. No big deal. By not answering them, I thought it added to my coolness. The girls wanted *fotos*, so I put my arms around them and let them take as many as they wanted. I also signed autograph books and scraps of paper.

Finally, I separated myself from them and told the security guard who I was. He opened the door and let me in.

The backstage area wasn't anywhere near as fancy as the Ox Mulligan Pro Wrestling Factory, but it had fitness equipment, showers and rows of lockers with compartments, where we could hang our clothes.

Most of the wrestlers were Latino, although I did spot a couple of white guys and a black guy. And I counted four Latina women.

My opponent, Gerónimo Chávez, was sitting at a card table, playing poker with three other men. He had on black tights with red jagged lines on the sides, black boots, but no shirt. His long hair hung over his face.

A locker room attendant handed me a key and told me in Spanish that my locker was C32. None of the wrestlers were wearing masks, so I figured it'd be all right if I removed mine.

I place it in the locker, along with my garment bag and backpack. Then I walked around and introduced myself. A few *luchadores* tried to engage me in a Spanish conversation, but I excused myself with a smile and a "*con permiso*."

I made my way toward the non-Latinos, with whom I felt more comfortable. The black guy's name was Michael Lazarus. The white guys were Blake Cooper and Sebastian Flynn.

"Do you speak Spanish?" I asked them.

"*Un poquito*," Michael said, making a tiny-amount gesture with his fingers. "But almost everybody here speaks English."

"All we really need to know when we're wrestling are the names of the holds and moves in Spanish," Blake said. "For example, if a guy calls for a *plancha*, I can expect a type of crossbody. Or if he says *tope suicida*, I know that as soon as I slide out of the ring, he's going to come at me with a suicide dive."

I wasn't familiar with any wrestling terms in Spanish. I hoped Gerónimo knew them in English. If not, it was going to be a long afternoon.

When he finished his card game, I walked over to him. "Hi, if you don't mind, I'd like to talk to you about our match."

"Okay," he said.

"Do you prefer to lay it out beforehand, or do you want us to call it as we go?"

"I just need to know the finish," he said. "*Lo demás, pues a ver qué pasa*."

I took his answer to mean that he liked to play it by ear. Goose and I often wrestled the same way, taking our cues from one another.

"Well, Mr. Reyes suggested that I win the first fall, you the second and me the third."

He shrugged with indifference. "Okay."

"Anyway, I was thinking about using the spear as my finisher for the first fall."

He gave me a confused look.

"You know." I motioned the spear tackle.

"*O, sí, una lanza*," he said. "*Está bien*."

"And you?"

"A . . . *¿cómo se dice?* A power bahn."

"You mean a powerbomb?"

"*Sí, ése*."

"And for the third fall, I want to end it with a brain buster. Do you know what that is?"

"*Claro. Un brain buster*."

"But the commentators are going to call it *El sueño profundo*."

"Okay," he said, unimpressed. I wondered if Gerónimo had wrestled for so long that he'd lost his passion for the business. Or maybe, like Dale Mulder, he wasn't particularly interested in working with a new talent. At any rate, I planned to give him everything I had.

We shook hands and wished each other luck. Then I grabbed my backpack from my locker, sat on the floor in a corner and tried to get some studying done.

Mr. Reyes came in and took a head count to make sure everyone was present. Then he went over the order of the matches with us. Gerónimo and I were second.

After Mr. Reyes left, I heard music playing and people talking, as the arena began to fill. Wally texted me, saying she had arrived and was sitting at ringside. She didn't mention anyone being with her. She may have felt the same way I did about not wanting to invite friends, in case something went wrong.

One of the female wrestlers pulled the drape that hung on a rod across the top of a row of lockers to give the women privacy while they changed. The men switched into their gear, too. Most of them wore masks. I got dressed, then returned to my corner.

Before long, I heard Mr. Reyes's voice coming through the curtains, welcoming the audience to Extravaganza de Lucha Libre. Then he introduced the first match, a six-man tag. The *rudos,* El Cartagenero, Anubis and Voodoo King, were going up against the *técnicos,* Sebastian Flynn, Aldo Alemán and Perico Saldaña.

A monitor in the back allowed us to watch the show. I gave up trying to study and pulled up a chair in front of it to see my new coworkers in action.

The bout was a best two-out-of-three falls. What I found interesting was that the match had two referees; one, a *técnico,* the other, a *rudo.*

Ultimately, the heels won, when Voodoo King smashed Sebastian Flynn over the head with his scepter, while the *rudo* ref distracted the *técnico* ref.

When the match was over, Gerónimo and I stood behind the curtains in what is known as the Gorilla Position and waited our turn. Because Gerónimo was the *rudo,* Mr. Reyes wanted him to walk out first, so that when I made my appearance, the fans would accept me as a *técnico.*

Gerónimo's entrance music sounded, and he headed toward the ring, as boos rained on him.

I took a deep breath to steady my nerves. *You're not Jesse Baron*, I told myself. *You're Máscara de la Muerte.*

Next, an eerie tune, with a combination of a piano, violins and a bass guitar, began to play. My very own entrance music!

I stepped through the curtains to the entrance ramp. With my chest puffed and my fists on my hips, I paused for the crowd's reaction. They didn't know who I was, but they gave me a huge pop, anyway.

I swaggered down the aisle toward the ring. Then I hoisted myself over the top rope, as I'd seen some of the *luchadores* do, and walked across the mat to measure the distance.

Mr. Reyes introduced Gerónimo first. All I understood was, "*Damas y caballeros . . . blah, blah, blah . . . de San Luis Potosí, México . . . ¡Gerónimo Cháve-e-e-z*!"

Gerónimo yelled at the audience as they jeered him, then climbed out of the ring and continued to argue with them. An old man with a megaphone heckled him mercilessly. An old woman cranked a noisemaker at him, while other fans hurled Spanish cuss words I'd heard at school, plus a bunch of new ones.

Gerónimo stepped back inside the ring and waited for Mr. Reyes to introduce my name.

"Blah, blah, blah . . . de Oaxaca de Juárez, México . . . ¡Máscara de la Muerte-e-e-!"

I thrust my fists in the air and soaked in the cheers.

Gerónimo snatched the microphone from Mr. Reyes and hollered something at me. I didn't understand what he said, but it didn't matter. He was playing his role as a *rudo*.

Then unexpectedly, he shoved the microphone against my chest. I froze. I didn't know what to do. I couldn't respond to him in English. I was supposed to be from Mexico!

Come on, Baron, think of something. Anything!

I took the microphone from him, the blood draining from my masked face. The crowd started going crazy. They wanted me to fire back with a clever barb. But what? I didn't know any Spanish insults. Mr. Reyes kept waiting for me to answer, so he could start the match. I couldn't put it off any longer. I had to say something. Finally, out of desperation, I shouted, "*¡Tú eres . . . tú eres una vaca!*"

The audience howled with laughter. "*¡Va-ca! ¡Va-ca! ¡Va-ca!*" they chanted.

I looked at Mr. Reyes. He was biting his lip to keep from laughing. I gave him the microphone, and he climbed out of the ring.

"*¡Va-ca! ¡Va-ca! ¡Va-ca!*"

I felt like a complete idiot. Of all the things I could've said to Gerónimo, I told him he was a cow.

The referee sent us to our corners, then called for the bell.

Gerónimo and I locked up in the middle of the ring with a collar-and-elbow. I switched it to a waist lock and shoved him against the ropes. When we bounced back, I rolled him up with a Sunset Flip, but he kicked out. He took me down with a clothesline and began stomping my chest, until the ref pulled him away, and I was able to fight back.

After five or six minutes, I leaned into Gerónimo and called for the spear. I swung him against the turnbuckles, then tackled him as he teetered toward me and knocked him off his feet. I hooked his leg, and the ref made the three count. Mr. Reyes declared me the winner of *la primera caída.*

I didn't know about Gerónimo, but except for me blowing it on the mic, I thought we'd gotten off to a good start. We were given a minute to rest. Then the ref signaled the timekeeper to ring the bell, and we began the second fall.

Gerónimo rushed out of his corner and hit me with three consecutive dropkicks. He grabbed me in an armbar submission hold, and I sold it as if it were causing me excruciating pain. I kicked out, and our match continued. Overall, I thought Gerónimo and I were working well together, almost as if we could read each other's minds.

Until I committed my second major mistake.

While I was on my back, he picked me up and whispered, "*Desnucadora.*"

I didn't know what that meant. He put my head between his legs and lifted me over his shoulders. Instinctively, I flipped him over with a hurricanrana.

"*¡No, pendejo!*" he growled in my ear, when I went to grab him. "A power bahn! A power bahn!"

I felt like an idiot again.

I let him punch his way out of my grasp. He kicked me in the stomach, then put my head between his legs once more, lifted me over his shoulders and slammed me on my back with a powerbomb. The ref counted to three, and Mr. Reyes announced Gerónimo as the winner of *la segunda caída.*

During the third fall, I messed up again when Gerónimo called for a *cruceta*, which I didn't know was a Figure-Four Leglock. He yelled and cussed at me when we got our legs tangled up awkwardly. To the audience, he was acting like a heel, but I knew Gerónimo was genuinely upset. I also botched a *quebradora*, a backbreaker, and we both fell down next to each other. He, on the other hand, didn't have any trouble understanding me when I whispered "brainbuster" to finish our match.

My mind spun deliriously, listening to the cheers, as the referee raised my hand, and Mr. Reyes proclaimed me, "*El ganador de la tercera caída y el combate.*"

Things were a lot different backstage.

Perico Saldaña and some other *luchadores* were waiting for us. As soon as I walked through the curtains, he pointed at me and screeched, "*¡Eres una vaca-a-a-a!*" Everyone busted out laughing.

"*¡Muuu! ¡Muuu!*"

When Gerónimo showed up, they broke into a chant of, "*¡Va-ca! ¡Va-ca! ¡Va-ca!*"

Wrestlers are used to ribbing one other, but Gerónimo didn't think it was funny. More than the silly taunting, he was angry at me for screwing up our match.

He glowered at me, baring his teeth. "You make me look bad! You no know what you doing!"

"Listen, Gerónimo, I'm really sorry about what happened. I know the botches were my fault and . . ."

"*¿Qué demonios estás haciendo aquí?*" he bayed. "You not a *luchador*! You just a gringo with a mask!" He pointed to the door. "*¡Vete!* You no belong here!" Then he turned and walked away.

Seconds later, Wally texted me.

You were fabulous, Jessup! Let's go somewhere and celebrate!

The last thing in the world I felt like doing was celebrating, but I wanted to talk to her.

Give me a few minutes. I'm going to take a quick shower. Drive your car around the back. I'll meet you there.

I didn't tell Mr. Reyes I was leaving. As soon as I got dressed, I went out the back door, wearing my mask, as I'd been told to do. Thankfully, there weren't any fans lounging outside.

Wally jumped out of her car and threw her arms around my neck. "You did it, Jessup! Máscara de la Muerte was a huge hit!"

I peeled her off me. "Let's get out of here," I said.

"Is something wrong?" she asked, now looking worried.

"I'll tell you in the car."

I didn't take us anywhere to celebrate. I just drove around the city and explained what happened.

"I'll bet you Gerónimo's never told the white guys and the black guy that they don't belong there," I grumbled.

Wally gazed out the window at the yellowing fields of grass on the sides of the rural road we were on, listening quietly, while I complained. At last she said, "I'm going to be real honest with you, Jessup. When you first told me that you wanted to promote yourself as a *luchador,* I was afraid something like this might happen. I don't mean to be critical, but you've never really embraced your Latino heritage."

"Why do you say that?" I asked, my face burning with resentment. "Because I can't speak Spanish like you?"

"No, but I think it would help," she said. "Look, a lot of Latino kids at school don't identify with their ethnicity, and that's fine. I'm not judging them. It's how they were brought up. You were probably raised the same way. But being a *luchador* is more than simply putting on a mask. You've got to feel it in your heart. You've got to take pride in who you are as a Latino because that's who you represent when you step inside the ring. The Latino audience looks up to someone like you. So if you're going to call yourself a *luchador,* then you need to be more accepting of your culture. Otherwise, Gerónimo's right. You *are* just a gringo with a mask."

I'd never been ashamed of being Latino. I'd just never given it any thought. My parents spoke only English to me. So did the Latino kids I hung out with. Wally would tease me sometimes about not being able to speak Spanish, but she did it light-heartedly. I'd never been confronted about my background until today. I wondered if I would've been better off wrestling as Jesse The Red Baron.

I made it to my dorm that evening, still baffled over my unbelievable streak of bad luck. It seemed that no matter what I did, I kept hitting a brick wall. I felt as if God was punishing me for trying to wrestle on the sneak.

Temp asked me about my match. I told him it went well, and that I'd won it, but that I was exhausted and wanted to take a nap. I'd fill him in on it later, when I was in a better mood.

Before I shut my eyes, I checked my phone for messages. I groaned when I saw one from Mr. Reyes. Undoubtedly, he was writing to tell me that he didn't have any use for me. But to my surprise, he sent me a pleasant email that lifted my spirits.

Jesse,

You were sensational today! The audience loved you! I'm sorry you had to leave before you got paid. You can pick up your check next week. I'll let you know later who you'll be wrestling. Glad to have you on board!

Santiago

CHAPTER THIRTY-SIX

Tuesday evening, I drove to the Guadalupe County Center. Despite all the work I had to do for school, I decided to enroll in Mr. Reyes's *lucha* classes to show him I was part of the team. I began by apologizing for my *vaca* blunder. I'd watched my match on YouTube, and I cringed when I heard myself on the mic. The way everyone was laughing, I thought I'd lost my credibility as a wrestler.

"Are you kidding?" Mr. Reyes said. "That was the best part. I mean, here you are, this mysterious figure with a skeleton mask who comes out to scary-sounding music. The fans have never seen you before. They don't know anything about you. I didn't write a promo for you, so I didn't know what you were going to say. I thought you were going to speak in poetry form, like your papi does." Mr. Reyes's eyes crinkled with delight. "God, I had to do everything I could to keep from laughing. *Eres una vaca* is such a stupid insult, especially coming from someone who looks like your character. That's why the fans ate it up."

"Well, Gerónimo didn't see it that way," I said. "He chewed me out backstage and told me I didn't belong here."

"Ah, don't worry about him. He's bitter because he's been with me a long time, and he's still a jobber. He was probably mad that he was going to have to put you over, when he thought he should've won against a newcomer. Don't get me wrong. Gerónimo's a good wrestler, but he doesn't put butts in the seats." Mr. Reyes wrapped an arm around me in a fatherly fashion and added, "Still, it wouldn't hurt for you to work on your Spanish. He told me about your miscommunication in the ring."

"Yes, sir," I said, embarrassed. "I googled wrestling terms in Spanish, and I've been trying to memorize them."

"*Buena idea.* The thing I noticed was how quickly you recovered from your mistakes. It takes a lot of ability to do that. But just to be on the safe side, Sunday, I'm putting you in a match against Michael Lazarus. He'll be here Thursday. You can go over it with him then."

What a relief it was to know that Mr. Reyes hadn't given up on me. From now on, I was going to do everything I could not to disappoint him. To start with, I'd have to remember to bring my mask. All the *enmascarados* wore theirs to the training.

Mr. Reyes opened the session by having us do warmups—stretching exercises, push-ups, squats, jumping jacks, rolls, running the ropes and such. We spent the rest of the evening going over holds and moves, which I could already perform, but it was a big help to practice them with a new group of wrestlers. And I tried to nail down the terms in Spanish as I heard them: *estacas*, *pescado*, *cavernaria*, *guillotina* and, of course, *desnucadora*, *cruceta* and *quebradora*.

Back at my dorm, I texted Wally, asking her if she could write a promo for me in Spanish. Even though I'd be wrestling Michael Lazarus, and he wouldn't understand what I was saying, I felt I needed to redeem myself by addressing the audience in my character's native tongue. Wally said she was busy with homework and musical rehearsals but would try to have something for me by Saturday.

Juggling wrestling and school was demanding, but I managed to maintain an A average in everything, except for Rhetoric and Writing, where I held on to a steady B. One of my motivations for keeping up my grades was that if my parents ever discovered I was wrestling, I didn't want them to claim that my side job was causing me to do poorly in school.

By Saturday afternoon, I still hadn't heard from Wally. I was about to text her when she called.

"Jessup, guess what? You're about to get a manager."

"What are you talking about?" I asked.

"I wrote to Mr. Reyes this morning and told him that I'm a theater arts student, and that I speak Spanish fluently. I asked him if I could play your manager on his show. That way, I could cut your promos, so you wouldn't have to. And I told him I'd be willing to do it for free. Anyway, he just wrote back. He said it'd be okay with him, if it was all right with you."

"Are you serious?"

"As a toothache."

"I don't know, Wally," I said. "I mean, I just started working there. I'm still trying to figure out how they do things."

"Jessup, the owner said it'd be fine. What more do you want? Trust me. I'm going to make a star out of you."

Cassandra Richardson used to play my father's valet, Spirit, until my mom put a stop to it, accusing my father of being a little too friendly with her. I don't know if there was any truth to her suspicions. Regardless, the Angel of Death and Spirit were super popular. I wondered what the fans would think of Máscara de la Muerte and . . .

Perséfone. That's what I'm going to call myself, Wally texted me a few minutes later. *In Greek mythology, Perséfone was the queen of the Underworld, so I think the name is perfect for me, since your character is supposed to represent Death.*

Máscara de la Muerte y Perséfone. I could get used to that.

CHAPTER THIRTY-SEVEN

On Sunday afternoon, Wally looked just like she did at my prom. She wore her short, sequined, turquoise dress, her gold bolero jacket and gold high heels. She also had on a feathery, turquoise-and-gold Mardi Gras mask that she made.

I took her backstage and introduced her as Perséfone. No one asked if that was her real name, which wasn't surprising. Unless they're close friends, wrestlers often address each other by their ring names.

My match with Michael Lazarus was third on the card, following a women's singles bout between Silvia Santana and Baby Blue Eyes.

"Do you know what you're going to say?" I asked Wally, as we were getting ready to go out.

"No worries, love. I'm in my element. But I would like to try something." She whispered it in my ear so no one could hear.

"Are you sure about that?" I asked.

"Don't question your manager," she said.

Michael Lazarus was a tweener, who played both a *técnico* and a *rudo,* depending on what his role called for. That day, he was a *rudo.* He walked out first, yelling at the audience and pretending he was going to hit them.

Next, my entrance music sounded, and Wally and I stepped through the curtains. She was holding a microphone.

"*¡Buenas tardes, Seguin!*" she shouted. "*¿Cómo están?*"

The crowd responded with loud cheers.

"*¡Mi nombre es Perséfone!*" That's about all I understood. The rest sounded like, "*¡Blah, blah, blah . . . Máscara de la Muerte . . . blah, blah, blah . . . Michael Lazarus . . . blah, blah, blah . . . El sueño profundo!*" She paused, then said, "*Y una cosa más . . .*"

She handed me the microphone. I looked at Michael and hollered, "*¡Eres una vaca-a-a!*"

The crowd laughed uproariously. "*¡Va-ca! ¡Va-ca! ¡Va-ca!*"

Wally had the bright idea to turn my gaffe into my catchphrase. And it worked. The audience went crazy over it.

Michael and I had rehearsed our match on Thursday, so we knew what we were going to do. Wally wasn't there, but like she said, she was in her element. Whenever Michael got the upper hand, she pounded on the mat and called him names in Spanish, making the audience laugh. After fourteen minutes, I defeated Michael with my finisher, *El sueño profundo.* Wally jumped in the ring, and along with the ref, raised my hand in victory.

During the show's intermission, Wally and I were assigned to a table in the arena, where we posed for photos and signed autographs. Wally did most of the talking, although every once in a while, I slipped in a "*Buenas tardes,*" and "*Hola, chicas,*" and "*¿Cómo te llamas*?"

A woman nudged a little boy around five years old toward me. "*A ver, mi amor, dile,*" she prodded him.

The little boy looked up at her shyly, then at me. "*¡Eres una vaca-a-a!*" he shrieked. The crowd around us hooted with laughter.

Never in a million years would I have imagined I'd be wrestling for a *lucha libre* promotion. Yet there I was, having the time of my life, meeting and greeting a most unlikely fan base.

Gerónimo was wrong. This *was* where I belonged.

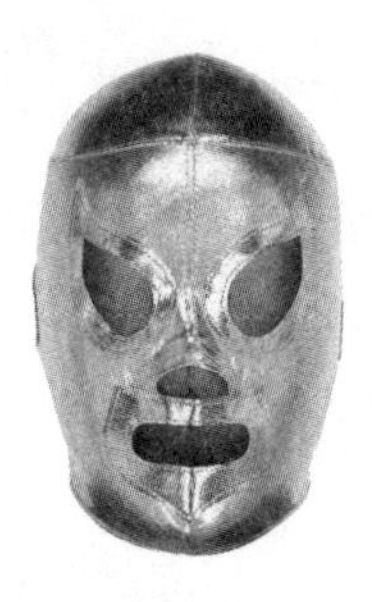

CHAPTER THIRTY-EIGHT

The following Saturday was Wally's musical. Temp couldn't make it because UT was playing the University of Houston in a night game, and the Longhorn band was performing.

My father didn't have a show that evening, which worked out for Wally. In addition to selling tickets at the Factory, she helped at the concession stand and the merchandise table. Three times a week, she swept and mopped the floors and cleaned the restrooms. My father paid her a decent salary, but she could always use more money. Hopefully, if her Perséfone character took off, Mr. Reyes would consider compensating her for her appearances.

I'd watched the old, black-and-white reruns of the *Addams Family* TV series, and it was fun seeing the characters come alive on stage. As Morticia Addams, Wally dressed in a long, tight, low-cut, black gown, with a black wig. Her friend Brandon played her husband, Gomez. The rest of her theater arts group did a good job portraying the roles of Uncle Fester, Grandmama, Pugsley, Wednesday, Lurch and others.

I knew Wally could act, but I didn't realize what a great singing voice she had. I was astounded, listening to her belt out tunes like, "When You're an Addams," and "Just Around the Corner."

After the show, Wally allowed me to buy her dinner. She chose another hole-in-the-wall restaurant, this one, a seafood place called The Grinning Alligator, and she convinced me to try the fried alligator tail. I'd never eaten alligator, fried or otherwise. It wasn't bad, though. It sort of tasted like chicken.

As we were eating, Wally rehashed the details that went into putting on the musical. I tried to listen, but my mind kept drifting off to my upcoming match. On Sunday, I'd be wrestling Voodoo King, one of Extravaganza de Lucha Libre's top performers, and I was feeling nervous about it.

Wally snapped me back to attention when she said, "I meant to tell you this earlier, but I forgot. My mom wanted to know where I was going last Sunday when she saw me in my prom dress."

I gulped. "What'd you tell her?"

"The truth."

"What do you mean, the truth? Did you tell her about us?"

"She didn't ask about us, Jessup. She asked about me. I told her I'd gotten an acting gig as a wrestling manager at Extravaganza de Lucha Libre."

"You didn't!"

"I can't lie to my mom," she said. "I told her about how you and I had gone to the *lucha* matches a few weeks ago, and that I met Santiago Reyes, who used to be one of my dad's patients."

"A-a-a-and," I said, bracing myself.

"And that I told him I was an actress and would it be possible for me to play a *luchador*'s manager, and that I'd be willing to do it for free. And that he said yes, because he had a lot of respect for my dad. I even showed my mom your match when it came out on YouTube."

"What?"

"No worries. She didn't know it was you. All she saw was me working as a manager for a *luchador* from Mexico named Máscara de la Muerte."

It amazed me how Wally was so secure in herself that she could get out of a tight spot by sticking to the truth. My natural instinct was to fib.

"How does your mom feel about it?" I asked.

Wally shrugged. "She knows how much acting means to me, so she tries to be supportive whenever I get a gig, even if it's one she doesn't necessarily approve of."

"I wish my parents felt the same way," I said glumly.

"How do you know they don't? I mean, your dad never said that you couldn't be a wrestler. The only reason he didn't want to put you in his shows was because he was afraid you wouldn't go to college. But the semester's almost over, and you're acing all your classes."

"Yeah, well, I'd still have to contend with my mom," I said, then turned the situation around. "If *your* mom had told you that you couldn't work for Extravaganza de Lucha Libre, would you still do it?"

"Jessup, we're not doing anything illegal or immoral," she said. "If wrestling as Máscara de la Muerte is the worst thing you're guilty of, I'm sure your parents can live with it."

Wally made sense. Maybe after the semester ended, and I went home for the holidays, I'd come clean with my parents about how I was spending my Sunday afternoons.

CHAPTER THIRTY-NINE

Voodoo King's real name was Carlos Ponte. He lived in Luling, not far from Seguin. Originally, he was from the Mexican border town of Reynosa. His character was similar to my father's in that he painted his face to look like a skull, except that he shaved his head. He wore a robe of fake animal pelts and a necklace supposedly made of human bones. And where my father carried a scythe, Voodoo King had a "magic" scepter. He spoke English well enough, but when we went over our match, we used the Spanish terms for the holds and moves.

Sunday afternoon, he walked down the aisle with Anubis at his side, to a verbal assault of boos and jeers.

When Wally and I came out, we received a massive pop. On the way to the ring, she went into her spiel. "*¡Buenas tardes, Seguin! ¿Cómo están*?" Then after the expected loud response, she began badmouthing Voodoo King. She finished with, "*Y una cosa más . . .*"

I took the microphone from her and looked around, letting the anticipation build. The fans knew what was coming. They whistled and cheered and stomped their feet. Waiting. Waiting. Waiting.

"*¡Eres una vaca-a-a!*"

The crowd exploded with laughter. "*¡Va-ca! ¡Va-ca! ¡Va-ca!*"

Voodoo King won the first fall, when he "blinded" me with a flash of light from his scepter that he grabbed while his partner distracted the referee. Outside the ring, Wally went after Anubis, attacking him with hilarious insults, as the fans egged her on.

I came back and took the second fall with a stunner, and the third and final fall with *El sueño profundo.* As before, Wally climbed inside the ring and raised my hand. I couldn't tell who was getting the most cheers, her or me. It didn't matter. We were a team.

When the match was over, Wally and I signed autographs and posed for photos. I asked Mr. Reyes if it'd be possible for her to start getting paid. He told me he didn't have money in his budget for her at the moment, but that if she wanted, she could have 8x10 photos of herself made that she could sell.

I told Wally about it. She thought it was a great idea. She said she'd also have prints made of the photo Temp had taken of me.

* * *

In the weeks that followed, my undefeated streak continued, and Máscara de la Muerte and Perséfone became insanely popular. People brought homemade signs to the arena with captions that read: ¡TE AMO PERSÉFONE! ¡CÁSATE CONMIGO, PERSÉFONE! ¡VIVA MÁSCARA DE LA MUERTE! ¡ERES UNA VACA-A-A!

Fans brought me all sorts of toy cows, and little kids gave Wally and me pictures they'd drawn of us. She had T-shirts and buttons made with our likenesses on them, which we sold, in addition to tons of photos.

Video clips and images of us soon turned up on every form of social media. We also started getting offers from *lucha libre* promotions across the US and in Mexico. We couldn't accept them, of course. Nevertheless, it got me wondering if there was any way Wally and I could go on tour in the summer.

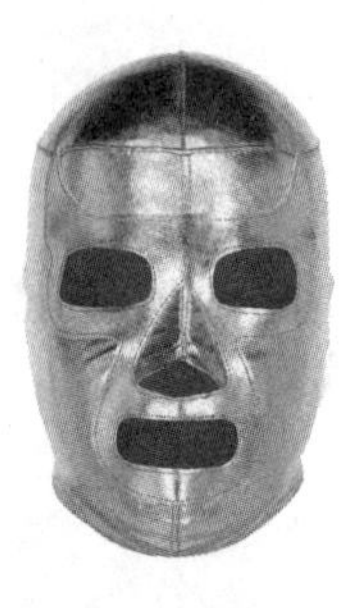

CHAPTER FORTY

December twelfth was the last day of classes. It was also my birthday. My mom wanted to have a big party at the house with lots of friends and relatives. My father proposed a smaller gathering at Belmondo 51. I told them I wanted to celebrate my birthday at Casa Guanajuato, with just us and Wally and her mom, and maybe Aunt Gracie and Uncle Ryan.

My parents were curious to know why I'd chosen Casa Guanajuato, of all places. They'd driven by the restaurant but had never tried it. I told them about the times Wally and I had eaten there, and how much we enjoyed it.

My mom called Aunt Gracie and Wally's mom to invite them. She also bought a birthday cake to take to the restaurant.

Friday night, my parents and I were the first to arrive. The mustachioed big man I'd seen the first time Wally and I ate there, the owner perhaps, welcomed us at the door. He asked how many we had in our party. My mom told him seven, but that we would wait to be seated until the rest of our group showed up. She handed him the cake to save for later, saying we were celebrating my birthday. The man told her the mariachis would be in shortly, and he'd make sure to send them our way.

Wally and her mom and Aunt Gracie and Uncle Ryan arrived soon after. Uncle Ryan looked around the dining room and wrinkled his nose. "Whose idea was it to eat *here*?" he asked.

"Mine," I said. "Trust me, Ryan. You're going to love their food."

The restaurant didn't seem ratty anymore. It felt . . . homey. I nudged Wally, then turned my eyes toward the counter. On the corkboard was a flyer for Extravaganza de Lucha Libre, and our photos were on it.

After we were seated, a server came by. "*¿Qué les gustaría tomar*?" she asked.

I waited for everyone to tell her what they wanted to drink. When it was my turn, I answered, "*Una coca de dieta, por favor*." And after she brought our drinks and asked for our food order, I pointed to the menu and said, "*Quiero el Huachinango Entero al Mojo de Ajo*."

Wally gave me a subtle smile and a wink.

As we visited, Uncle Ryan commented on my physique and wanted to know if I was involved in sports. Images of me wrestling raced through my mind, but I said no.

"If I had your muscles, I wouldn't let them go to waste," he said. "You should think about getting into weight-lifting or body-building competitions."

"Jesse's too busy with school for that, Ryan," my mom said. "Did you know that he finished the semester with straight As? And that's with taking calculus and chemistry."

Everybody clapped.

"Well, let me show you what my crazy daughter's been up to," Wally's mom said. She pulled her phone from her purse and opened the YouTube app. A few clicks later, she found a video of Wally and me at Extravaganza de Lucha Libre. In it, we were walking toward the ring, and Wally was belittling my opponent, El Cartagenero.

My mom smiled at first. Then as she looked closer, her face tightened. "Oh, Jesse, please don't tell me this is you!"

"What are you looking at?" Aunt Gracie asked. She sidled next to my mom and watched several seconds of the video. "Are you saying that's Jesse?"

"Of course, it's him! Don't you think I recognize my own son?" My mom held the phone to my father's face. "Is this what you spent the summer training him to do?"

He glanced at it but didn't say anything.

"I'm sorry, I didn't realize that was Jesse," Wally's mom said. "I've been to the matches, but I didn't recognize him, and Wally never mentioned a word to me about it."

"I would have, if you had asked," she said innocently.

"Let me see." Uncle Ryan took the phone. "Which one's Jesse?"

"The one with the skeleton mask," Aunt Gracie said.

He snorted. "Well, like they say, the apple doesn't fall far from the tree."

My mom glared at him. She didn't need Uncle Ryan adding fuel to the fire, especially with the attitude he and Aunt Gracie had about my father's career.

"How long have you been doing this?" she asked me.

"I don't know," I muttered. "A couple of months, I guess."

Turning her anger toward my father, she said, "I can't believe you didn't tell me that Jesse was wrestling!"

"Don't blame him, Mom," I said. "Dad didn't know anything about it."

"Yes, I did," he said quietly.

My heart jumped. "You did? Who told you?"

He shrugged. "Word gets around."

"Then why didn't you make him stop?" my mom lashed out at him.

My father collected his thoughts. Then he said, "Because it would've been hypocritical of me to tell him to quit when I wasn't willing to do it. Look, I could never get you to understand this, Molly, but there's something about the profession that gets in your blood. For some people, it almost becomes an obsession. Now if Jesse had been doing poorly in school, or if he'd started talking about dropping out, I would've confronted him about it. But like you said, he made As in all his subjects. And as long as he can handle both school and wrestling, I don't see a problem with it."

"When did you find out?" I asked, still reeling from the surprising revelation.

"I got a call from Mitch Green at Capital City Wrestling," he said. "He wanted to know if I had a son named Jesse who was trying to break into the business. After that, I started hearing from other promoters."

I should've known better than to think they'd keep quiet about it. "So if you knew I wanted to wrestle, and you weren't against it, why didn't you put me in your shows?"

"I thought about it," he said. "Many times. But if I brought you in, I don't know that you would've been a good fit. I mean, the boys would always see you as my son, and that wouldn't be fair to you. Anyway, Santiago Reyes says that you're way over with the fans in his promotion. I've seen your matches on YouTube, and he's right. Both you and Wally. And you did that on your own, without my help. That says a lot about you."

My mom huffed in frustration. "So you're just going to sit back and let him get hurt?"

"Mom, Aunt Gracie told me that you were super excited when Dad got drafted by the Dallas Cowboys," I said. "He could've been hurt doing that, too."

Aunt Gracie put her hands up. "Hey, don't drag me into this argument."

Uncle Ryan tried covering for her, saying, "Yes, but the thing is, Jesse, pro football's a respected sport. It's a national pastime. No offense, but wrestling is more on, shall we say, the unseemly side."

"Stay out of this, Ryan!" my mom yelled at him. "Keep your comments to yourself. This is between Mark and Jesse and me."

"Excuse me, Mrs. B.," Wally broke in. "May I say something?"

Everyone turned and looked at her.

"Jessup's wrestling this Sunday. I think you should go see him. He's an amazing wrestler. I know you'd be real proud of him."

Her mom patted my mom's arm gently. "I can appreciate how you feel, Molly, but Wally's right. When you think of the heartaches a lot of parents have to deal with, we should count our lucky stars that we have smart, talented teenagers, who simply want to pursue their dreams. I plan to be there. I hope you will, too."

A long silence followed. Finally, my mom looked at me. "Oaxaca?" she said, cracking a smile. "How in the world did you come up with the idea to wrestle as a *luchador* from Oaxaca? And why did you call your opponent a cow?"

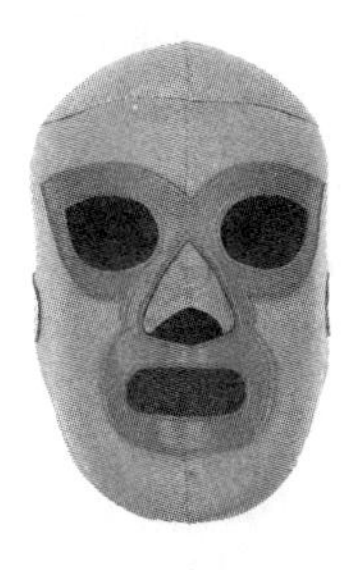

CHAPTER FORTY-ONE

Would my mom ever be comfortable with me being a wrestler? Probably not. But in the end, I think she decided to support my decision, because she didn't want it to come between us, as it had with her and my father. If it was any consolation, I promised her that no matter what, I was going to finish college. Of course, I didn't tell her what I was thinking about doing after I graduated. No need to. I'd cross that bridge when I came to it.

Sunday, she attended the matches with my father and Wally's mom. Aunt Gracie and Uncle Ryan passed on the invitation.

Before the start of the show, Mr. Reyes took my father backstage and introduced him to everyone. The wrestlers were elated to meet the legendary icon and asked if they could take photos with him. Mr. Reyes then revealed that the Angel of Death was my father. I'd already developed a good reputation among my peers, but now they held me in higher esteem. They told him what a great performer I was and how much they loved working with me, even Gerónimo. Although I think he was just trying to kiss up to my father, so he could claim that he knew the Angel of Death.

"Jesse and Wally have definitely boosted our attendance, Mark," Mr. Reyes said. "The fans are wild about them. You'll see what I mean when they come out."

My father beamed with pride. "Mom and I are looking forward to seeing your match, Jesse," he told me. "I know you're going to be great out there."

"Thanks. I'm third on the card, after the tag bout."

"*We're* third on the card," Wally corrected me. "Don't forget about your manager."

"Sorry. Wally and I are third on the card, Dad."

My father returned to his seat. Wally went to her side of the locker room to change from her Yells at Eels T-shirt and jeans into her Perséfone/prom dress and Mardi Gras mask. I switched out of my clothes into my white tights and boots, my cape and finally my skull mask.

Out in the arena, Mr. Reyes welcomed everyone to Extravaganza de Lucha Libre. He made some announcements, most of which I didn't understand. Then he acknowledged my father as the Angel of Death. My father stood and waved at the crowd.

The show opened with a one-fall bout between Gerónimo Chávez and Aldo Alemán. Both men were jobbers, so the crowd wasn't into the match, despite the men giving it their all. A lot of fans chatted throughout it, others spent time at the concession stand.

Eight minutes or so later, Aldo won the match with a 450 Splash.

Next was a tag-team bout. Blake Cooper and Sebastian Flynn were facing the masked *rudos,* Gran León and Dr. Cíclope. The *rudos* took the first fall. The *técnicos* came back and won the second and third fall, and the match, when Blake caught Gran León in a Triangle Choke and forced him to tap out.

Backstage, the men congratulated one another on their performance. In the ring, they were enemies. Outside of it, they were respectful coworkers.

As our time grew near, I started getting antsy. I always did before a match, but with my parents in attendance, I was feeling more nervous than usual.

"*No te preocupes, 'mano,*" my opponent, Calixto Camacho, told me. "I'll make you look real good in front of your family."

Calixto was a thirty-year-old, bilingual kindergarten teacher from Waco. He wrestled as a masked *rudo,* known simply as Calixto. For him, wrestling was a way of releasing the stress he dealt with all week. Playing a heel, especially, allowed him to say and do things he never could in the classroom.

He and Wally and I were standing behind the curtains in the Gorilla Position.

"Are you going to do that *vaca* thing?" Calixto asked me.

"*We're* going to do that *vaca* thing," Wally piped in.

"Excuse me, Calixto," I said. "Perséfone and I are going to do that *vaca* thing."

He gave us a thumbs up. "Awesome. I love it!"

Soon, his music began to play. He walked out and headed to the ring, as the crowd showered him with boos.

Moments later, my haunting entrance music sounded. I could hear the crowd roaring for us. I took a deep breath, then let it out slowly. "You ready?" I asked Wally.

"Always," she said confidently. She pulled my mask above my mouth and kissed me on the lips. "Let's rock this house!"

We stepped through the curtains to an incredible ovation.

"*¡Buenas tardes, Seguin! ¿Cómo están?*"

"*¡Perséfone! ¡Perséfone! ¡Perséfone! ¡Perséfone!*"

Wally trash-talked Calixto, ending her promo with, "*Y una cosa más . . .*"

I looked up at the crowd, taking my time before delivering my line. My father often talked about how he enjoyed manipulating the audiences' emotions.

"I can make them love me or hate me, boo me or cheer me."

Now I understood what he meant. I snatched the microphone from Wally and yelled at Calixto, "*¡Eres una va-ca-a-a!*"

"*¡Va-ca! ¡Va-ca! ¡Va-ca!*" the fans chanted,

We walked down the aisle, slapping hands along the way. When we reached the bottom, my mom got out of her seat and wrapped her arms around me. "I love you, Jesse," she said.

"Love you, too, Mom."

Under other circumstances, I might've thought that showing affection toward someone in the audience would've been an uncool thing for Máscara de la Muerte to do, but when I hugged my mom, I heard a loud "*Aw-w-w*!" from the fans.

My father stood and pointed at me. "*¡Éste es mi hijo!*" he shouted.

The crowd erupted with more cheers.

Like the previous match, Calixto's and mine was a best two-out-of-three falls. When we were going over it, we used terms like chin lock, arm bar and cross face, but also *candado*, *tijeras*, e*stacas* and *tornillo*.

I won the first fall when I hit Calixto with Travis's finisher, the Spinning DDT.

Calixto came back and took the second fall with a Springboard Elbow Drop off the top rope. He hooked my leg and the ref made the three count.

While I was on my back, I happened to look at my parents. My father was telling my mom something, no doubt, assuring her that I was fine.

For the third fall, Calixto and I went all out, striking each other with punches and kicks, dropkicks, clotheslines, sentons and crossbodies. We had lots of near pins, whipping the crowd into a frenzy with the story we were telling. The entire time, Wally paced outside the ring, pounding on the mat, rooting me on.

Finally, with Calixto down, I picked him up by his mask, grabbed him in a Front Facelock, lifted him vertically and dropped him with *El sueño profundo*. I pinned his shoulders, and the referee made the three count.

As Wally and the ref raised my hands, and Mr. Reyes declared me the winner of the third fall and the match, I could hear thunderous cheers from the audience, but none sounded louder than the ones coming from my parents.

Later, when Wally and I had our autograph session, they waited in line with everyone. From time to time, fans approached my father to ask for his autograph, but he politely declined, saying he was there for Máscara de la Muerte and Perséfone.

My mom bought a dozen photos to give away and asked us to autograph them. She also bought a T-shirt and a button, which she put on immediately.

After the autograph session, my father took me aside. "Listen, Jesse," he said. "I'm having a Super Saturday Clash show at the Crockett Field House in February. I'd like for you to be part of it."

"That'd be awesome, Dad," I said. "Would it be okay if Wally worked it with me?"

"Of course. She's a tremendous asset to your character. In a way, she reminds me of Spirit." He looked around to make sure my mom hadn't heard him. "Anyway, I'm thinking about putting you in a match against someone like Kendric Scott or even Mace McKeon."

"I have an idea," I said. "How about Goose Guzmán?"

"Goose? Are you sure about him?" My father sounded as if he didn't have enough trust in Goose's wrestling abilities to book him for a high-profile event.

"Yeah, he and I work really well together," I said.

"All right, I'll think about it. Maybe I'll change his name to Ciclón Suárez and have him wear a mask. That way, I can promote both of you as *luchadores* from Mexico."

I thought it was weird how my father had made Goose's vision come true. And I laughed to myself, thinking how much fun Wally would have ripping Goose apart during her promo.

My father didn't say anything about using me in his shows regularly. Even if he had, with school keeping me super busy, I wasn't sure I'd have time to work in both promotions. Besides, I liked making a name for myself, rather than wrestling in his shadow.

CHAPTER FORTY-TWO

Wally and I were sitting in her den, watching my match with Goose on YouTube. We'd already seen it, but she got a charge out of hearing herself tell Goose, in English and in Spanish, that he was living proof that humans can function without a brain. And that I had planned to kick his teeth in, except that he didn't have any. As always, she ended her promo with, "*Y una cosa más . . .*" to which I bellowed, "*¡Eres una va-ca-a-a!*"

A lot of PWF fans were familiar with our characters, so they knew how to respond. "*¡Va-ca! ¡Va-ca! ¡Va-ca!*"

"*¡Va-ca! ¡Va-ca! ¡Va-ca!*" Wally's parrot Orpheus squawked.

Samson looked up from his doggie bed where he'd been napping and started barking at him.

"*¡Va-ca! ¡Va-ca! ¡Va-ca!*" Orpheus continued, until Wally draped a towel over his cage. We could still hear his muffled squawks, but after a few seconds, he stopped.

Goose and I had put on what I thought was one of the best matches of the evening. As Ciclón Suárez, he wore a silver mask with black trim that Shirley Washington had designed, at my father's request and expense. His grandma changed the name on his vest to CICLÓN. Clyde Conner introduced him as coming from Mexico City.

If my father had any doubts about Goose's in-ring skills, they were erased within minutes. Even with me defeating him with *El sueño profundo,* Goose proved he had the makings of a top-tier wrestler.

I encouraged him to talk to Mr. Reyes about wrestling for Extravaganza de Lucha Libre, and he said he might once he had more experience.

After our match was over, I turned off the TV.

"The *vaca* catchphrase isn't going to work forever, you know," I told Wally. "Eventually, the fans are going to get tired of hearing it and want something different."

"What if we talk to Mr. Reyes about turning us heels?" she suggested. "I'd love to do that."

"Me, too. The thing is that it could affect our sales."

On some Sundays, we make more money selling T-shirts, buttons and photos, than we do by performing. Heels usually sell less merchandise than baby faces.

"Well, if Mr. Reyes keeps paying us the way he has, that's not going to be a problem," she said.

I smiled. "You may be right."

My booking fee has been increased to three-hundred dollars per match. Wally gets seventy-five. She was able to negotiate our salary hike after telling Mr. Reyes that my father was luring us to his promotion, and that we were strongly considering it. What she didn't mention was that my father's offer was a one-time appearance. I guess she really is my manager.

Mr. Reyes is getting his money's worth, though. In the time Wally and I have been with his company, ticket sales have skyrocketed. So have the show's YouTube views.

Wally uses her earnings from working for my father and Mr. Reyes to help her mom with household expenses, in addition to making her car payments. She's also bought several outfits for her Perséfone character, so she's fully invested in her gimmick.

"All right, Jessup," she said. "Let's go over your promo again."

I groaned. "Do I have to?"

"You still haven't learned it. Come on, you can do it."

I picked up the script she had written for me, looked it over, then placed it back on the coffee table.

"*Damas y caballeros . . .*" I began halfheartedly.

"Stand up. You need to use your whole body when you speak. Here." Wally handed me TV the remote. "Use this as your mic."

I took it from her and rose from the couch. "*Damas y caballeros, éste va a ser el ano . . .*"

"No, Jessup, it's *año*."

"What'd I say?"

"You said *ano*. *Ano* means butt hole. *Año* means year."

I laughed. "Sorry."

Wally has been helping me cut a promo in Spanish. So far, she's done all the talking for us, but Mr. Reyes wants me to speak for myself during our interviews. He says I need to connect with the audience more.

"*Damas y caballeros, éste va a ser el año de Máscara de la Muerte*," I recited. "*Primeramente, voy a ganar el Campeonato Intercontinental de América Latina. Después, el Campeonato Mundial de . . . de . . .*"

"*De peso completo,*" Wally prompted.

"*De peso completo*," I echoed, then stopped. "You know what? I need my mask. It'll help me get into my character better."

"Your mask isn't going to teach you Spanish," she said. "Now keep going."

Sometimes I think it'd be easier for me to leave Extravaganza de Lucha Libre and find an American promotion to wrestle for, where I can conduct my promos in English. Now that I have tons of YouTube videos of my matches, and I've developed a huge following, I could probably get booked just about anywhere. But I don't know if other companies will hire Wally and me as a package, and I'm not ready to go at it alone.

Then I think, after everything I've had to overcome to get where I am, learning to speak Spanish should be the least of my worries. Anyway, I'm perfectly happy working for Mr. Reyes. Plus I enjoy wrestling in the *lucha libre* style. American Championship Wrestling isn't even on my radar anymore.

I plan to wrestle for Extravaganza de Lucha Libre until I finish college. And if I get a job as a mechanical engineer in the San Antonio area, who knows? I may keep wrestling there for years to come.

As for what the future holds for Wally and me, I can't say. We aren't officially dating anymore, and the only times we see each other is on Sunday afternoons at the Guadalupe County Center, and we go home afterwards. I've been on spring break this week, so I've had a chance to hang out with her, but I'll be leaving for Austin after my match.

Wally's going to be graduating from Erastus Deaf Smith High School in May. She's applied to the University of Texas, which would be awesome if she were to get accepted, because we could be together. She's also filled out applications for Texas A&M and the University of Houston. Both schools are about two-and-a-half hour's drive to Seguin, so she could still make the shows on Sundays.

Unfortunately, she's also applied for scholarships at Juilliard in New York and the Carnegie Mellon University

School of Drama in Pittsburgh to study acting. If she goes to either of those schools, it'll surely be the end of us as a couple.

I hope not.

I've been reluctant to tell Wally how I feel about her, especially with the uncertainty of our relationship, but I've finally realized that I love her. I love her with all my heart. I suppose I've always known it. Too bad it took losing her for me discover just how much she means to me.

Wally said she loves me, but I don't know if it's to the extent that she'd turn down a chance to attend an out-of-state university just to be with me. The selfish side of me would like for her to do that, but I'm not going to say anything to persuade her to stay. I want what's best for her, even if her future doesn't include me.

Mr. Reyes told us he believed that fate had brought us to him. Maybe that same higher power has destined Wally and me to be together. I'd like to think so. But I guess only time will tell.

For now, I'm content to entertain the Extravaganza de Lucha Libre fans with Wally at my side as the mysterious masked couple known as Máscara de la Muerte y Perséfone.

Also by Ray Villareal

Alamo Wars

Body Slammed!

Don't Call Me Hero

My Father, the Angel of Death

On the Other Side of the Bridge

Who's Buried in the Garden?